off list

cate ashton

Off List

Cover Design: Abigail Owen | Authors on a Dime
Character Illustration: Anastasia Novikova
Edited by: Dolly Jackson

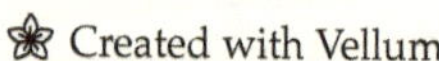 Created with Vellum

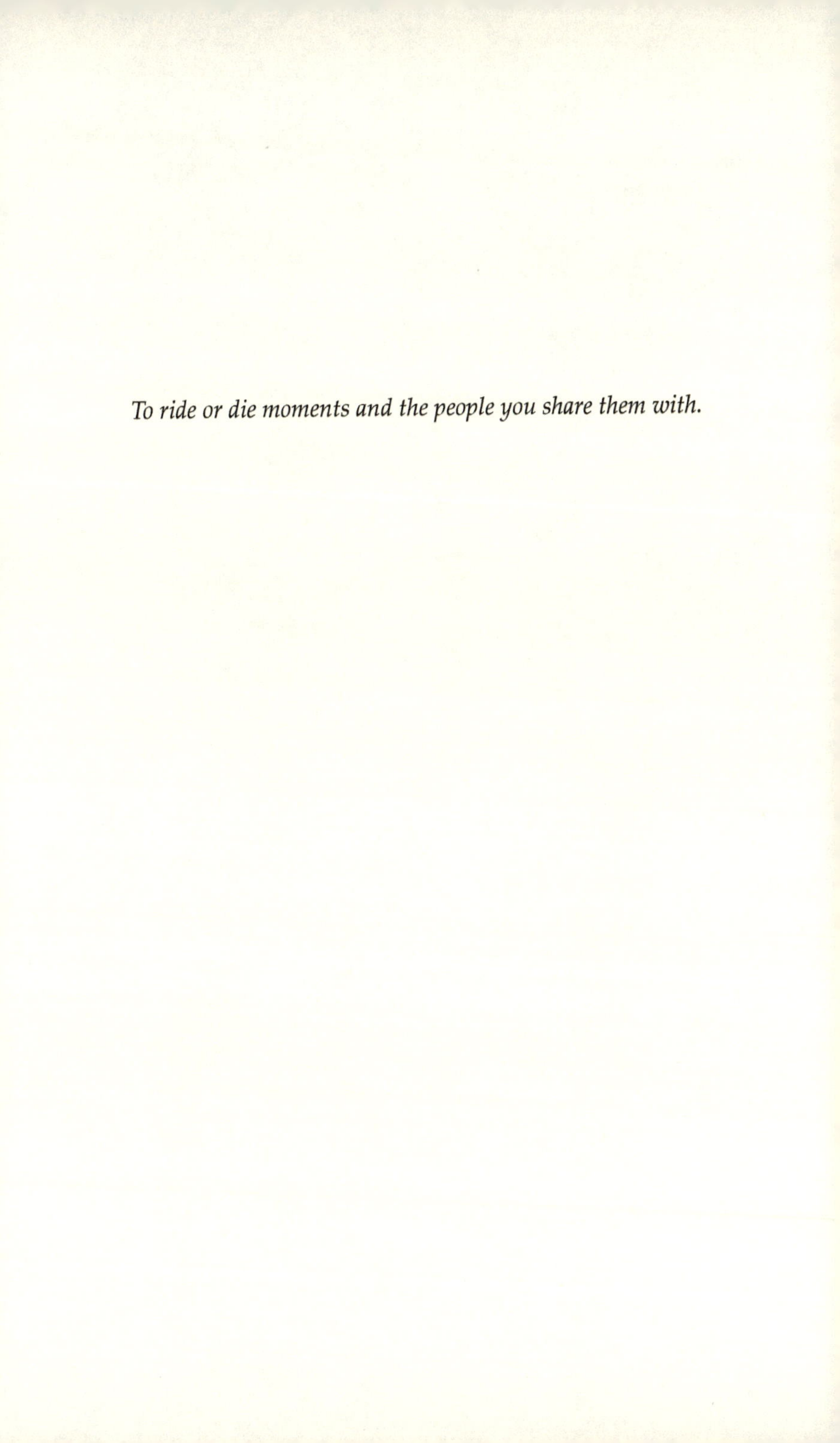

To ride or die moments and the people you share them with.

author notes

For the list of Trigger Warnings, please visit my website here.

www.cateashton.com

Off List contains images which could affect the book formatting depending on the platform it's read on. And while the story is set in Austin, Texas, some aspects of the setting have been fictionalized to fit the story.

chapter one

As I stare at the sex toys that just spewed from my bag onto the bright yellow tile in my personality psychology class, it's like my brain and body stall, my mind hung somewhere between *condoms, cocks, and kink, oh my!* and *why the hell are these things in my purse?*

My brain fires back to life as a sharp pain zips through my head like a pinball.

I'm. Never. Drinking. Again.

But first, I'm going to kill Ginny. It isn't humiliating enough I'm so hungover I tripped over my own two feet, but my best friend apparently made the Marc Jacobs bag I got for Christmas an accomplice to her sick humor. Marc is hosting an all-out orgy without my knowledge, and if I don't shut the party down, the whole class will file in and join the fun.

I sink to the floor between the rows of stadium-style seats. This isn't exactly how I saw myself starting off the first day of my last semester of college. Thankfully, no one else has sat in this row yet to notice the sex stash or the bright neon pink vibrator. *Freaking Ginny.* I went over to her place last night to laugh at the goodies she received for her latest money-making attempt as a "romance" consultant. Oh, we laughed alright— as we got wrecked on margaritas and made a sex list.

Oh God, the list.

At least I don't see *that* among the carnage. It's embarrassing enough to have made it in the first place, but the last thing I need is for someone else to get their hands on it. The thought turns my stomach. I can already see the headline: *Central Texas University President's Daughter Has Naughty Sex List.*

Unfortunately, I know all too well how quickly the internet pounces. How it turns your mistakes into life-altering disasters. How it twists your vulnerability into something ugly. And that's exactly what would happen with my list, which started out as a funny and mostly innocent graduation bucket list—until Ginny and margaritas took it over.

"Really, Ally? This list is way too boring for someone who has spent most of her college years in the most boring relationship ever," Ginny says as she generously refills my glass.

"Hey, not all relationships are passion and fireworks."

"They should be," she responds with a waggle of her eyebrows.

I shrug. Joel knew me before. Before the big horrible thing. He was my safe space. When we crossed the line from friends to lovers, I wasn't looking for passion, just comfort and release.

"You know I'm right. Joel found his passion now you need to, too."

Her words sting. Maybe we weren't the hottest couple around, but we were committed. So, when I let myself in his apartment, the last thing I expected was to find him half naked with someone else. Yet another betrayal by someone I trusted.

"Come on, this list needs less college bullshit and more sex." Ginny grabs the pen out of my hand.

The margaritas tell me Ginny has a point. I'm a single girl with less than five months until graduation, and I've never taken advantage of the "wild and crazy" college days. For a good reason, but still.

"I guess we can spice it up a little," I say, reluctantly. "Like a dash of pepper."

"Fuck that. We're going to ghost pepper this thing," Ginny's lips curl into a Cheshire cat smile that scares me a little.

From there my list took on a life of its own. We were so hammered by the end of the night I can't even remember what's all on it. I do remember thinking if I did everything, the only thing I'd gain before graduation is an STD.

I try to ignore the pounding in my head as I wrap my hand around the pink vibrator and stifle a sigh at how irresponsible I was last night.

"Missing something, Ally Cat?" comes a familiar voice from the row below me.

I close my eyes as my heart speeds up. I'm on the floor, on all fours, and it's *Clark.*

I haven't seen him since Halloween, since…I stop myself from going further.

What happens on Halloween, stays on Halloween.

I repeat the mantra we created my freshman year in my head when we first bonded over our mutual misery of the holiday and look over my shoulder to see Clark's deep blue eyes sparkling with laughter behind his rounded-square-framed glasses. As always, he steals a little bit of my breath. His real name is Logan, but thinking of him as that always feels like this personal line I can't cross, so I don't.

Besides, I've always loved his Clark Kent look with his

sexy frames and unkempt golden-brown hair that has just enough curl to make my fingers itch to touch it. Our first Halloween together, I nicknamed him Clark and haven't looked back since.

His hair is longer than it was the last time I saw him, and my fingers instantly start to tingle. I ignore the sensation and don the mask I wear with him on every other day except Halloween.

"If I was as graceful as a cat, I wouldn't be in this situation," I say, glad I've managed to recapture most of the errant toys.

The right side of his mouth lifts as his gaze shifts to my upended ass. A sudden flash of heat consumes me. You would think I'd be used to my reaction to him by now, but nope, every time it's a scorching shock.

"I kinda like your current situation, Ally Cat."

That flash of heat settles into a slow burn. He says it in a teasing way, but there's an edge of interest behind it that makes me wonder if he really means it. There's always been this unspoken electricity between us, though we do our best to ignore it or disguise it as playful banter.

He bites his bottom lip as if he's trying to not laugh out loud at me. Then, I notice what's in his hand. My birth control pills. Perfect.

"A girl's gotta be safe, right?" I sit back fully on my heels and pluck the case out of his hand with as much of a saucy grin as I can muster.

"Well, then, you really like to be safe." He nods his head at the two flavored condoms on the floor. *Ugh, Ginny!*

"Um, yeah, a girl's gotta be prepared as well."

His grin widens to panty-melting proportions. "I like a girl who's prepared."

Oh God, this feels good, and I'm not talking about the hot

tingles firing up in all the right places of my body. I've missed him and our playful conversations. As strange as our friendship is, it's been one of the most important ones of my college career.

"So, we get to spend our last semester together, huh?" Clark is a sociology major, and with me being a psychology major, this isn't the first time we've had a class together.

His sexy smile transforms into a friendlier one yet maintains its panty-melting status. "Looks like it."

Then his gaze falls to the pink vibrator in my other hand. Surprise and something a little darker comes over his expression before he meets my eyes and amusement takes over. "A pink dick? Really?"

I shrug and try to not let my mortification show. "What color would you like it to be?"

"I don't know. Not neon pink. I mean, wouldn't you want something more realistic?"

"It's a vibrating cock, Clark. There's nothing realistic about that. Why not give it a fun color?"

His mouth falls open as his sapphire eyes go from my face to my purse to the vibrator in my hand. He quickly gets over his shock and throws his head back and laughs. We garner some looks and I shove the vibrator in my purse.

He leans further over the seat back and peers into my open purse and the sexual cornucopia inside. "What exactly are you up to with a pink cock, fuzzy handcuffs, lube, and a book of the Kama Sutra?"

My cheeks burn.

"Don't forget the dick pen." I pick up a pen with the head of a penis as a clicker. Maybe I can use it to make a list of the many ways I can kill Ginny.

"Definitely can't forget that."

"Clearly I'm stockpiling for the sex-pocalypse."

Clark laughs loudly. The stares people give us are full of

curiosity. The class is starting to fill up now, so I zip up my purse and put it on my shoulder.

"Sex-pocalypse, huh? Are you expecting this to happen soon? Like during class? Because that sounds way better than learning about...well, anything really."

"Why do you think I have all this with me?"

His smile widens and, holy moly, if I wasn't already on my knees, I absolutely would be now. I've always been a little obsessed with his smiles, so much so I started labeling them that first Halloween. I'll have to call this one his Holy Moly smile.

"Okay, class, it's time to start," the professor says.

I stand and move down a couple of seats when I see another scattered item from my spilled purse. I grab it, take a seat and quickly realize I have nothing with me to take notes on. Since I was too wasted to go home last night, I stayed at Ginny's and woke up with only enough time to go straight to campus. I have no laptop or notebook, not even a pen. Okay, I guess I have a pen, but I really don't want to use it.

"Hey," I whisper as I slink closer to Clark who has already turned back to face the front of the room. He looks back, amusement still on his face. "Do you have any paper I can borrow?"

His grin widens. "It's not the Middle Ages, Ally Cat. I have a laptop. Where's yours?"

"I spent the night away from home last night and didn't have time to go back to my place for my backpack."

Clark's eyebrows raise as his grin fades. "I think the bag of sex is starting to make sense now." His mouth quirks up again, but this time it's different. I can't really explain how though.

"Uh, no. Trust me, that wasn't the case. Come on, help a girl out. Hey, if the sex-pocalypse hits during class, I promise to rock your world first." I move my eyebrows up and down suggestively.

The fire in his gaze flares back to life, but it's darker…more dangerous. Suddenly, I can't breathe properly. I feel reckless, and I'm not sure if I like that. It's been so long…

I don't know if I moved, or if he did, but somehow we're closer. "Promise?" He says, his voice deeper, thicker, and touching me in places I haven't been touched in…maybe ever.

He lifts his hand, his pinky finger extended toward me. I don't even hesitate. I wrap my pinky around his. "Promise."

He blinks at our intertwined fingers and suddenly yanks his hand away, looking at his hand as if he didn't understand how it got twisted up with mine. With a shake of his head, he turns and digs into his backpack and hands me a notebook. As I reach to grab it, he pulls it out of my reach. "After you rock my world, I'm using the fuzzy handcuffs and your little pink friend to rock yours."

My cheeks burn, and suddenly a little devil takes over my mind. I lean all the way down until our faces are mere inches apart. "Promises, promises."

Oh my God! Have all the sex toys in my purse deluded me into thinking I'm some sort of seductress? Clark's pupils are now so large his eyes are almost all black, and I'm so turned on I'm aching. His gaze drops to my mouth, and my breath cracks in this embarrassing moan as the professor makes a very loud *harumph* sound. I snatch the notebook out of his hand and scurry to my seat.

Since a sinkhole isn't going to appear and take me down with it, I try not to think about what just happened. I flip open his notebook and instantly admire his handwriting. It's neat, printed letters, some with a slight slant to them. There's something pretty about it, yet completely masculine. I move my finger over the words, feeling the dips in the paper from the writing. It's mostly notes, and while I'm dying to pore over the pages to see if there is anything personal to read, I quickly move to an empty page. It wouldn't be right to snoop. I pull the penis pen from my purse and turn my attention to the professor.

Twenty minutes later, I'm fidgeting in my seat. Though I haven't once looked at Clark, I also haven't truly heard one word the professor has said. My notes are filled with phrases like: *Why did I flirt? I'm such an idiot. What is he thinking? Did he think I was serious? Was I serious? I'm an idiot. I'm going to kill Ginny.*

I must still be drunk. That's it. After class, I'll tell him that. Or maybe I'll run away. I do have class across campus after this. My gaze flicks to him, and disappointment grips me when I see he's angled away from me and hunched over his tiny desk.

As Professor Martin drones on, I lean back in my seat and gnaw on the end of my pen. After a while, I glance over at Clark again and he's looking at me. I freeze. His eyes are huge and appear even darker than earlier—and zeroed in on my mouth. Realization hits me. I have the dick pen in my mouth. And it's not the first time I've done it. No, I've been sitting here the whole class giving my pen a blow job.

Kill. Me. Now.

I yank the pen out of my mouth so hard I bobble it, but quickly catch it before it flies across the room. Clark's gaze locks with mine and his whole expression cracks. I bury my face in my hands, my embarrassment giving over to laughter. I can't believe I spaced on what kind of pen I was using. I glance over and Clark's shoulders are shaking, and his hand is over his mouth to cover up his own laughter. We catch each other's gazes, which only makes us laugh harder. Heads turn—the class isn't that big—so I force myself under control, but for the rest of class we keep sneaking amused glances at each other. I don't pick up my pen again.

When the professor dismisses class, I tear my pages and a few more out of his notebook. The last thing I need today is more embarrassment. I look out of the corner of my eye to see Clark bending down to pick something up. I stand and head his way.

"Here," I say as I hand over his notebook. "Hope you don't mind, but I tore out a few pages for my other classes. Not that I plan to take any more notes with that pen."

He grins as he takes his notebook. "I have to say, this is the best first day of school I've ever had. Except it's a real shame the sex-pocalypse didn't happen."

"It didn't, but hey, it's not every day you get a little live porn action in class."

His eyes widen, shocked, then he doubles over in laughter. Clark laughing…well, it's a beautiful thing. It reminds me of our first Halloween, and how easy and natural it was between us though we were essentially strangers. He meets my gaze again and that same ease from three years ago slips through me. Does he feel it too? I mentally shake myself from the silly sentimental thought.

"I'm glad my humiliation has entertained you, but me and my purse of porn have another class to get to." I heft the strap over my shoulder and give him a wave.

"Oh wait, is this yours? I found it on the floor."

I look at his extended hand with a folded piece of paper in it. My heart slams into my chest and my whole body seizes up. My list.

I snatch it out of his hand then realize how crazy I must seem. "Um, yeah, thanks. You just found it?" I try to come off casual, but I know I'm failing. It doesn't matter, I need to know if he read it.

"Yeah, saw it on the floor when I got up." He gives me a quick smile of reassurance and my panic eases some, though my heart is racing so hard it would leave a Formula One car in the dust.

"Thanks. I gotta run." I head down the aisle in the opposite direction and stuff the list in my pocket. My stomach seizes and churns with every step.

Pushing a fellow student aside, I dart into the nearest bathroom and lock myself in a stall moments before I lose the contents of my stomach. Afterward, I sit back against the stall door and run a shaky hand through my hair. How could I do something so stupid? And for Clark to find it…the man is a football celebrity on campus, not to mention he has a big social media presence. It would be so easy for him to share it to his thousands of followers.

I learned the hard way that even the most trusted people in your life will turn on you. I pull the list out of my pocket and start tearing it into pieces until it resembles confetti then toss it in the toilet and flush. I wait and flush again to make sure all evidence of it is gone.

I lean back against the door, close my eyes, and let my head hang. When I open them again, I move aside the wrap bracelet I'm wearing and rub the simple sun and ocean wave tattoo on the inside of my wrist. I take a few breaths. It was foolish to think I could let loose. That I could recapture some part of that girl I used to be. I need to focus on school and my internship at a local high school before I enter grad school in the fall. An internet scandal would ruin everything. I can't let that happen. Again.

chapter two

Logan

I slam the locker door shut, and it bounces back as if to mock me. Then I notice my glasses are still in there. So, I rip off my sports glasses and toss them inside, but I throw them too hard, and they fall back out. Fucking hell! I can't do anything right today. I blow out a breath, and with a calm I definitely don't feel, I put my regular glasses on and make sure my sports glasses are securely on the shelf. Then I shut the door with more control. Control I clearly didn't have on the field today.

I shouldn't have an invite to the NFL Scouting Combine in six weeks. Not after quitting football when my mom died my senior year of high school. I never thought I'd ever get football back, didn't even think I wanted it back. Then Nate and Wes, two of the CTU Toros top defensive players, my friends and current roommates, encouraged me to train again. I tried out for the team as a walk-on to play my junior year. Unbelievably, I made it. Getting that little piece of my life back was huge, I didn't even care if I ever actually made it on the field during a game.

Then Nate, our star edge rusher, went down with a shoulder injury in the second game of this past season. It was the fourth quarter, and we were ahead by ten, so I got put in his place. I sacked the quarterback three times. The next game I got the start. I sacked the quarterback eight times and broke the collegiate record for number of sacks in a single game. Suddenly, the media was on me like a cheap suit.

The last three games of the season weren't as impressive, but my season was unheard of for a walk-on that had only been on the team for two seasons. Now here I am with an invite to the NFL Combine and I can't seem to play for shit anymore.

I book it out of the locker room and straight to my truck before the rest of the guys file in and give me shit. I'm not in the mood. After my classes today, I realized how busy this semester is going to be. Let's just hope I can get through the psych class with Ally Worthington sitting a few seats down from me.

If I'm truly honest about what has me distracted today, it's Ally. Ally and her purse of porn. Ally and her sex-pocalypse.

Ally and her list.

My body instantly tenses with a raging hot need, which has pretty much been my state from the moment I saw Ally Cat on all fours with a pink dick in her hand. Why did she have all that stuff in her purse? The birth control pills and the condoms seem plausible, but the rest? And if all that wasn't enough to send me into a lust-filled frenzy, then she wrapped her perfectly plump lips around her cock pen. All I could think about was how I wanted my much larger, much harder, cock in its place. As I was trying to hide my raging hard-on behind the tiny desktop, I spotted a folded piece of paper on the floor.

Never in my wildest dreams did I think that piece of paper would be a sexy college bucket list from the daughter of the university's president. I snapped a picture with my phone, and I know I shouldn't have, but I wanted the chance to read it closely. It reminded me too much of my own college bucket list I made freshman year that has a bunch of similar stuff on it—that's still not crossed off.

It's not that I've been completely boring my whole college career. I definitely stepped up my social game my sophomore year, but most of it ended up being within the football community. I know Ally has struggled in the past with putting herself out there, but I don't know how much of that is true anymore. Our Halloweens together tend to be extremely personal—to a point.

What happens on Halloween, stays on Halloween.

I pull into the driveway at the off-campus house I live at with Nate and Wes, head straight to my bedroom and open the drawer to my nightstand. I shift through the junk, but don't find what I'm looking for. I know it's here somewhere. I remember finding it when I moved into the house. I finally find it in my bottom desk drawer. I carefully open the folded-up piece of paper and at the top it says, FRESHMAN YEAR BUCKET LIST.

I snort at that. I was determined to party hard enough that I'd forget the nightmare my life had been in only two semesters. Then that first Halloween came and...I just stopped. I didn't want to be around anyone anymore. Glancing at the list, I can only say I've crossed off a handful of items.

I swipe my phone screen and bring up the picture of Ally's

list. It's clearly a collaborative effort since there's two sets of handwriting on it.

I know Ally's handwriting is the cursive one and it sounds like she's over her ex if one-night stand is her number one item. That one is on my list too, but it definitely got crossed off —multiple times. Out of the others, I haven't done number two. While I've been to plenty of parties, none were at a frat house. Her list goes on with some basic items until number ten.

Whoever wrote that last bit, I like her. And wholeheartedly agree. I honestly can't remember if I've ever banged a girl against a wall. Maybe I should add it to my list.

15. Take spring break trip
16. Try a new sport
NO MORE BORING STUFF!!
17. HAVE CRAZY HOT SEX IN PUBLIC
18. GET TIED UP DURING SEX
19. Make out in library
20. ~~THREESOME~~ Nope!!
20. SEX WITH VIBRATOR AND MAN
(OR WOMAN)

A certain pink cock comes to my mind at that last one.

21. Break a campus rule
BY HAVING SEX!!
22. Netflix and Chill
23. Sex in shower
24. Body Shots
25. Sext someone
26. Talk Dirty to Me!!

I glance at my list, and the similarities are eerie. Her list gets more incoherent as it goes until I'm squinting to make out the words. I have a feeling Ally wasn't sober when she made this list. The last one sticks out though, and it's something I could totally get on board with.

40. Multiple Orgasams!!!
lots and lots of orgasams

What kind of vanilla relationship did she have with her boyfriend?

"You made better time leaving the locker room than you did on the field."

I jump at the sound of my roommate Wes' voice. I quickly blank the screen on my phone, refold my list, and stuff it into my pocket. I look up to see my other roommate, Nate, crowding Wes at the entrance to my room, giving him a shove into the doorjamb.

"Fuck off."

My insult only makes Wes grin wider. I roll my eyes and push past him and head into the kitchen to grab a beer. Unfortunately, the guys follow me.

"You made more mistakes than the freshman edge today," Nate says, his voice matter of fact, as he grabs a beer for him and another for Wes. Of course, he wouldn't pussy-foot around the real issue.

"He's a four-star recruit out of high school. He should be on point."

Nate gives me a pointed look. "Don't act like you weren't a top recruit out of high school either."

"Yeah, years ago. I'm only a college player now because you got hurt." Thankfully, Nate's shoulder is fully healed from his surgery.

"Stop making excuses. It doesn't matter how you got on the field, what matters is that you took care of business when you did." Nate shakes his head. "What's going on with you? You're missing more cues now than you did when you started training after almost two years off the field."

I wish I knew. My last few games weren't my best, and I still got the combine invite. I don't get it. Or maybe I don't feel like I deserve it.

"I guess I'm letting school stress get to me," I say instead of admitting that I might be unconsciously sabotaging myself.

"You don't have to push yourself to graduate this May, Lo," Wes offers.

"No. I have to graduate." My tone leaves no room for question. Football isn't guaranteed for me, and my plan has always been to get out of Austin as soon as I can. A degree helps me do that.

Wes doesn't give a shit about graduating. If he hadn't redshirted his freshman year, he'd have declared the draft this year as a junior. But considering his competition as a free safety, he knew his chances would be better if he stayed in college another year. Nate should have the combine invitation instead of me, but since his season ended in that second game, he earned a medical redshirt and is staying on for his senior year too. I don't think he's upset about it though. Nate is the studious one of us all and actually made the dean's list.

"I'll snap out of it. I'll train more," I say. "I just need—"

"To get laid," Wes finishes for me. "You desperately need to get laid."

I roll my eyes at him. "Is that your answer for everything?"

"Well, yeah, but I'm being dead serious. You've been on this celibacy kick for a while now and it's not working."

"I'm not on a celibacy kick." At least, I haven't thought about it that way. I just haven't hooked up in a while.

"Dude, you've had a stick up your ass ever since Halloween."

I stiffen at the mention of last Halloween. That day is never a good one but spending it with Ally always makes it better. Except that day…well, everything got fucked up.

"When's the last time you've even been out?"

"We went out last weekend."

Wes rolls his eyes. "We went to a bar and ate. That's not going out, that's dinner."

I open my mouth to argue, but I honestly can't remember the last time I went out. I look over at Nate to see if he'll back me up. He looks curious, and that's never a good thing.

"The last party I remember you going to is when you hooked up with that Trish chick," Nate says.

The mere mention of her name sends a cold shiver down my spine. Trish and I had some no-strings sex which she totally agreed to that night then slid into my DMs wanting to get together again two days later. I'm not a complete asshole, I replied that it was fun but I wasn't interested in a girlfriend or another hook-up. But her DMs didn't stop. I finally blocked her.

"Wait," Wes says. "That was during the summer. You haven't fucked anyone since summer?" Wes' expression is so incredulous you'd think it's been five years not five months.

"No, but can you blame me? I've needed that much time to exorcise her bad ju-ju from my dick."

After a beat of shocked silence, Nate and Wes fall over laughing. "Don't say that. It sounds like she gave you an STD."

"Thank God, no! I was wrapped up, but I got myself checked out to make sure."

"Look, you've been attacking drills like crazy, and you're still wound up tight. I think Wes is right. You need to get laid."

I stare at Nate in shock while Wes sports a shit-eating grin.

I refuse to admit it, but I can see their point. I'm so sick of rubbing it out. It's not the same as sliding inside a woman. I miss the softness, the breathless moans as I touch her. Taste her. Take her.

A pair of gorgeous green eyes full of desire suddenly flash in my mind.

"You need a fuck buddy," Wes says breaking into my thoughts. "You've got to have someone in your phone who'd be DTF."

"Nah, I don't do repeats." Or any kind of relationship beyond a few hours.

My parents got married straight out of high school with my mom two months pregnant with me. In the end, their marriage became a bunch of broken promises so I'm not interested in getting tangled with anyone until my life is set. I still can't believe I had Ally make a pinky promise today. What the hell was I thinking?

"There's got to be someone looking for something temporary. Hey, what about your Halloween 'friend'?" Wes does air quotes around the word *friend*. "I know you still have her in your phone."

The sexy image of Ally floats back to the surface of my mind, sparking my body to life. Shit, what has she done to me today? I don't talk about Ally with the guys—with anyone, really. Wes and Nate actually know Ally, but they don't know she's my Halloween girl. I eventually fessed up that there was a girl with a mutual dislike of Halloween that I hung out with so they would stop pestering me to party with them.

"That's because I haven't slept with her."

"You might not have banged her, but you want to," Wes says.

I roll my eyes but don't deny it. "We have a class together this semester. Plus, she got out of a relationship not long ago. It's too complicated."

"Even better. Easy access and rebound sex. That's the best fucking kind." Wes perks up like he's the one about to get laid. "That means she's ready to go wild. This is your chance."

Shit, he's right. Ally does want to go wild, and I have the sexy list to prove it. Plus, I have my own list currently burning a hole in my pocket. We could tackle our lists together, and there's even a built-in deadline with graduation. A list-only relationship. It's perfect.

chapter three

"This will be the best fucking Halloween ever!"

I suppress the urge to roll my eyes as I pass two frat-wannabes dressed as superheroes on the sidewalk. They're the third set of Avengers I've passed since leaving the corner store, so I hope they don't think they're being original. My phone buzzes, and I pull it out of my pocket and look at it.

> Wes: Where are you? Did you know there's a sexy version of an astronaut? I got the perfect line: I'll boldly take you where no woman has gone before. Get it?

I shake my head. Wes is a year younger than me, but we met years ago at a football camp we both attended in high school. I never really knew him outside football but have quickly learned the guy is a big flirt and determined to fuck his way through freshman year. Not that I blame him, that had been my plan too last year. And I'd started off doing pretty well. Until Halloween.

I adjust the plastic bag in my hand so I can type out a response.

> Me: I told you I wasn't coming out tonight.

> Me: And please don't use that line. It's bad. Really bad.

> Wes: It's fucking brilliant! Come on, it's Halloween! And we won our last game. You gotta come out and celebrate with us.

One: I fucking hate Halloween. Two: I'm really happy for the Toro football team, but I can't help feeling a pang of jealousy. If I hadn't quit football my senior year, I'd be on the team myself. I was days away from signing a commitment letter to Central Texas University when my mom died. Honestly, it hadn't bothered me at all until this year when Wes and Nate joined the team and sparked the interest back in me.

> Me: Nope. Gotta watch the floor.

> Wes: Bullshit! RAs party too. Get ur ass here

I ignore that, black my screen, and stuff the phone back in my pocket. He knows my mom died but doesn't know it was two years ago today. And that the nightmare still replays through my mind daily.

My phone starts buzzing in my pocket, and I pull it back out to see Wes is now calling me. I should send it to voicemail, but he'll just keep bugging me.

"Hey," I answer. Loud music and chatter fill the background.

"I can't believe you've made me call you."

"I didn't make you do shit."

"Lo, come on. You should be here. It's fun."

I don't have fun on Halloween anymore. I don't say the words though. "Then have fun without me, I'm good."

Wes grumbles then I hear him say, "Talk sense into him," before the phone switches over to his roommate, Nate.

"Hey man. One sec, going to get somewhere quieter."

I met Nate at the same football camps as Wes, and we both play the edge position. I wanted to hate him because I can get super competitive, but the guy is too likable. He and Wes immediately sought me out when they got on campus and got me working out with them. They really want me to try out to be a walk-on next semester. It's a crazy idea that I immediately dismissed. But after hating not being on the field this year, I might be crazy enough to do it.

"Okay," Nate says, all the background noise now muted. "Look, don't worry about Wes. He's got his buzz on and just wants everyone to join the party."

Nate is pretty much Wes' opposite. More stoic and down to earth as opposed to Wes' life of the party ways. I honestly don't understand their friendship most days.

"Thanks, man. Y'all have fun."

"Hey, Lo. Are you okay?"

For a brief second, I want to tell him. That he senses this is about more than me being a wet blanket makes my chest suddenly feel tight. But now is not the right time.

"Yeah, I'm good. Just not up for it. Besides, I should probably be on point in case I have to deal with floor drama later."

"Okay." He pauses and I'm certain he knows I'm lying. "I'll get Wes off your case. See you tomorrow."

I end the call and let myself into the co-ed dorm I live in.

The elevator opens and an angel and devil appear before me. They're no ordinary angel and devil; they're the hot college girl variety in tight, barely there costumes. I'm pretty sure people have been arrested for indecent exposure for wearing more than these two, but hey, I'm not complaining. My gaze lingers over Angel's plunging neckline longer than it should, especially since the two girls live on my floor and darken my door with a "question" at least once a week.

"Hey, Logan," Angel says with a devilish smile.

"Hey Angel." I can never remember which one is which. It's Casey or Kelly.

She gives me fuck-me eyes as she leaves the elevator, and the devil brushes my arm with a sexy smirk on her lips as I enter. It's tempting to say fuck it and follow them for a night fueled by alcohol and sex. I could probably cross threesome off the bucket list I abandoned last year, but there's no way I'm hooking up with any girl living on my floor. That's just asking for drama, and those two definitely have trouble written all over them. I let the doors close without saying a word. The pungent smell of spilled beer penetrates my senses. By the end of night, it'll smell like piss and vomit, which is a good reminder why I should stay locked in my room tonight.

I get to my floor and fumble with my keys as I approach my room when I hear the door across the hall open. A pair of legs in lace-up heeled sandals enters my view. My heart kicks up, and it has nothing to do with sight of tan bare legs, not completely at least, but it has everything to do with the woman the legs belong to. I let my gaze roam up those gorgeous legs to short black shorts and a fuzzy black cropped sweater that hugs her in all the right places. A set of cat ears sit on top of her dark brunette hair that hangs down her back in waves. I brace myself for her to turn around after locking her door. I might not have plans to hook up with anyone on my floor, but this girl is the only one that truly tempts me.

She turns, her bright green eyes immediately find mine, and the now familiar one-two punch hits my gut. I think Angel and Devil could be standing in front of me buck-ass naked and it wouldn't be as potent as one look from Ally Worthington.

I lean against my door frame and take in her thick bangs, dark cat-eye make-up, painted nose and whiskers. "Let me guess, you're an *Ally* cat," I say, relieved I sound cool and collected instead of hot and bothered.

Her vibrant eyes widen, and suddenly she's laughing, and I have to consciously stop myself from groaning. Her laugh has gotten to me since the first dorm floor meeting. This time it's loud, a little gruff and throaty, and a whole lot of sexy.

"Oh my God, that's perfect! I probably should have thought of that, huh?"

I shrug and pretend my body isn't shifting into overdrive from the sound of her laugh. "Heading out?"

Her smile dims. "Uh, yeah, I guess."

"You guess?" I gesture toward her costume. "If that's not a Halloween costume then you must have a really big cat fetish."

She laughs again, it's softer this time, but no less powerful. "No, I'm going out. I am," she says the last bit with more conviction, though it sounds like she's trying to convince herself. "I…" She opens her mouth then closes it then repeats the action before shaking her head.

"What?"

"I haven't done the college party thing yet. And it's *Halloween*," she practically spits out the last word, immediately piquing my interest. She shakes her head. "I don't know. This whole costume thing is stupid." She tugs at her shirt then wraps her arms around her waist.

I've only hung out with Ally when there's a group around, so I don't know her well. I have noticed she tends to stick close to the dorm. She actually reminds me a bit of myself last year.

Sometimes I feel like there's this sadness that's always clinging to her. Maybe that's what draws me to her. Like my sadness recognizes hers.

She does have a guy that visits her often, guessing a boyfriend. I haven't seen her interested in anyone and pretty sure she shot down Wes. The guys live in another dorm with the football players, but they're here enough that I think they know the whole floor by now.

"You look…great. Really." I bite my tongue, so I don't tell her what I really think, because great doesn't begin to describe her. She looks like my every fantasy come to life.

"Thanks." She blushes and glances away. "Thinking I should change my top—"

"Don't!"

Her gaze snaps back to mine.

"I mean…I like your top." My gaze dips to her chest watching the not so steady rise and fall of her breathing. As my stare lingers, her nipples tighten. Fuck. I swallow and speak without thinking. "I want to pet you."

She makes a sound and my gaze jumps to hers. Her bright eyes are dark—turned-on dark. And yet she also looks panicked. Probably because I just said I wanted to pet her. Like a fucking psychopath. What the hell was I thinking?

I start laughing because there's no other way to fix this. "I'm sorry. Ugh, I sounded like a total perv."

Her face relaxes and she bites back a smile.

"I meant it's fuzzy like a cat and you pet cats so…"

She puts a hand over her mouth, but it does nothing to stop her burst of laughter.

I close my eyes briefly, mortified. "Okay, yeah, I'm not making it any better so I'm going to stop now."

Her hand falls and I'm gifted with her joyous laughter again, but this time I join her. Our laughter escalates to the point that we have to hold onto our door frames so we don't fall to the floor. Then there's a sudden change in her laughter, and I look up to see she's crying. Not laugh crying, but full out sobbing. That sobers me up immediately.

"Uh, are you okay?"

She covers up her face and nods then shakes her head in denial. I'm at an utter loss as to what just happened, and the longer I stand there and watch her cry, the more I feel like an ass. I cross the space between us and pull her into my arms.

"Shit, Ally Cat, please don't cry." I give her back an awkward pat.

"I'm sorry." The words are muffled from her hands covering her face.

"It's okay." I relax and let my arms rest comfortably around her waist. "Actually, go ahead and let it out." She nods and eases into my chest and continues to cry. When it looks like she isn't going to settle any time soon, I decide it's best if we get out of the hallway.

"I'm going to take you into my room. That okay?"

She nods, her tears still coming, but her sobs have lessened. I do my best not to let her go as I unlock my door. Thankfully, my room isn't a total disaster. I steer her to my desk chair, tossing the bag from the corner store on my bed then grab a tissue box from my closet and hand it to her.

She takes it, not meeting my eyes. I sit on my bed opposite her and just let her get it all out. I feel awkward as fuck. I want to help, but I also want to run away. I don't do well with crying females, but as RA it's probably my responsibility to make sure she's okay. Thankfully, the crying seems to be coming to an end and she's mostly wiping her eyes and blowing her nose. Her make-up is all shot to shit now, but there's no way I'm saying anything.

"I'm so sorry. That was a lot. I don't...Ugh, I'm so embarrassed."

"Don't be. Do you want to talk about it?"

She blows out a breath. "I don't know what happened. I was laughing and it felt really good then…then I remembered. It's Halloween and I'm supposed to be at a party and the last time I was at a party on Halloween, my life went to shit. And suddenly I wanted to go back in time to when Halloween was about candy and junk food and watching cheesy horror movie marathons with my parents, but…but…" Ally's face turns into this mixture of pain and anger. "That life is gone."

She closes her eyes and a few tears seep down her cheeks. Then she groans and wipes her cheeks. "I'm so sorry I'm such a mess. I…I *hate* Halloween."

My heart pounds at her confession while a commiserating anger rushes forward. "I get it, Ally Cat. I *fucking hate* Halloween too." The venom in my voice snaps her gaze to mine. Her face softens and somehow brightens at the same time. Like I just told her the best thing she could have ever heard. Her delight isn't joyful though, it's compassionate.

Her gaze falls then she smirks. "And yet, you still got dressed up."

"What are you talking about?"

She leans toward me and touches the center of my chest. I try not to jump at the rush of heat that spreads from where her fingertip rests. "Come on, Clark, your secret identity is showing."

I glance down then remember the Superman T-shirt I'm wearing. It's my laundry day shirt since it's a little on the snug side. "You think I'm dressed up as Clark Kent?"

"You are Clark Kent." She looks back at me with a lopsided smile and taps my glasses. "You even have the button-down shirt over your logo." She tugs on the flannel I threw on over it. Damn, I'm a fucking superhero and didn't even realize it.

"I don't dress up for Halloween." Not anymore.

She gives me a teasing look and taps my glasses again. "Sure, Clark, whatever you say."

"Listen, Ally *Cat*," I bop her cat ears, "you better cut it out or I won't tell you how I'm going to make your night better."

She raises her eyebrows at me, and I grab my bag from the store.

"Doritos?" she asks when I turn back to her.

"Yeah, Doritos make everything better." I toss the chips out and pull out the next item. "And Reese's Peanut Butter Cups. And last, but not least…ramen!" I hold up two of the microwavable cups of ramen.

Her eyes light up. "How did you know I loved ramen?"

"What college student doesn't? And that's not even the best part."

"What's the best part?"

"*Scream* is on Netflix."

"Oh, that's nineties cheesy horror at its best."

"So…want to skip the party and watch it with me?" This is probably a huge mistake, but she needs a distraction as much as I do.

She looks back at me and there's a softness in her eyes, a vulnerability that makes me want to kiss her. I want to taste this sweet soft side of her, but I also want to kiss her until I spark the fire back inside those gorgeous green eyes. I want to devour those red smeared lips until I erase her sadness. Until I erase mine.

"Are you sure?"

I've never been more unsure of anything. This girl has had me in knots from the moment I laid eyes on her, and getting tangled into any sort of relationship is the last thing I want. But I can't turn her away. She needs this. I do too. One thing has become startlingly clear in the past few minutes: I don't want to be alone tonight.

"I'm sure."

She nods. "Okay, I'd love that. So, ramen first? Or are the Doritos the appetizer?

"Ramen first. The Doritos are movie munchies."

"Sounds perfect," she says as she stands and holds out her hands for the ramen cups. "I'll add the water."

I hand them to her, and she heads to my bathroom to get water. I get up and grab some of the clothes that are on my floor then I hear a loud screech. I round my bed as she comes from the bathroom.

"Oh my God! Why didn't you tell me my face looks like Catwoman and Joker smashed their faces together?"

Suddenly I see exactly what she sees and it's the best fucking thing ever. I laugh so hard I collapse on my bed.

She glares at me and puts her hands on her hips, which makes her look more ridiculous and I lose it all over again. I can tell she's trying not to laugh, but quickly failing.

"Seriously, Clark," she says as a laugh escapes her. "You should have said something. I mean, come on, look at me!"

My stomach is cramping I'm laughing so hard. She comes over and gives me a shove and being on the edge of my twin sized bed, I start to slide off. Out of instinct I grab her, but she isn't expecting it and gravity is stronger than the both of us so I end up taking her down with me. She lands on top of me, and our laughter renews until our gazes lock and the realization that our faces are inches apart hits. My arm comes around her waist and I wonder if it has a mind of its own, because I definitely shouldn't have done that, but now that it's there I add pressure, pulling her into me a little more.

Her eyes fall to my mouth and I inhale sharply.

She cracks a smile. "I almost forgot I look like a clown."

"The Joker is not a clown," I say. "There's a difference. You know, the Joker and Catwoman are my favorite comic book villains."

She tilts her head, a faux frown on her lips. "Awww, you and Lex Luther have a falling out?"

"I'm *not* dressed up!"

She rolls her eyes. "Whatever, Clark."

I probably should let her go, but I don't. She isn't pulling away either, instead she settles in and lays her head on my shoulder. We're simply holding each other and it's oddly comforting considering we're virtually strangers.

"I played a game of Truth or Dare last Halloween," she says, her voice barely above a whisper. "I took a dare that went too far. Further than I even knew." My stomach knots at her confession while my mind goes to dark places. The thought of her experiencing any of them makes me want to punch something. Repeatedly.

"After that night, I broke. And as much as I thought I'd pieced myself together…I don't think I'll ever be whole again."

Fuck. I pull her in even more then stop, now wondering if it'll make her uncomfortable. But instead of recoiling, she curls into me. I want to tell her it's all going to be okay. That even broken, she's beautiful to me. That I'll fill her missing pieces.

Except I have no right to say those words. Not when I'm broken myself. But maybe I can make her feel less alone, so I give her my own confession.

"My mother died on Halloween two years ago. I understand what it's like to walk through life with missing pieces and barely held together with glue."

This is the first time I've told someone who didn't already know that my mother died. The tension in my chest isn't gone, but it seems to ache a little less.

She burrows into me. There are no words. No awkward apology or sorry for your loss. Just two people holding each other, taking care of our barely held together pieces. It's perfect. I'm not sure how much time passes, but I absorb every second.

"Is this weird?" she asks after a while.

"It should be."

"But it isn't," she confirms.

"No." I want to tell her this is the best fucking thing I've felt in a long time. I want to tell her I could stay like this all night. I even want to ask her to stay with me tonight, and the thought twists my stomach even as it makes my heart race. I need to put some distance between us and yet...I don't move. Maybe for tonight, it'll be okay to just let go. "Hey, how about we let what should be weird not be weird. What happens on Halloween, stays on Halloween."

I feel her smile form against my chest. "I like that."

"That'll be our mantra."

She nods and snuggles closer. Damn, she feels good. I love the feel of her soft curves pressing into me, the weight of her leg draped over mine. All I would have to do is pull her a few inches and she would be fully on top of me, her legs straddling me. My arm starts to tingle with the urge to do exactly that. It would be so easy. Then we'd be pressed fully together. Her mouth would be right where I could take it and I would finally know how soft those incredible lips are. My body tightens with need, and I silently curse myself. My horny ass mind is going to ruin everything.

She pushes up, our gazes instantly catch, and there's something in hers that makes me wonder if she's been thinking the same thing. Then her gaze falls to my mouth.

Fuck. Me.

I'm going to kiss her. And I don't even care if she looks like the Joker and Catwoman's love child. As soon as the thought crosses my mind, I snort a laugh.

She groans and starts to laugh as well. "I really need to wash my face, huh?"

"Maybe."

She pushes off me. "Okay, I'll be back. You cook the ramen and get the movie ready."

I have everything ready, and the movie queued up when she comes back. She's in a university crop sweater and pair of plaid pajama bottoms, now barefoot with her face completely washed of make-up. There is only a slight bit of black leftover around her eyes that gives her that smudged supermodel look. I didn't think it was possible for her to look sexier, but she's done it. We settle on my bed with our ramen and the bag of Doritos between us. Her phone dings right as Drew Barrymore answers the phone on screen. She picks up her phone and fires off a text. I notice a guy's name. Probably the same guy who regularly stops by her room.

"Were you supposed to go to that party with your boyfriend?"

She looks at me quizzically.

"I assume the guy I've seen visiting you is your boyfriend."

She twirls noodles around her fork. "He's not my boyfriend."

"Fuck buddy?"

"No, we haven't had sex. He's pledging a fraternity so I was supposed to be his date tonight."

"Is he going to be upset that you bailed?"

She shrugs. "Doubt it."

"I thought you two were high school sweethearts."

She looks at me then. "Why did you make that face when you said that?"

"What face?"

"You scrunched up your nose like you just smelled something terrible when you said high school sweethearts."

I didn't even realize I'd done that. "My parents were high school sweethearts. They weren't exactly the poster children for that working out. No one should get married young. Live life first."

Her brows furrow. She clearly disagrees. "Okay, I get it about living life, but what if you fall in love in college?"

"I won't."

She gives me a thoughtful look. "My parents met in college, got married at twenty-two, and they're still going strong."

"I'm not saying there aren't exceptions, but it's not for me."

She nods. "I suppose I understand. I'm not really interested in relationships at the moment either."

"So, you and that guy aren't dating?"

"No, we've kissed a few times. I don't know what that makes us. Friends that kiss sometimes? Joel and I did go to high school together but didn't know each other well. He was really nice to me after...everything, and we reconnected through one of the university's freshman forums in August."

She takes a sip of her broth then looks at me. "I see Kelly knocking on your door all the time."

I cringe. "Yeah, she's not very subtle. But I have no interest in going there with her. Besides, fraternizing with someone on your floor is highly discouraged."

"So, what are we doing? Are we fraternizing right now?" Her voice has a teasing lilt to it, but when I look at her, I don't feel anything amusing. My gaze zeroes in on her lips. I want to fraternize the hell out of those lips. I want to fraternize her whole body.

"I don't know what we're doing," I say honestly.

I watch her throat move through a hard swallow. I bring my gaze back to hers only to see she's looking at my mouth. I stop breathing. It would be so easy. Just lean in.

A scream comes from the television and we both startle and look over to see Ghostface take his first victim. The moment broken, I focus on the screen more. Ally's phone lights up a few more times until she turns it off. I pretend I don't notice, and she doesn't say anything. We barely watch the movie and instead talk about our majors and how she even hopes to go to grad school here at CTU since their psychology program is one of the best in the country.

Our attention moves back to the TV when Ghostface has Rose McGowan trapped in the garage, her death imminent. I glance at Ally and she's cringing. Without thinking, I take her hand and the tension in her body instantly releases. After McGowan's body is broken by the garage door, Ally looks at me and starts laughing. "This movie is so ridiculous. I don't know why it freaks me out."

I should let her hand go now, but I don't want to. I glance down at our linked hands and notice for the first time a tattoo on the inside of her wrist. It's a delicate line drawing of a sun and a single wave. I adjust my hand and rub my thumb over it. She jerks and pulls her hand away. I glance at her face, and she almost looks panicked. I want to ask, but it's clear the tattoo is an off-limits topic. So, I steer the conversation back to the movie.

"It's all pretty gross, but seriously, wouldn't the garage door just come back down once she hit the top?"

"I know! This is the nineties though, so maybe that's before they did that. We should look that up. We could fact check all the ridiculous deaths in horror movies. You know, see how plausible they are."

I laugh. "When you're cut in half, I think it's pretty plausible."

"Come on, Clark. You know cutting a person in half is not as easy as it is in horror movies."

"So, are you going to call me Clark all the time now?"

She smiles. "Yep. I've always thought you had a Clark Kent look anyway." Her cheeks turn rosy as if she didn't mean to confess that.

"Oh really?"

"Well, yeah, there's the glasses and, well, you're all huge and muscley. It's the whole nerdy-sexy package." As soon as the words are out she immediately slaps her hands over her mouth then she drops them, seemingly mortified she did so. I can't help it, I burst out laughing and her cheeks go from rosy to bright red.

"You think I'm sexy, Ally Cat?"

"Um, that's not what I meant... I was talking about the real Clark Kent. Not that Clark Kent is real, I just...oh, whatever," She rolls her eyes to me. "You know you're good-looking."

"But I didn't know *you* were looking."

"I'm not, but I'm not blind."

I smile and she blushes again. "You sure do blush a lot."

Her cheeks redden more. "You know, a gentleman wouldn't point that out."

"What makes you think I'm a gentleman?"

"You hugged me while I ugly cried and have provided me with junk food and a cheesy horror movie in my time of need."

I snort at that. "I suppose." Then I lean in close until my mouth is an inch from her ear. "Be careful, Ally Cat, a gentleman is simply a patient wolf."

She inhales sharply and turns toward me. Our lips are close, only a breath apart, and I'm suddenly feeling very wolfish and very very impatient. She swallows and her gaze falls to my mouth again. I'm not sure I'll be able to resist this time.

Another high-pitched scream comes from the television, and we jump apart. Fucking movie. She settles back, creating some distance between us, so I do too, and we watch the rest of the movie in mostly silence. I'm surprised when she suggests another movie. I put on a classic, *The Texas Chainsaw Massacre*.

A banging sound from the hallway jars me, and I glance at the TV to see that it's gone to screensaver mode. We fell asleep. My movement rouses Ally because she seems equally confused. Then I hear it again. Banging and all sorts of commotion in the hallway. I glance at the clock and see it's almost two in the morning. Pumpkin time for the partiers.

"Open up, Al!"

Ally groans, and I realize she is Al. What a horrible nickname.

"Ally, please."

It hits me this must be the friend she sometimes kisses. He bangs again, and now I'm worried.

"Is he pissed?"

"Probably drunk," she answers as she gets off my bed and heads toward my door.

I don't like to get into other people's business, but there's no way in hell I'm letting her face her irate friend alone, so I follow her to the door. She opens it and another Avenger whirls around. His eyes briefly meet mine before they go back to Ally. I can't see her face, but whatever her expression is, it immediately softens his.

"I just couldn't do it, Joel. I'm sorry, but..." Her voice breaks and he immediately pulls her into his arms. I almost step forward to wrench her away but stop myself. She's not mine.

"I know. It's okay. I should have been here." He pulls back and frames her face in his hands then kisses her on the forehead.

He says something softly to her. I can't make it out, but she nods and sinks back into his arms. Their bond is stronger than I anticipated. She hands him her key from her pocket, and he opens the door.

She turns to me. "Thanks for tonight. I needed...a friend, I guess."

I know what she means. She needed someone who under-stood the pain. And I suppose after tonight we'll be considered friends. Just what I need—a friend I have very unfriendly feel-ings for.

"Yeah, me too."

She gives me a small smile then disappears into her room

with Joel, and I ignore the pang piercing my chest at seeing her leave with him.

The elevator dings and a rush of loud students spill into the hallway, Wes and Nate in front. I should have known they'd end up here.

"Hey, Lo! Look at my party favor!" Wes holds up a bottle of tequila as he sways my way.

"It's not a party favor when you steal it," Nate says with a shake of his head.

I take the bottle from his hand. "You've had enough." Then I spin the top off and take a big swig. "But I haven't."

chapter four

Ally

3. Day Drinking
5. Eat at The Hub

Clark: Meet me at The Hub at 2

I glance at him a few seats down.

Me: Why?

Clark: Lunch. A celebration of getting through the first week of our last semester. See you there.

I stare at my phone for a few seconds, fully prepared to say no, then I silence it and stuff it in my backpack. Clark and I have barely spoken since my sex stash disaster on Monday, and today I'm apparently having lunch with him. Our few previous lunches together have always been at the student union and always spontaneous, but The Hub is a restaurant and bar right off campus famous for their burgers. Not that I can attest to how good their burgers are because I've never been there. It's literally on my list—or it was until I tore it up.

This will be the first time Clark and I have met off-campus outside of Halloween. My stomach does a flip-flop and doesn't stop through the rest of my classes. By the time I'm standing in front of The Hub, I'm such a bundle of nerves I think I might throw up. Why am I so nervous? It's just Clark. Except Clark has never been just Clark.

"Hey!"

My gaze is drawn to the wooden patio where Clark is leaning against the railing with a crooked smile on his lips. Heart Skipping smile. That has to be what this one is called since I'm pretty sure that's what just happened to mine. I wave and head his way. I have to say, I'm pretty jazzed about finally being here. I've always longed to join the fun-filled patio, but every time I convinced myself it wasn't my scene. Not that I really have a scene.

"Well, you picked the perfect day for the patio," I say as I approach him. Texas winters are like Forrest Gump's box of chocolates, you never know what you're going to get. Temps can be in the forties one day and seventies the next. Today is one of those wonderful spring-like days.

"I know, right? Do you know what you want? I'm starving."

"I've never eaten here before." I hate how dull that sounds.

His mouth twists in this odd smile. "Can I confess something? He leans closer and my heart takes a hard jump. "Neither I have."

"Are you kidding? I thought I was the only person on campus that hasn't eaten here yet."

He shrugs. "I've drank here before and stolen a fry or two but haven't had a burger."

"Well, I guess we get to cross it off our list today…uh, so to speak."

There's that odd smile again. "We sure do." He holds out a menu to me. "I grabbed this and already know what I want."

I look it over. "Oooh, I'm getting this one." I point to a burger that sounds like a huge cheesy mess. He looks at it and his eyes widen as a huge smile spreads across his lips and my stomach flutters. I'll simply call this smile, Beautiful.

"That's the one I'm getting. Why don't you snag a table and I'll order for us?"

He heads inside to order, and I find a table. There's a part of me that wishes I still had my list so I could feel the satisfaction of drawing a line through this one. Maybe I could make another list with non-sexual stuff like this on it. As soon as the thought enters my mind, I dismiss it. This is not the semester for distractions. Now that I know exactly what my course load is, I'm not sure how I'm going to keep my head above water to graduate.

I look up to see Clark talking to a table full of students. They're all laughing then one of the guys gets up and aims his phone to take a selfie of all of them, with Clark leaning in to get in the shot. I look away as the table erupts in laughter. When I see him on campus like this, with people surrounding him, it always surprises me. I'm so used to Halloween Clark that I don't know what to think of football star, Logan Mackenzie. But man, watching him this past season was electrifying.

A salt-rimmed pint glass is set in front of me. "What's this?"

"Please tell me you know a margarita when you see one," he says as he sits across from me.

"Yes, I know what a margarita is. I meant, why did you get it for me?"

"Because it's Friday and it's happy hour and it's one of the best margaritas in town, which is saying something considering how many amazing Mexican restaurants there are."

"But…I, um, was going to go study after this."

"It's Friday."

"So?"

He watches me as he takes a sip from his own margarita. "I probably know the answer to this since you're graduating early, but do you ever take a break?"

"Of course, I do." My statement is far more adamant than the truth.

"Great! Then you can enjoy this beautiful Friday afternoon with a little happy hour."

I open my mouth to protest, but I don't have a reason. He's right. And this is exactly why I made that stupid list. Since I started the semester off with margaritas, might as well finish the first week with one. I pick up my drink and take a sip and immediately cough.

"Holy tequila, Batman!" These are stronger than Ginny's homemade ones—and that's saying something.

Clark laughs. "It's good, right?"

"Really strong, but yeah, it's tasty. Thanks."

He lifts his glass in toast. "To kicking off our last semester with a little day drinking."

I clink my glass to his. "Crazy, huh? I can't believe we're graduating. Not that I don't have grad school ahead of me, but still…"

"Yeah, as much as I'm ready to put college behind me. I'll definitely miss some things, especially stuff like this."

He's always talked about how he can't wait to graduate, though he's never said why.

"So, how have you been, Ally Cat? You and your ex still broken up, or did you reconcile?"

"No, we're done for good."

"What happened?"

"He fell in love."

"Whoa, did he cheat on you?"

"Yeah, I really don't want to talk about it." Joel and I have barely spoken since I walked in on him and Matthew. The fact that he was with a man wasn't a surprise. I'd always known Joel was bisexual. He dated both men and women before we started dating. No, it's the fact that he broke the trust between us that I can't quite forgive.

"You okay? Want me to rough him up?" he asks, clearly teasing though I imagine he's the kind of guy who would go to bat for you.

I laugh at that. "Nah, it's okay. I would hate for you to mess up your precious football hands."

He snorts a laugh. "Yeah, wouldn't want to mess up these gnarly digits." He holds up his hands and I laugh and take them in my own. His hands aren't pretty by any stretch. His nails are short and blunt, and his fingertips are rough with calluses. I turn over his hands and his palms are equally rough. I gently rub my fingers over the firm skin. He inhales sharply and I glance up at him.

"Did I hurt you?"

He's utterly still and he's looking at me intensely. He gives his head a small shake and I fight the urge to move my thumb over his palm again so I can see his response this time. Though, if I'm honest with myself, I'm not sure I'm ready to experience it.

I gently put his hands down. "You do have pretty gnarly hands."

The right side of his mouth quirks up. "Not pretty, but talented."

His gaze falls from my face to my chest and now I'm imagining those rough hands moving over my skin, feeling every crack and dip in his palm as he cups my breast.

I clear my throat and his gaze jumps to mine. My face must

reveal my thoughts because the smile forming on his lips now says, *I know what you're thinking.*

"Um, so, guess since you're talking about graduating then you aren't staying on for another year of eligibility." I need to get us away from this hot tension between us, and I was sure he'd stay on to play another year since he didn't join the team until his junior year.

"I ended up declaring for the draft and got invited to the NFL Combine next month."

"No kidding! Clark, that's amazing!"

He nods. "Yeah, it's pretty exciting." His voice sounds nowhere near excited though. He looks downright pissed about it.

"And you're not excited, because…?"

He breaks my gaze and shrugs. "I'm in a slump. Making mistakes. My times are off. If I show up there with my latest stats, I'll be laughed off the field."

"Do you know why things aren't clicking?"

He glances back at me and a searing smile forms on his lips. I don't know what to name this one. It's a combination of several smiles—all the dangerous ones. It's a Sexy Danger Combo.

"My roommates think it's because I need to get laid."

It suddenly feels like someone cranked up the heat inside me. "Oh. Um, do you think that's what it is?"

He shrugs and picks up his margarita. "It's been awhile."

I want to ask what *awhile* is. I shouldn't. Or should I?

"You want to ask how long, don't you?" he asks after he takes a drink.

I cringe. "Kinda. My 'awhile' is pretty big, so I'm curious as to what 'awhile' is to you."

"I'll tell you mine if you tell me yours. When exactly did you and Joel break up?"

"A couple weeks before Halloween. But the last time we

were together was probably just after school started. Maybe August." His brows shoot up as if surprised by that. "Your turn," I say, not wanting to dwell on the fact that my boyfriend and I didn't have sex for six weeks before we broke up.

"End of July."

My jaw drops. Am I hearing him right? I've seen Clark walking around campus with girls plenty of times and hardly ever the same one. He's a freaking football player and just had a killer season. "Are you serious?"

"Yep. Is it any wonder that both of us were so ready for the sex-pocalypse, Ally Cat?"

My cheeks burn with embarrassment. I was really hoping we would pretend Monday didn't happen.

"So, you gonna tell me about your bag of sex? Because I have to be honest, if the sex-pocalypse is a real thing then I definitely want to get on board."

I laugh again. "The story isn't as exciting as you'd think."

"Humor me."

"My friend Ginny is starting to host those adult toy parties to make money, and Sunday night she got all her stuff in, so she invited me over to check it out. In the process, we got wasted and after I passed out, she stuffed my bag with some of her freebies as a joke."

Clark thinks this is hilarious and declares he has to meet Ginny right as our burgers are delivered, and I'm thankful for the distraction. I lift my bun and take in the juicy burger smothered in tomatoes, guacamole, and queso. I look at him with a huge grin.

"If this tastes as good as it looks, I might become a regular here."

He looks equally ravenous. "I'll be here with you."

I pick up the massive burger and already have grease sliding down my hands. I take a big bite and groan as my eyes flutter closed. Now I see why they're famous for their burgers.

I know my mouth is covered in guac and queso, and I don't care. There's no way I'm putting this burger down to wipe my mouth.

I fully expect Clark to laugh at me, but when I look at him, there's no smile. His gaze is intently watching my mouth. I dart out my tongue to clean it up as best as possible and his gaze shoots up to my eyes. The way he's looking at me reminds me of the way he looked at me in class when we were flirting. Desire tightens my stomach, but I'm not sure I'm ready to deal with these feelings so I cross my eyes at him and take an overly huge bite of my burger to break the tension. It works. He laughs then picks up his own burger. We don't talk again until we've both devoured every bite.

"Oh my God, I can't believe I ate that whole thing." I press a hand to my stomach, a little afraid the button on my jeans might pop.

"It was worth it though." He throws his napkin on his plate in surrender.

"Absolutely. Hands down the best burger I've ever eaten."

He leans forward with a satisfied smile on his lips. "Now you can say you've crossed two things off your list."

At the word *list*, I freeze. My gaze snaps to his, and his own eyes go wide—with guilt. Oh my God, he read my list.

"You said The Hub was on your list," he says quickly.

"That's one thing." I sit up straight. "You just said I crossed two things off my list. What's the other thing?"

He opens his mouth then closes it and my stomach sinks.

"Day drinking," he finally says. His shoulders slump in guilt, but he meets my gaze straight on.

Oh no no no no no no.

My stomach twists and I'm afraid my burger is about to come back up. He saw my list, my very private list, full of embarrassing and explicit things. Things he can exploit.

Things, if they were to become public, could ruin my life. Again.

Panic starts building inside me, and I feel the burn of tears behind my eyes.

"You had no right," I finally say.

"I didn't know what it was when I picked it up."

"But you still read it!"

"I know and I'm sorry, but it's no big deal."

"No big deal?! It's personal and private and *mine*. It isn't even serious, but it still wasn't meant for anyone else's eyes but mine."

"Are you going to do the list?"

The question jars me out of my red haze momentarily. "What? None of your business!"

"I don't think you are," he says, his expression challenging me.

"What does it matter? I was drunk when I made it. It was a joke. Can you please just forget you ever saw it?"

He leans forward, his hot gaze holds me captive. "There's no way I'm forgetting that list."

I swallow at the rough intensity in his voice.

"I think you need me," he continues. "Look, I've already helped you cross off numbers three and four."

"You know the numbers? Do you have a photographic memory or something?"

He glances away, looking guilty as hell.

"Clark?"

He cringes and my stomach jumps into my throat as I wait. "Okay, don't freak out, but I snapped a picture of it."

I lose it. "You did what!? Delete it! Right now."

"Ally Cat—"

"Right now!" I yell as fear claws at me.

"Will you sit down and lower your voice, please, or

everyone is going to be interested in what we're talking about."

It isn't until that moment that I realize I'm standing, my hands balled up in fists as I lean across the table in a threatening manner. I glance around, and the table full of Clark's fans are looking at us with shocked or amused expressions. Great! Our fight is probably already trending. I take a quick sweep of their hands and thankfully no one is recording us. I take a breath and calmly sit down, but I'm nowhere near calm. My whole body is shaking. This is way more than him reading something private—he has proof. He has leverage. He has the key to my ruin.

"Why would you take a picture of it? What are you going to do with it?" I whisper harshly.

He leans in and matches my volume. "Jesus, nothing. I wanted more time to read it, that's all."

"Why? Why do you care?"

"Because I want to help you cross off the items on your list." He inches closer, his gaze falling to my lips. "Every. Single. One."

Time seems to stay still. I watch the flash of heat in his gaze as his words slowly sink in. He wants to do my list. *All* of my list.

I'm suddenly very hot. Then everything hits me like a bucket of cold water.

I narrow my gaze at him. "Oh my God, you think you do this list with me, and you'll suddenly get your football mojo back."

He, at least, has the grace to blush before he aims a determined expression my way.

"Look, you have a lot to get through in a short amount of time. Going out and trying to find someone you actually want to do those things with takes work. Trust me, bar hook-ups are rarely as good as they seem. And some of those things are pretty personal, so you need to be with someone you can trust."

"Trust! You think I trust you after what you did?"

"Can we put the picture aside, please? We can help each other out here."

"Are you seriously trying to tell me you're doing this out of the kindness of your heart and not because you want easy sex?"

"Of course, I'm in it for the sex. Hot and kinky sex at that. Your list is fucking hot."

My cheeks flame, and I quickly turn my gaze away before he sees my interest.

"Okay yes, your list is perfect for me right now. I'm going to be busting my ass to stay afloat with all my classes, my internship, and training. And I'm sure you're going to be stressed to the max with your classes, too. This makes sense. We need sex, and you have a sex to-do list. Do you really want to put in the effort to find someone to do those things with when you have someone right here who's willing and able?"

I roll my eyes. "You're missing the point of the list, which is to be wild and spontaneous. I'm not exactly doing that if everything is planned out."

"We can do spontaneous, and we can definitely do wild." His smile is positively wolfish.

I shake my head. "I don't know why I'm having this conversation with you. I don't want to do the list. I tore it up and flushed it down the toilet."

"What!? Why would you do that?"

"Because it wasn't serious!"

"Are you telling me you aren't interested in doing any of it?"

"No." I can hear the lie in my voice, and I didn't even realize I was lying until that moment.

"Liar. You made that list for a reason. And I don't blame you."

"What do you mean by that?"

He shrugs. "I'm just surprised you and your boyfriend didn't knock some of those things out."

Now he's throwing in my face that my sex life has been lackluster. Yeah, maybe it's the reason I made the list, but it's still a dick move. "You know what, screw you."

He smiles slowly and leans forward. "Honey, I'd love for you to. I'll show you exactly what you've been missing."

A traitorous spike of heat slices through me as I see red. Smug asshole! I grab my margarita and toss it in his face.

He blinks and looks at me in shock. I grab my stuff and pick up his margarita as I get to his side of the table. He doesn't even try to avoid it as I pour it over his head.

I cringe as a wake of jeers and cheers follow my exit, but I'm too furious to care right now.

chapter five

"Damn, it's colder than a witch's tit in a brass bra. Can we please have last week's weather back?"

There's a shiver to Ginny's voice as she huddles further into her coat though I use the word *coat* loosely. What she has on is made for fashion, not warmth.

"What does that even mean? Why a witch's tit and not any tit in a brass bra? And who wears brass bras?"

"Sheesh, Ally, I don't know what it means. *Tit* is just a funny word to say."

I laugh at that. "I guess so. You wouldn't be so cold if you wore a proper coat."

"It's Texas! How often do we need a proper coat? Besides, this is my favorite coat. It's too cute not to wear."

"Says the girl freezing her tits off."

She barks out a laugh. "See! It's funny!"

I shake my head at her. I met Ginny Ellis my sophomore year when we shared a class together. She plopped into the seat next to me, her almost black hair piled on her head in a messy bun and her face flawlessly made up, giving her this comfy chic look that I could never pull off. She immediately grabbed my hand and said, "Fuck me, our professor is hot." We've been friends ever since.

"Come on," I take her elbow. "We're almost there."

We pick up our pace and when we get to Cafe Jolt, it's packed with people forcing us to squeeze our way in and take our place at the end of a very long line.

"Maybe we should've gone to Starbucks," I say, though I prefer Cafe Jolt's coffee.

Ginny makes a face of disgust. "It'll be just as crowded, and it doesn't nearly have the view this one does."

"View? What are you talking about?" Starbucks is literally three doors down. The view is the same.

Ginny nudges me and nods her head toward the barista taking orders. His name is Ben and he's almost too pretty to look at. Seriously, he puts Bradley Cooper to shame with his chiseled jaw and baby blue eyes. He's a huge flirt, but I think he does that to keep his tip jar full.

"I suppose you have a point."

"You're going to ask him out today."

"What?!" I say it so loudly the guy in front of us turns and looks at us.

"Asking a guy out is on your list and you two eye-fuck each other every time you're in."

The guy in front of us snorts and I feel my cheeks burn. "Will you keep it down? And I have not."

I've never really thought about going there with Ben. Either because I was with Joel or because Ben is the kind of charming

I immediately don't trust. Even if his flirting has always given me little zings. Zings I never really got from Joel. But I wasn't looking for them from him either.

"Whatever. He's always trying to get you to go out with him so he's perfect for the list."

"I flushed the list down the toilet."

Ginny grabs my arm and spins me toward her, her amber eyes full of shock. "What? Tell me you're fucking with me right now."

"I'm not. And will you shush!" I whisper not as quietly as I intend.

"Ally! Why would you do that?"

"Because we were drunk when we made it."

"So?"

"It was a joke."

"No, it wasn't. You were seriously excited about it."

"I was excited, Because. I. Was. Drunk."

"Nope, not buying it. You wouldn't have flushed it without a better reason."

I sigh. I might as well fess up. Ginny found out about my past one drunken night so she'll understand and maybe leave this whole list business alone. "Remember when I spilled my purse on the first day of classes?"

Ginny bites back a smile. "Yeah."

"Don't you dare laugh. I'm still plotting how to kill you for that." Ginny's smile widens though she does her best to keep it from fully forming. "Well, the list was one of the items that fell out, and a guy in my class found it."

Ginny's mouth falls. "No way! Did he read it?"

"He said he didn't, but I flipped out and flushed it. Then I found out he did read it. He actually took a picture of it and now he wants to 'help' me with it."

"He didn't! Oh my God, are you okay? This must be freaking you out. Has he deleted it?"

"I don't know, though he seems to have memorized it."

"What a perv!"

I shrug. "It's Clark so I really don't know what to think."

"Wait." Ginny clutches my arm tightly and forces me to meet her eyes. "Clark? Your Halloween guy?"

"Yeah." Ginny smiles and I don't like it. It reminds me of the smile she wore the night we made the list. "What?"

"Um, the guy you've had a serious crush on for the last three years wants to help you with your list. I'm seriously not seeing a problem here."

"I haven't—"

She puts up her hand, stopping me. "Don't even deny it. What did you tell him?"

"I dumped my margarita on him."

Ginny looks at me, incredulous. "Are you serious?"

I shrug. "I found out he had a picture of my list. He deserved it."

"Wait. You dumped your margarita on him? Were you at The Hub?"

"Yeah, how did you know?"

A pained expression comes over her face and my stomach knots. "I hate to tell you, but your little stunt is making its rounds on social media."

"What?"

"Don't worry, your back is to the camera so you don't know who it is. I didn't even realize it was you."

I close my eyes and pray I don't throw up. "Show me," I say though I really don't want to see it.

Ginny digs out her phone and starts typing and swiping away. "By the way, you didn't tell me Clark is really Lo-"

"Stop. Don't say his name."

She looks up at me. "Um, surely you know who he is."

"I try not to think of him by his real name." I shrug. "It feels too personal. Our Halloween aliases work for us."

Ginny looks at me like I've lost my mind before she holds up her phone and plays a video. It starts after I threw my margarita on him so he's already soaked. It shows me standing next to him pouring his glass on him as he sits there and takes it. The title of the video reads, *Logan Mackenzie had no defense against that margarita.*

I cringe. Damn, I didn't mean for him to be humiliated online.

"I'm so impressed," Ginny says. "That was badass. And yes, he totally deserved what he got, but I still think you should take him up on his help."

"First off, having him embarrassed online was not my aim and I feel pretty shitty about it. And second, are you crazy? He took a picture, Gin. Of all people, I wouldn't think he would do that. Though I don't know why I'm surprised at this point. I've been so mad I haven't even approached him to make sure he's deleted it. I've just wanted to hide and forget it all happened."

My therapist even helped me work through different options on how to address the situation and I've done none of them. What a great psychology student I am.

"Okay, forget him for now." She tucks her phone away. "You need to ask out hot coffee guy."

"Ginny—"

"Come on, it's easy and harmless, and what's the worst that can happen? You don't have a good time? At least you get a free dinner out of it."

I glance at Ben and our gazes catch. His expression perks up and he smiles. My heart kicks up a little. Not like it does with Clark, but it's still a good feeling.

"See," Ginny says as she elbows me. "He's totally into you."

My stomach flutters. I've never asked out a guy before. My high school relationship started with him pursuing me, and

Joel and I went from friends to more, completely skipping over the getting-to-know-you flirty stage.

"I suppose a date is harmless."

Ginny bounces on her toes as she lets out a little squeal, and I nudge her to get her to calm down. A few minutes later we're finally at the counter and my stomach is in a thousand knots.

"Hey there," Ben says. "Have a good Christmas break?" He gives me a friendly smile, nothing label-worthy.

"Yeah, it was good. You?"

"I had to work so wasn't much of a break. You want your usual?"

"Yeah, that would be great."

He rings it up, and Ginny gives me a not-so-subtle kick to the leg from where she stands at the next cashier. I glare at her then take my card out. I lean over as I hand it over to him. "You haven't asked me out this time."

His eyes go wide with surprise then presses his hand over his heart. "A guy can only take so many rejections."

"Maybe I won't say no this time."

Okay, maybe I'm technically not asking him out, but this still counts, in my opinion.

He raises an eyebrow. "Oh yeah? My fraternity is having a party next Friday. Want to be my date?"

A fraternity party isn't exactly what I had in mind. I school my expression to not show my disappointment though. I suppose a party would be an uncommittable way to ease myself into the dating world. And if I remember correctly, I had frat party on my list. Two items in one. Not that I'm doing my list.

"Yeah, that would be great."

"I'll put my number on your cup. Text me so I have yours." He winks at me and my stomach flutters. I'm not sure if it's because I'm excited about the date or dreading it.

"Great," I say, suddenly feeling awkward so I move out of the way and join Ginny as we wait for our orders.

"You didn't ask him out," Ginny whispers to me.

"Sure, I did. I gave him the go-ahead before he asked. It totally counts."

She rolls her eyes. "Fine. You have a date and that's all that matters."

My order is called out, and sure enough, Ben's number is on it. I glance up and he's looking at me with a flirty smile. Another smile flashes in my mind and instantly sends a fire to my nerves. No, I don't want to think of Clark. This date with Ben couldn't come at a more perfect time.

chapter six

I'm in full-out grovel mode. I handled everything wrong with Ally the other day. I didn't even mention my own list, and now she won't talk to me. I try to sit next to her during class, but she has a bag in both seats on either side of her. She doesn't even look at me. My texts apologizing go unanswered. I decided to back off, thinking if I kept pushing, I'd drive her further away, but now it's getting harder and harder to deny Nate and Wes' theory. While running practice plays, I got my ass handed to me by an offensive lineman because I was late off the snap. Then the fucking QB evaded my tackle in a simple move I should have predicted, leaving me flat on my stomach. I need Ally and her list.

Me: Hey Ally Cat, want another margarita? I might have some still left in my shirt to fill two pint glasses.

I watch as her phone lights up from where I'm sitting in class. She glances at the screen then goes back to making notes.

Me: Okay, okay, I get it. Shirt margarita doesn't sound very appealing. How about we get a fresh one with a side of epic groveling?

Me: If I don't win you over then you can douse me again. This time maybe we can go with a house marg. I'd hate to waste the good tequila on my shirt again.

Finally, she picks up her phone and my screen lights up.

Ally Cat: Stop! We're in class

Me: Let's get lunch after

Ally Cat: Running to my next class

Me: I can run with you

Ally Cat: You can't do epic groveling while running. That's a cop-out.

Me: Pls start talking to me again. All jokes aside, I need to properly apologize.

She glances at me and this time our gazes hold. Her expression softens and, for the first time in over a week, I start to breathe easier.

Me: I have an idea. I'll pick you up on Sat morn. Wear something sporty and a light jacket.

Ally Cat: Why?

Me: #7 + epic groveling

Ally Cat: I don't know what #7 is. And nope.
Pls delete and leave me alone.

Me: I will. Promise. Just come with me. Hear
me out. Let me prove I'm not a complete
asshole.

After I hit send, I cringe at the word promise. I hate that word and try to never use it and yet I've thrown it around several times since the sex-pocalypse class day, plus I did that stupid pinky promise. All my life, my parents did pinky promises with each other, with me. It was basically our way of saying I love you. I still don't understand why I did it without thinking. I don't make promises, not when they're too easy to break.

She doesn't respond, but when I show up at her place Saturday morning, she's thankfully waiting for me.

"I'm only doing this because I need you to prove that you deleted the picture," she says as she gets in my truck.

"Fair enough."

She looks at me, the anger on her face loud and clear. "Am I appropriately dressed?"

I glance at her again, not that I need to. Her skin hugging yoga pants and fitted long sleeve shirt are burned in my brain. So simple but looks super sexy on her.

I clear my throat. "You look good, Ally Cat."

We head downtown and as we get closer to Lady Bird Lake, she perks up.

"Are we SUPing?" I love the excitement in her voice.

I glance over and smile. "She remembers!"

It isn't long before we're standing on a floating dock, waiting our turn to get our stand-up paddleboards. Ally keeps fiddling with her life vest, which is awkwardly big on her. I can't help but laugh because she's only making it look worse.

"You look ridiculous, too," she says defensively.

"I know. Don't worry, we can take them off as soon as we push off."

"Oh good."

"Didn't you go to high school here? How have you never done this?"

"We moved here after…Halloween. My mom was already hired to take over for President Bradbery when he retired mid-year."

As with every time she mentions that particular Halloween, her eyes fill with sadness. And that's the last thing I want her to feel today.

"So, how cold do you think the water will be when you fall in?"

She looks at me with wide eyes. *"When?"*

I shrug. "All first timers fall."

"What? Clark! Why the hell would you take me to do this in January then? And why not tell me to wear a swimsuit? No, we're not doing this. It might be seventy degrees today, but that water is going to be fucking freezing."

I start laughing and she stares at me like I've lost my mind.

"I'm totally fucking with you. You shouldn't fall."

"Shouldn't?" She looks over at the paddleboards with a worried gaze.

"Look, I can't guarantee it won't happen, but if you fall then I'll let you push me in too."

The tension eases in her stance, and an all too delighted expression comes over her face. "Deal." I'll gladly dip into frigid water to see that smile on her face.

She starts fiddling with her life jacket again, and my gaze catches on a man on the hike and bike trail behind her. I freeze, realizing why. It's my dad. He's bent over with his hands on his knees, catching his breath, and a woman is jumping up and down in front of him. He's smiling at her, and when he stands fully, she throws her arms around him and gives him a kiss on the lips. He pulls her in and kisses her back. His girlfriend. My stomach tightens, and this churning anger starts bubbling within me.

After everything that happened, why the fuck does he get to be happy? Why does he get to move on when *she's* gone?

My dad laughs, and they slowly separate. His gaze turns my way, and I quickly turn around. When I glance back, they're heading toward the parking lot, arm in arm.

"Who is that?"

I look back at Ally, and she's looking between me and my dad.

"My dad."

We're called over to our paddleboards. I can't even enjoy watching Ally cautiously get her balance as she gets on it on her knees. All I can see is my dad and that woman. Once we're both on the water, I stand, and Ally does get a laugh out of me as she works on finding her balance to stand. Once she's up, we get going. I put all my effort into paddling, and it isn't long before my arms are burning. But the pain still doesn't get my dad out of my mind.

"Clark! What the hell?!"

The words jar me out of my thoughts, and I look around to see that Ally is way behind me. I can't fully see her expression from her, but I know a hundred percent it isn't happy. She balances her paddle on the board then sits.

Shit. I can't believe I left her like that. I turn around and paddle back toward her. When I get back to her, she's hugging her knees, glaring at me.

"You know I'm glad I'm not really doing the list because if this is your idea of doing it together, you suck at it."

"I'm sorry, Ally Cat. It was like I was on autopilot. I didn't even realize I was going that fast."

She looks away, still pissed.

"Come on, we'll do it the right way now. Together and slowly."

She tips her head back up. "I'm not going anywhere with you until you talk about your dad."

"I don't want to talk about him."

"You blame him for your mom's death."

I stiffen. I suppose she knows enough about what happened that night from our Halloweens together to piece that together. "I'm not talking about this."

"Too fucking bad! I'm tired of bearing the brunt of your anger every time you see your dad."

She's referring to last Halloween and how I treated her. When I lied to her.

"You blame him. Just admit it."

"Fine! I blame him! If he'd just kept his damn promise that night, she wouldn't be dead. But no, he was more interested in fucking another woman."

She sucks in a breath. "Oh no…"

I sigh and sit on my board and set my foot on hers to keep us from floating apart. "He turned off his phone. I couldn't get a hold of him. I tried and tried, but it kept going to voicemail." I take a breath. "I had to deal with the ambulance, the hospital, everything…all by myself. It was a good thing I was already eighteen. Finally, I went to the apartment he had during their separation and there was a woman there with him."

"What happened when you told him?"

I shrug. "He was devastated, but I was too angry to care."

Still am. Ally's expression softens, and I know she hears the unspoken words. I turn my gaze away. I don't want her pity.

"Is that the same woman?"

I shake my head. "That woman was a one-night thing. But

two weeks before Halloween my parents had gotten together. I'd played hooky from school and saw my dad leaving our house." I watched them interlock their pinkies and press their foreheads together before sharing a kiss. I couldn't even remember the last time I'd seen them do it. I shake off the memory. "Just another broken promise. That woman today was the same one I saw last Halloween."

She leans forward and takes my hand in hers. I want to tell her the truth about last Halloween, how I lied to her. How all I wanted was to take her comfort, but didn't trust myself not to take it too far.

"Okay, I'll start paddling again."

I laugh. "Glad my trauma assuaged your anger."

She laughs. "Let's see how long it takes us to get to the Congress bridge."

"Let's do it."

We both stand and grab our paddles. We let our competitive nature kick in and go balls out to get to the bridge as fast as we can. Conversation is light, and I'm mostly laughing at how terrible she is at going straight. Once we get to the bridge, we both let out exhausted breaths and immediately drop down so we're lying on our boards.

"Everything burns. My arms. My legs. My abs."

"I'm Jell-O," I say, the same burn flowing through my whole body.

We don't say anything for a while; we simply float and catch our breath. Finally, she sits up, leaning back on her hands as she takes in the skyline. Unable to resist, I pull out my phone and open my camera. I frame the picture so it's mostly the lake and the Austin skyline, but it also includes part of Ally's outstretched legs, ponytail, and shoulder, her face completely hidden. I want to post the picture, but even though you can't see who it is, I don't. I know she wouldn't like it. It'll just be for me.

"This is great. Thank you." She turns to face me, a happy smile on her face. I return her smile, loving that I was able to do this for her.

"I'm glad you're having fun." I dig into my backpack and pull out two water bottles and toss one to her.

She mutters a thanks, her cheeks turning pink. "So, is this part your epic groveling?"

"Is it working?"

She takes a drink, but I can see a hint of smile that tells me I'm winning her over. But I do still need to grovel.

"Hey, I didn't mean to judge your relationship with Joel. I deserved to get margarita thrown in my face."

She dips her head. "No, you didn't. Or at least, you didn't deserve to be made fun of online. I'm sorry about that."

I wave off her apology. "It's old news now. And it wasn't so bad. I can handle a little razzing."

She sighs. "Clark, you took a picture of my list. It's an extreme invasion of privacy."

I grimace. "Yeah, not proud of that. You're right, it was out of line. It was only so I could have time to read it."

"You haven't...shown it to anyone, have you?" I hate the fear and uncertainty in her voice. Hate that I put it there.

"No. Of course, not. I know it wasn't meant for my eyes, but I feel as protective about your list as you do. I would never share it. Promise."

Fuck. There's that word again. At least this one I know I'll have no problem keeping.

"You'll delete it?"

"I'll delete it." I pull out my phone and bring the picture up, but before I delete it, I text it to her. I hear her phone ping and bring up the picture again. I show it to her with the delete button hovering over the image. I press it and she releases a huge breath.

"Thank you. It's completely deleted?"

"I swear. I did send it to you first." She opens her mouth, but I hold my hand out to stop her. "You should have it. I think it's more important to you than you're letting on."

She shakes her head and turns her gaze away from mine. "It was a joke."

"That doesn't mean it has to stay that way. Look, another reason I took the picture is because I wanted to compare it to my own list." I dig into the waterproof bag in my backpack and pull out my list and hand it out to her.

She looks from it to me before she takes it and slowly opens it.

"I made it freshman year, and it's been stuffed in the bottom of my desk drawer gathering dust ever since. I started out wanting to live it up, but I've barely scratched the surface."

She scans it. "Oh my God, it has a lot of the same stuff on it."

"I know. You helped me cross off *eat at Hub*."

She looks at me. "There's no way you haven't done a keg stand."

"Nope, never."

"Or played beer pong?"

"I've played once, but my list says win and I've never won."

She looks at me suspiciously. "You're a football player. How did you lose?"

"I'm on defense. And I played against the quarterback."

She shakes her head and looks at the list again. "You seemed to take care of the sex stuff pretty well."

I shrug. "I didn't say I've been a monk."

"You actually have threesome on here."

"Hey, that's on your list, too. And, as you can see, it's not crossed off on mine."

"Ginny added that one, and I promptly axed it."

"I'm perfectly happy for my threesome to be with you and your little pink friend." I give her a teasing wink.

I can't see her eyes through her sunglasses, but I know she just rolled them at me.

"Ally Cat, we can help each other out here. I have a list, you have a list, it's our last semester so let's tackle it all together."

"All of it?" There's an unmistakable yearning in her voice and the energy between us immediately intensifies.

I lean in, holding her gaze. Making sure she sees every bit of interest in my eyes. "Yes, all of it."

There's a charged beat of silence before she says, "We're friends. Sex complicates things."

"Ally Cat, there's been sexual tension between us since that first Halloween, and you know it. What happens on Halloween, stays on Halloween? Wasn't that just our excuse to push the boundaries between us? That's why we barely saw each other outside of Halloween. Now we have every reason to give in to what we've always wanted."

Her breath catches and holds. Yes, I put the truth out there. She can't deny it. Me either. Not anymore.

"Listen, this will be the least complicated our relationship has ever been. Our lists simplify everything. We stick only to the lists, and we already have a built-in deadline. After graduation the lists are void."

"You mean we're void."

I shrug. "When would we see each other anyway? I could be in the NFL, and if I'm not who knows where I'll land. You'll be in grad school here. Our lives are going in different directions."

She sighs. "I suppose you're right. But I need to bust my ass this semester. My internship, my thesis."

"Exactly! Me too. We'll be so busy this semester that we only have time for a list only relationship."

"List only," she repeats, but she seems to be considering it. Or does she not want that?

My original doubt that Ally can't do only the list comes back. "You aren't wanting an actual relationship, are you?"

She looks at the skyline as she shakes her head. "No," she says solemnly, yet definitively. "I don't."

It's the exact words I want to hear, so why are they tying my stomach into knots? No, it's good knots. Anticipation knots. She's interested.

"Okay, maybe I do want to do the list."

My heart immediately jumps to my throat. Oh my God. We're doing this. We're really doing this.

"The stuff like this. The sex part…that was us being drunk and silly."

"Okay, we can—"

She holds up her hand, stopping me.

"But…"

"No, no buts."

Her lips form a tiny smile. The kind of sad smile you get before you're delivered bad news. "You see, there tends to be a pattern of me trusting the men in my life then getting the rug pulled out from under me." She looks at me, and the pain I see there has my heart plummeting down to my feet. Shit. Not only did I fuck up, I hurt her. I hurt her bad.

"I can't do my list with you. I just can't."

Her softly spoken words pierce me like an arrow right to the heart. Ally is the last person in the whole world I'd ever want to hurt. And I did so much more.

"I'm so sorry, Ally Cat. I shouldn't have taken that picture. It kills me that I hurt you. I deserve your distrust. I should probably accept it and walk away, but I want to earn it back. List or no list, I hope you'll give me that chance."

She gives me another tiny smile, and this one feels hopeful. "Thanks for today."

I don't know what that means, but I'm going to take it as a positive. I have to. I nod and we get back to standing and start making our way back to the dock. It takes longer since our muscles are already tired. We talk some, but about nothing of consequence. While I drive her back to her condo, we pass by the Bull & Horn Pub. I was going to suggest going there as a list item.

"Every Friday the Bull & Horn has a beer pong tournament. You should go. For your list."

"A tournament for my first time? Probably not a great idea. Actually, I'm going to a frat party on Friday. I'm guessing there will be beer pong there."

"A frat party, huh? Two items at one time." I do my best to ignore the jealousy that fills me at the thought of her doing the list without me.

"Three." She glances at me then out the windshield. "Ginny encouraged me to ask out the barista at Cafe Jolt a few days ago. He picked his frat party as the date."

Frat barista at Cafe Jolt? "Please tell me it isn't with Ben Kelley."

"Yeah, Ben."

"Um, you don't trust me, but you'll go out with Ben *fucking* Kelley?" Over my dead body is Ally going out with him. "He once bragged about banging four girls in one day. He only wants to fuck you."

She flinches. "For one, Ben didn't steal my list away from me and has given me no reason to distrust him. And who said I was going to sleep with him?"

I pull into her complex and slam into park. My body is practically vibrating with anger. "Cancel the date, Ally Cat. I mean it."

"Are you kidding me? You can't tell me what to do, and it's none of your fucking business anyway. If I want to be one of Ben's one-night stands, then I will be! Hey, it'll knock something else off the list. Go to hell!"

She yanks the door open and gets out then slams it shut so hard it rocks the whole truck.

I'm so damn pissed I can't see straight, but for some strange reason, I start laughing. I've fucked this all up. But it's nowhere near over. There's no fucking way Ben Kelley is getting his hands on her. Only me.

chapter seven

Ally

2. Go to a frat party

7. ~~Go Stand Up Paddleboarding~~

"So, this is a frat party."

I wish I could say I'm impressed, but I'm not. There is no elaborate theme or crazy party decorations like you see in the movies. It's a bunch of people surrounding kegs in a court-yard. There's music pumping, but no one is dancing. This is what I got so mad at Clark about?

"Yeah, it's never as cool as it looks in the movies," Ginny says. "The main attraction is always the keg."

I laugh. "I was just thinking that movies totally oversell frat parties. Since I'm technically here, I can cross it off my list. Wanna go? It's not too late to go home and pick an 80's rom-com to watch. We can make a drinking game out of it and take a drink every time someone does something totally toxic."

Ginny eyes me. "That's cheating and you know it. Besides, we're not here for the party. We're here for your date."

Right. A date I insisted I keep. Ben texted me yesterday, and we decided I would meet him here. I was so close to canceling. I'm not really interested in going out with a fuck boy, even for one night. But I didn't want to give Clark the satisfaction, so I enlisted Ginny to come with me.

"Come on, it'll be better after a beer." She grabs my hand, and we weave through the crowd until we get to the keg.

"Ally, hey!" I turn to see Ben making his way toward us. "You made it."

He's hot, there's no denying it, but there's something missing. Maybe if he was a little taller, less blond and wore glasses. Ugh. I need to forget Clark. I need to forget about how I really want to do my list with him. How I wanted to agree, but I kept thinking, what if I'm wrong? What if I trust him again and it backfires on me? Maybe what he did wasn't on the same level as Danny, my high school boyfriend, but it has the power to do as much damage. I would be an idiot to forgive and forget so easily. Even if I want to.

"Look like you're happy to see him," Ginny mutters under her breath, so I shake out of my thoughts and paste a smile on my face.

"Hey, Ben." Gah, even my voice sounds fake.

He gives me a hug then keeps his one of his arms around my waist and pulls me to him. I stiffen. I wasn't exactly prepared for him to be so close so soon. It feels weird. It has to be because we don't know each other, and I'm not really a touchy-feely person.

Except I was that first Halloween with Clark.

Nope. Not thinking about Clark. Ben is a flirty guy, and I shouldn't read too much into it. I do my best to relax and give his red Solo cup a tap with mine. Tonight, I'm going to party like it's freshman year.

Two beers later, I can admit I'm having a good time. Ben pulled me into a group of his friends, and we've been talking and joking around for I don't know how long. The party is now raging and the courtyard is a sea of people. I've completely lost sight of Ginny. She was chatting up some guy the last I saw her.

The group surrounding Ben has gotten a little bigger. It's clear that he's a popular guy. Several girls have flirted with him, and while he was charming back, he's kept an arm around me pretty much the whole night. He might be a fuck boy, but at least he's a focused fuck boy.

"Whoa, whoa. Look who we have here," Ben says, looking over his shoulder. He takes his hand away from my waist and steps away, giving another guy a bro hug. I turn fully and freeze when I see who it is.

Wes Russo. And next to him is Nate Standen.

My stomach tightens. Where Wes and Nate are, Clark isn't far behind.

Nate greets Ben the same way, then they part and there he is—and his intense gaze is on me. All the tingles and heat I should have been feeling with Ben all night suddenly start firing inside me. Damn him.

I hear Ben greet him, and he tears his gaze from me and gives Ben an easy smile though it doesn't remotely reach his eyes. They do the bro hug thing too, and Clark's gaze is back on me, hot and angry. And fuck me if it doesn't turn me on more.

"Ally!"

I rip my gaze away from Clark as Ben comes back to me and takes my hand. "Come meet my friends."

My steps are heavy and slow, and I wish I could put on the brakes and slip out of his grip as easily as my old dog did with his harness when we took him to the vet.

"Hey guys, meet Ally…"

"Ally!!" Wes says and immediately pulls me into a hug. I can't help but smile. Wes is impossible to hate. He's just too charming and happy.

"Hey, Wes, it's good to see you again."

He pulls away. "Damn girl, you've gotten even hotter since freshman year."

Nate and Clark both slug his arm.

"Don't be an ass," Nate says and gives me a less enthusiastic hug, but it's comforting and friendly. "Hey, girl," he says affectionately. Nate's super easy to like too. He immediately became like a big brother figure to me. He was always friendly and kind and ready to help with anything.

"Hey, Nate," I say with a smile, and then he steps aside, clearly for Clark to come up and greet me too.

It's like time goes into slo-mo, except my heart is racing in two-x speed. Clark steps forward. "Hey, Ally Cat, long time no see," he says with a smirk then his hand slips along my waist, his touch leaving a scorching trail until it comes to a stop at my lower back. Then he presses his hand into me, and this intense heat shoots up my spine then spreads through every nerve. He has my whole body tingling in what is hands down the sexiest hug ever.

When he pulls away and steps back, his sapphire eyes are dark with desire and practically glittering with satisfaction of knowing exactly how he's affecting me.

Ben immediately pulls me to him, and I snap my gaze away from Clark. "So, guess you all know each other, huh?"

I can't tell if he picked up on the tension between me and Clark since his expression is still open and friendly. I glance at Wes and Nate, and it's clear they noticed, though Wes quickly answers Ben's question.

"Logan was her RA freshman year, and we were constantly crashing his place."

"Oh yeah? What a coincidence. Man, it's really good to see

y'all. It's been forever. That bowl game was fucking awesome."

They all say their thanks, but Clark's comes out tight before his gaze flicks to Ben's hand around my shoulder. I swear if he really were Clark Kent, he would have put his Superman heat vision power to work. It takes all my willpower not to shrug his hand off.

"Ben!" Someone shouts from behind us, and we both turn around to see some guy standing on top one of the kegs, pointing at Ben. "I challenge you to a keg stand."

The crowd immediately starts cheering.

"Are you sure you know what you're getting yourself into?" Ben shouts back, laughing.

I'm not sure what that means.

"I'm taking you down once and for all," the guy shouts back. The crowd collectively *ooohhs* at that statement.

"Bring it on," Ben shouts back, and then everyone goes even crazier.

Ben suddenly pulls me into him until I'm plastered against his chest. "Good luck kiss?" It might be a question, but he doesn't wait for an answer. His mouth presses against mine, quick and hard, his tongue immediately slipping through my surprised lips. He swirls his tongue around mine a couple of times before he pulls back. He smiles at me as if he thought that was good. "I can't wait to come back for my victory kiss."

He takes off toward the kegs as the crowd cheers him on while I'm still reeling from Ben's lip attack. I glance over at the guys and see that Nate has his arm across Clark's chest as if he's stopping him from jumping into a fight. Now Wes is looking between us with a curious gaze then suddenly his eyes go wide.

"Oh shit. You're Halloween girl!"

"Um..." I don't know exactly what that means. I mean, I

know I'm Halloween girl, but I don't know what Clark has said to them about me.

Nate pulls his arm away from Clark, shaking his head. "I can't believe we've known Halloween girl all this time."

Clark doesn't say anything, but he still looks furious that Ben kissed me. I can't deal with him right now. I turn back toward the kegs where Ben and that guy are shaking hands.

"So, what is all this? Are keg stands like a normal frat party thing?"

"Maybe. Apparently, Ben is some sort of keg stand champion. He's undefeated," Nate says, and I resist the urge to roll my eyes.

Ben and the other guy talk then shake hands again. They do rock-paper-scissors to see who goes first and Ben wins. The challenger goes first, and I watch as he grips the sides of the keg then two other guys lift up his legs so he's in a handstand position. Once the beer nozzle is in his mouth someone starts the counting then the crowd joins him. He lasts twenty-three seconds. I have no idea if that's good or bad.

Ben pumps up the crowd before his turn. Lots of cameras go up to video. His friends help him up, and then the counting begins. He goes past twenty-three seconds. He goes all the way to thirty-six seconds. The whole place erupts. I should probably be one of the ones cheering. He is my date, after all. I clap and give a lackluster woo-hoo.

Nate snickers, and Wes tells me that it was pathetic. I glance at Clark, and he's still looking all grouchy but smirks at my pitiful reaction too.

Suddenly, the guy that lost is taking off his clothes, all the way to his underwear. Even more cameras go up and my stomach twists. I don't like the direction this is going. "What's going on?"

"He lost to Ben. There's usually some embarrassing bet for the loser," Wes says.

"That's awful."

Wes shrugs as he brings his beer to his lips. "He agreed."

Someone hands Ben a marker and he starts writing on the guy's chest. When he steps back, it clearly says, *I have a micro penis*, on his chest. The crowd laughs. The guy raises his hands as if he doesn't care. And maybe right now he doesn't, but he probably will when he's sober and trending on the internet for having a micro penis. Ben jumps on a keg and asks if anyone else wants to challenge him.

I'm so over this party. I need to find Ginny and get the hell out of here.

"Ally!" As if she heard my thoughts, Ginny runs over. "There you are! This is insane."

"It's stupid."

"Ginny?" I turn to see Nate looking at Ginny with wide surprised eyes. Like he's seen a ghost.

I look back at Ginny and she's looking at Nate with the same horrified surprised expression then her eyes narrow. "What the hell are you doing here?"

The venom in her voice surprises me.

He blinks a few times then smirks. "It's a party, Gin & Juice."

Her mouth twists in anger and she charges him, shoving hard at his chest. *"Don't fucking call me that."*

Nate's so big though he barely sways. Ginny growls in frustration then slaps his cup out of his hand and it hits the ground hard, beer spraying everywhere. Before I can comprehend what just happened, she's already stomping away.

I look at Nate. "What the hell?"

He shakes the beer off his hands. "Yeah, long story."

Wes laughs. "Damn, dude. That was awesome."

Nate flips him off and Clark asks if he's okay. Nate waves him off as he looks in the direction Ginny went in.

I'm dying to know what happened between them to garner

this kind of reaction from Ginny. She doesn't let guys get to her easily. I need to go find her. But before I can take a step, I hear my name shouted over the crowd.

I freeze and look over to see Ben still on the keg and pointing at me. The crowd swings their collective gaze my way—and their cameras. Oh shit.

"Time for my victory kiss."

The crowd whoops and hollers as he jumps off, heading my way. My stomach churns. Oh my God, he's going to kiss me in front of all these people. And it's going to be on camera. Being shared all over campus. All over the internet.

Bile fills my throat as everyone starts chanting, *Kiss! Kiss! Kiss!*

All of a sudden, Clark steps in between me and Ben. "Hey, you're not done yet, Kelley."

Clark walks toward Ben, all the cameras following him as the chant dies.

"You're challenging me, Mackenzie?"

"Yeah, let's do this."

"You better make it interesting. I'd much rather get my victory kiss and call it a night."

Clark's jaw tightens, just enough for me to notice, but he never loses his grin. At the kegs they talk for a minute then Ben glances at me. He eventually shrugs and shakes hands with Clark. What the hell was that?

The guys go to help Clark, and I move closer, my interest now engaged. This time Ben loses rock-paper-scissors and goes first. His friends hoist him up and someone says *go* and starts the time. Ben stays up there for what seems like forever, but when he stops drinking the timer yells out his time as twenty-seven seconds.

Ben winces and looks a bit disappointed. "Not my best time. Let's see what you can do."

My stomach tightens. Clark has never done this before,

there's no way he'll beat Ben. What kind of stupid bet did he make?

Clark heads to the keg where Wes and Nate are now standing by. Clark takes a few seconds talking to them, and then suddenly he's taking off his shirt. The girls in the crowd go wild, almost everyone has a phone pointed toward him, and it hits me like a ton of bricks.

He's turning all the attention toward him on purpose. Away from me.

Clark looks up, his gaze catching and holding mine. My heart starts beating wildly against my chest as a flood of emotions churn through me. Then he takes off his glasses and hands them to Nate as a look of concentration comes over his face. He hoists himself up, and the guys help him get in a half stand. Once he has his balance, they let go. Clark slowly makes a handstand—completely unassisted. It's the hottest damn thing I've ever seen. The crowd roars, and once his balance is set, Wes yells, "Go."

"Fuuuccck," says Ben, now standing next to me. "How the hell can an edge rusher do that shit?"

I can't look away. Damn, the man is impressive. His back muscles, dear God. I can hear the other girls around me chattering away about them. I kind of want to punch them all in the face.

"Even if he doesn't beat my time, I might have to concede."

"What was the bet?"

Ben looks at me, a slightly amused expression on his face. "If I lose, I end our date and not touch you again. And I can't tell anyone what the bet is."

I open my mouth to respond but close it as the numbers close in on Ben's time.

"Twenty seconds!" And he keeps going, passing Ben's time. "Twenty-eight!"

At that point, Clark pushes back and lands on his feet with

a little stumble that Nate easily catches. The crowd closes in, all jumping around him. No one cares about me anymore. Not even Ben, who has gone to join the revelry.

I take the opportunity to find Ginny so we can get the hell out of here. I text her and head toward the house, hoping she escaped to the bathroom, but I can't find her anywhere. She still hasn't texted back when I look in the kitchen where there's a door leading outside. I open it and check, but the tiny patio is surprisingly empty. I turn to shut the door and run right into a hard chest.

Clark's hard chest.

Our gazes lock before he grabs my arm and pulls me outside, slamming the door behind him. He closes in on me until I'm flush against the brick wall. His hand cups my jaw, raising my face to his. Then slowly, with a little pressure, his thumb moves across my bottom lip and back again.

"What're you doing?"

"Wiping off his kiss."

My breath catches as tingles explode inside me, all pooling between my legs. His other hand comes up and he presses his other thumb across my lips too. "You didn't want it. Did you, Ally Cat?"

His blue eyes, intense and blazing, stay on mine. I say nothing, but I don't stop him. I want him to erase Ben's kiss. I want him to take it away until my lips are sore and swollen. And he does. Each hard swipe of his thumb stokes the fire burning inside me. And I want it to burn. I want it to consume me.

He tips my head more, his hot gaze studying my lips. "This mouth. It's mine. And I don't share."

He takes my mouth in a savage kiss that instantly lays claim. And I let him. His kiss is deep and consuming, and I'm drowning in it. Drowning in him. I've never been kissed like this. Where you feel it everywhere. And I don't think I'll ever be kissed like this again.

His lips trail down my neck. "Fuck, Ally Cat. You feel so good. Feel how good this is? How good we are together."

All I can do is feel. A strangled sound comes out of my throat as I arch into his touch. He takes my lips in another searing kiss before resting his forehead against mine. "I'm so fucking sorry for breaking your trust. I think it's the one thing I'll regret for the rest of my life. Please forgive me, Ally Cat."

God, how I want to. But I can't just let him kiss me senseless then say everything is okay.

"I want to. But you can't ask me to forgive you after kissing all my brain cells away. It's not that easy."

He grins. "Wasn't exactly my plan, but I don't regret it."

I find myself grinning back. I might not have wanted Ben to kiss me, but if it led to this moment—that kiss—then I can't regret it either.

"Thank you for what you did out there."

"I know you don't like the attention, and it was getting a little out of hand. Besides, you didn't want to kiss him. You never did."

I tilt my head. "I didn't want to kiss him, or you didn't want me to kiss him?"

Crooked Grin. Sexy as Hell Crooked Grin. "Both."

"He told me about your bet."

His grin lessens, but it's no less confident. "Well, did you really want to dodge his kisses all night?"

"You can't just…claim me like some caveman." Even if that's exactly what he did, and I loved every second of it.

He puts his hands on the wall above my shoulders, caging me in. "I've never wanted to claim anyone in my life. Then I saw you on your knees surrounded by sex toys. Then I read your list. And now the thought of you doing any of those things with anyone else makes me *fucking insane*." The intensity of his voice sends a spike of heat right in between my legs. He leans in and rubs his nose along my neck and jaw, and I suppress the urge to moan. "Why are you denying this? It's so hot between us."

I honestly don't know. Not with him so close. Not with his kiss still tingling on my lips. I'm feeling too much; I can't think straight.

"Ally? Oh whoa!" Ginny's voice tears us apart. I glance over and my friend is looking at me with wide eyes. "Um, should I go?"

"No."

"Yes."

Clark and I speak at the same time. Clark's stare pleads with me.

"Um, okay, my BFF said no, so I'm going to stick with her." Ginny looks at me. "I'm going to step inside and wait for you, okay?"

"I'll be right there." I look back at Clark. "I should go."

"Wait! Tomorrow, meet me at Lights Down Low at nine. Sit at the bar and I'll find you."

"Why?"

"I want to try something, and you can go along with it or not. It'll be totally up to you. You're going to call all the shots, just meet me. Give me a chance to start over and earn back your trust. Please, Ally Cat."

"I'll think about it."

His mouth flattens, but he nods, accepting my answer. "Okay. Thanks." He pulls away so I can leave.

When I get inside, Ginny gives me a once-over, but says nothing. She grabs my hand and makes a beeline for the door. Once outside and a good fifty feet away from the frat house, we both let out a big sigh. Who knew a frat party would be so emotionally exhausting?

"Are you okay?" I ask her. "I'm sorry I didn't run after you. Ben turned the spotlight on me."

"Yeah, I saw that. I'm sorry, I should have come back, but…"

"What happened between you and Nate?"

"Nothing I want to talk about." She glances at me then starts laughing. "Okay, what kind of kiss did Mr. Intense back there give you to make your mouth look like that?"

I touch my lips. "Like what?"

"You look like you just had a major make-out session with the Joker. Your lipstick is all over your face."

My cheeks burn as the memory of his kiss makes my lips tingle. "He wiped off Ben's kiss."

Ginny's mouth falls open.

"Then kissed the ever-living hell out of me."

She stops and blinks at me. "Oh damn, that's hot."

"It was. So fucking hot." We share a look for another second then start walking again. "He wants me to meet him tomorrow. He didn't say why, but I'm guessing it has to do with the list."

"Look, I know he really hurt you with the picture thing, and I get it. I really do. But the guy just grabbed the attention of an entire frat party for you. I think he might deserve a second chance."

I do too. I only hope I'm not wrong. He's the one man I'm not sure I can survive hurting me again.

chapter eight

Lights Down Low is a swanky bar in the newest hotel in downtown Austin. Even though it's only nine, it's already crowded. The bar hasn't been open long, but I've heard it's already the hot spot for all social media influencers. It's sexy and sleek with its retro modern look of dark-colored woods, deep purples and reds and elaborate chandeliers that give the whole room a golden glow. It reminds me of pictures of old Hollywood, like Marilyn Monroe could slip into the seat next to you at any minute.

I glance around the room, but I don't see Clark anywhere. My stomach has been in knots all day. I went back and forth on whether I should really meet him. I honestly wasn't even sure of my decision until Ginny showed up with the perfect little black dress an hour ago. I can admit I'm intrigued, and he said I'm calling the shots, so I decided to trust him that much.

I make my way to the bar and order a cosmo, glancing around the bar but still not seeing him. I swear if he stands me up, I'm going to kill him. The bartender sets my drink in front of me, and I pull up my purse so I can pay but he puts his hand out. "It's already paid for."

I open my mouth to ask by whom, but he moves down the bar to take care of someone else. I glance around again, but all I see are big groups or couples and no one paying me a bit of attention. Then I look across the bar and a lone man stops my perusal. He's looking right at me, and I know that face. I know those eyes. He's familiar, yet he's not. Then slowly the right side of his mouth inches up. Sexy Smirk. It's Clark. Except it isn't Clark.

No, this is Superman.

He's not wearing his glasses, but that's not the biggest change. He cut his hair. His shaggy, wavy locks are gone, and his hair is now short on the sides with the top slightly longer and neatly styled. While there's a part of me that's severely disappointed I never got to run my fingers through his hair, this look on him is so potent I can't breathe properly. No wonder Lois Lane was always so gaga over Superman. His power literally seeps into you and renders you stupid with lust.

His smile broadens as he gets out of his seat and makes his way to me. He's dressed differently, too. He's wearing a fitted, black button-down and slacks, and the look is lethal. I feel like prey in his path. Like it won't matter how far I run, I'm his.

"Clark," I say when he gets to me, my voice shaking. I've got to get a hold of myself. He's only a man. I can do this. "What did you do to your hair?"

His brows knit together as he leans against the bar next to me.

"My name isn't Clark, and what's wrong with my hair?"

"Of course it's not your name, and your hair is all gone."

Again, he looks at me perplexed. He reaches up and touches his hair. "Still there. If you know my name's not Clark then why are you calling me that?"

"Because…because it's what I call you."

"And what do I call you?"

Now I'm the one looking at him like he's lost his mind. This is Clark, right? I'm not talking to his doppelganger or something, am I? Then he smiles and I know this is the same man whose smile has been twisting me in knots since freshman year.

"You know my name." I say, but I feel on shaky ground.

He gives a small shake of his head as his gaze rakes over me heatedly. "Trust me, I'd remember if I'd met you before. I haven't been able to take my eyes off you since you walked in."

"Stop messing with me, Clark. I'm starting to wonder if I'm talking to your doppelganger."

His brows shoot up then he laughs. "Maybe that's it. I have a secret twin named Clark. Maybe you can introduce us, though it'll have to be soon. I'm only in town for one night." He holds out his hand. "I'm Logan."

I inhale sharply as my heart slams into my chest. His real name.

Give me a chance to start over.

Is that what he's doing? Are we starting over? I don't know, but I do know I've been wanting to say his real name for years.

"Logan," I repeat, finally saying it, and it feels so good on my lips. It's perfect. It's him. As much as I love calling him Clark, I'm not sure I'll be able to think of him as anything else but Logan from now on. I've been struggling to think of him as Clark after that kiss. We crossed that line we were so careful not to before, and I'm not sure what tonight is, but I'm pretty sure that line will only get further away.

His body relaxes as if he's been waiting years for me to say it. Maybe he has.

He leans in. "Say it again."

His voice is low and lusty, and it's filling me in all my private places. All the places I'm desperate for him to touch. "Logan."

Sexy Smirk is back. "I like my name on your lips. You're going to have to give me your name so I can test it on mine."

I search his face as if it will give me the magic answer as to what is going on. Why is he acting like he doesn't know me? And why did he say he's only in town for one night? *One night*. Oh my God, this is about the list. It was the first item on my list—one-night stand.

"You're in town for one night. One night."

He gives me a knowing look. "One night." He leans in even more and holds his hand out. "So, do I get your name now?"

You're going to call all the shots.

I get to decide if I want to play or not. He's giving me a chance to take ownership of my list—to take back some of the life I left behind after that Halloween.

His hand is warm as I slip my skin against his, and he immediately takes my hand into a firm grip. I take a breath and say a name I haven't uttered in over three years. "Allyson."

His eyes darken, and his grip tightens as he pulls me a little closer. "Allyson." There's almost an air of wonder to his voice as he says it.

I like my name on his lips too. Oh, to be that girl again. Maybe only for tonight…

He slowly, almost reluctantly, takes his hand out of mine and leans on the bar. "What brings you here, Allyson? Meeting someone?"

I nod. If we're role-playing then I might as well make it fun. "A date."

A brief look of surprise comes over his face before he schools it. "Boyfriend?"

"First date."

He smiles as if now he has a chance. He's playing the role of stranger very well. "A first date, huh? Why didn't you come together? Meet on an app or something?"

"No, he had to work late so meeting here is easier."

"Because that's how you want to start a first date—by making it easy." His voice is dripping with disdain.

"What's wrong with easy?"

"It's lazy. Is that really how you want a new relationship to start?"

I open my mouth to answer but shut it without saying anything.

"See? You don't. No, a first date should have something unexpected in it. Something that requires an effort. What's so special about having drinks at a swanky bar?"

"Says the man drinking at said swanky bar."

"Hey, when in Rome, you see what the fuss is all about, right? But me, I'm not on a date. I'm just visiting. No, if I was taking you on a date, I'd do it differently."

"Oh really? What would you do?"

A spark lights his eyes as he inches closer. This is exactly what he wanted. I'm putty in his hands, and I don't care. "Well, I'd try to find out what interests you before the date. Not in an obvious way, but I will want to try to do something you enjoy or something that intrigues you. Maybe something you've never tried before."

I take a sip of my cosmo to hide my smile. "And what do you think that is?"

He takes me in as if he doesn't know who I am. "I think

you're a woman who wants adventure but doesn't know where to start. Or maybe you've forgotten how."

Or maybe you've forgotten how.

My stomach drops. We haven't exactly gotten into the details of my past, yet somehow he knows. He knows I wasn't always the person too afraid to take risks.

"Is that so?" My words are like gravel in my throat even though I'm trying not to let him see how thoroughly he's shaken me.

"Yes."

"Then what do you propose for our first date?"

He thinks for a moment then snaps. "The graffiti park."

I blink. "What?"

"I heard there's a graffiti park here where you can bring spray paint and create your own art on all the walls. I would take you there. It'll feel a little dangerous because graffiti is usually illegal. And it's fun, because, well, playing with spray paint is fun. It would be a chance for us to get to know each other better without all the cliché small talk. We get to see what the other creates. I would get a glimpse of your inner self through your art."

Oh my God. He's slaying me yet again. This has to be the most perfect answer, and I never would have thought of it. I want this date with him. I want it now.

"How'd I do?"

I take a healthy sip of my drink. "You did well. What will we do next, or is that the end of our date?"

"No, this is an all-day date. It's an adventure, remember? From there we'd get lunch somewhere with a patio, good drinks, and amazing queso."

"Queso for lunch?"

"For sure. Best lunch ever."

I'm falling in love with this date, and it doesn't even exist.

"We'll have some standard date conversation, but it won't feel like that. It'll feel like we've known each other for years."

Like our first Halloween together.

"We'll keep finding ways to touch each other." He reaches out and grazes his finger over mine then shifts closer so his thigh brushes against my knee. My leg immediately falls open in silent invitation.

He notices and his gaze becomes so dangerously hot I can barely breathe. We stay like that, stuck in the heat of the moment before I finally come to my senses.

"Then what?"

He slowly works his way through our fog of lust and brings back his easy smile. "We'll definitely have to hit some live music. We're in the Live Music Capital of the World, after all. At the end of the night, I'll take you home and walk you to your door where I'll give you the most perfect goodnight kiss."

"And after the kiss?"

His gaze devours my lips. "Then you won't be able to stop thinking about me for the rest of the night. You'll even dream of me."

"Are you telling me you aren't going to try to charm an invite inside my place?"

"On the first date? Absolutely not. I'm a gentleman, after all."

"A gentleman, huh? That's funny. Someone once told me a gentleman is simply a patient wolf."

His eyes widen in surprise before his expression turns very wolfish. I tap the stem of my glass, suddenly very impatient. I don't want him to play with me anymore; I want him to pounce.

"Sound advice you should probably heed, Allyson."

His voice is warm and smooth, pulling me into its seduction.

"I have to say, this does sound like an amazing date. It's too bad you're only in town for the night."

"It is. But…since we just went through the whole date, it's basically like we've been on it. Maybe we can skip right to the second date."

"And what does the gentleman have in mind for a second date?"

His sapphire eyes glitter darkly. "Nothing gentlemanly."

"Your wolf is showing, Logan."

He leans in and I can't stop myself from grabbing his shirt and pulling him further into me. "And getting more and more impatient," he growls against my ear just before he gives it a gentle bite.

A feral feeling surges through me, and I tighten my grip on his shirt and feel a button pop. I want him so much I can't breathe.

"I'm already on a date." I somehow say, curious where he's taking this game.

"Not yet," he says then places a small nibble on the skin below my ear. "There's still time to stand him up."

"Now that wouldn't be very lady-like of me."

He runs a finger down my arm, leaving a trail of heat behind it. "Why don't you let your she-wolf rule tonight? Come upstairs with me."

I snap my gaze to his. "You have a room? Here?"

"I told you I was only in town for one night."

Okay, maybe this should have been obvious, but I never imagined he'd have an actual reservation at the hotel. It's several hundred dollars for a room at this place. Logan leans away, and I already miss his closeness. He gives me a small hopeful smile, and for the first time tonight the cocky stranger fades away and I see the guy from our Halloweens together— my friend.

"The night is yours. Yours, to spend however you want. It's

okay if you're not ready, if you'll never be ready. All that matters is what *you* want." He slips a key card in my hand. "But if you think you can trust me, I'll be in room ten-thirty-one."

"Ten-thirty-one?" Halloween. Did he do that on purpose?

He winks at me and slips away. I watch as he exits the bar and heads straight toward the hotel elevators. He doesn't turn around or look my way until he's in the elevator and the doors are about to close, but I feel his hot gaze from here.

He's leaving the decision to me. I either take this chance in trusting him, or leave my list behind. Because I know I don't want to do any of the sexy stuff with anyone but him. As scary as the thought of following him up to that room is, I want it with everything in me. But can I trust him? Can I trust myself?

chapter nine

I did a ton of planning in the past twenty-four hours to get to this moment. I chopped my hair and put in contacts that are so fucking irritating I'm ready to claw my eyes out. I got a last-minute discount from a travel site to get a semi-decent price on this hotel room. The question now is, will Ally trust me enough to cross one-night stand off her list with me tonight? Or will I spend the night in a hotel room alone feeling like the biggest idiot on the planet?

I glance at the Austin skyline outside the room's window. It's been ten minutes since I left the bar and she still hasn't shown up. Did I mess up by picking an item off her list without talking with her? Should I have picked a non-sexual item to start with? Slowly gain her trust instead of diving headfirst? But it was number one on her list, and I wanted to give it to her—even though I have every intention of having more than one night with her.

Why isn't she here yet?

Christ, I'm losing it. I turn away from the window and head into the bathroom. I take the contacts out of my eyes, put some eye drops in and immediately sigh at the relief. My vision is blurry, but there's no way I'm putting on my glasses and ruining the mood for her. I go back into the room and unbutton my shirt. And pace. I yank off my shoes and socks. And pace. I pull at my hair only to remember I have significantly less. And pace.

Shit, did I completely fuck up? No. She was having fun in the bar. If she doesn't come up, it's because she's not ready yet. I'll just need to keep earning her trust. I'll need to—

The slide of the card and click of the lock releasing fills the room.

I spin around as light spills in and her figure steps into the room. The tension in my chest immediately releases. She's here.

The door shuts with a definite click as she leans against it—unmoving. The only light filtering into the room is from the windows, and she's merely a shadow in the dark hallway. I don't move. I want to, but I need her to come to me. She needs to make the first move. Moments stretch as we stare at each other. I wish I could see her face clearly. I wish I knew what is going on in her head. Finally, she moves. She reaches behind her, and I see her dress loosen then her arms come back around as she slips her dress off her shoulders. I stop breathing. She keeps maneuvering her body until the top of her dress is at her waist and I can see the fairness of her skin contrasting with a dark bra. She lifts her hand again, and though I can't quite make it out, I know she's beckoning me toward her.

I don't hesitate. I cross the room, and once I'm directly in front of her I see her bra is black and lacy and perfectly pushing her breasts up.

"That's a pretty bra, Allyson, but I'd rather see it on the floor."

One side of her mouth lifts as she shifts and maneuvers then a few seconds later I'm staring at the most gorgeous pair of tits I've ever seen. Her nipples are hard and tight and begging to be touched—to be sucked. Fuck, I'm so turned on it hurts, and I haven't even touched her yet. I'm not sure if I can touch her without my hands shaking. This is Ally, beautiful and bare, standing in front of me.

Finally.

My gaze rakes over her again, and I know touching her won't be enough. I need to taste her. I lean down and suck a nipple into my mouth. A guttural moan escapes her as her fingers tangle in my hair. Fuck, I don't know how I'm going to last. I want her with such a fierceness that all my finesse is flying out the window. I want to take every ounce of pleasure from her, give her every ounce of mine.

I lavish my attention on her breasts as her nails dig into my scalp. I groan at the bite of pain and clamp my teeth around her nipple and pull. She digs her nails in more. Fuck, this woman is going to make me blow my load right now. I kiss my way up to her mouth. I've never kissed a woman where it instantly fell in sync like this. She knows when to let me be in control, when to give back and when to take over. I swear her lips are made for mine. When I finally pull away, I'm so hot and hard I think I might combust. I need to be inside her. Now.

"Bed," I say, my voice sounding more caveman than normal. I pull her further in the room, but she yanks my hand back.

"No. I want you to fuck me right here. Against the door."

"Damn, woman, you're going to be the death of me." I kiss

her hard then turn her around, pressing her hands against the door and sliding my hands down her arms, her shoulders, her back as my mouth takes the same path. She makes a strangled sound then bucks against me and turns around.

"No. Not like that." There's something in her voice that makes me pause, but before I can meet her eyes, she pulls me into her and wraps a leg around my waist. "Like this."

All concern disappears and I grind my cock into her hot center. "Like this, Allyson?"

"Yes," she moans. "Now, Logan. I need you now."

Fuck, the sound of my name on her lips almost makes me come. I've been waiting almost three and a half years to hear her say my name, and it's the sexiest thing I've ever heard. I want to hear it over and over again. I want her to scream it so loudly the whole fucking hotel can hear it.

I sink to my knees and slowly raise the hem of her dress. As soon as I get to the top of her thighs, I can smell her arousal, then I see why. She's not wearing any underwear.

"Such a naughty girl," I groan as I sink a finger inside her. "Fuck, so wet. Just for me. Isn't that right, sweet Allyson?"

She whimpers and I lean forward to taste her. Her legs start to buckle.

"No…wait," she says shakily. "Stop…please."

I do and stand up, panic clawing at my chest. "What? Did I hurt you? Are you okay?"

"I can't take it. If you touch me with your mouth…I'm too close and I need you inside me."

"Sweetheart, I'm going to make you come so many times…" I trail off when she starts shaking her head again.

"You said the night was mine, however I wanted it, and I want you inside me when I come for the first time. Please, Logan. This is what I want. What I need."

My heart pounds at her request. She reaches for me for the first time. Her hands slowly roam over my chest, down my abs, as if she's trying to memorize every dip and plane of my muscles. Then her touch goes lower until her hand grips my cock over my pants. I groan and thrust myself into her touch.

"Now, Logan. Don't make me wait any longer. I've waited years."

Fuck me. Even though I've known she's been as attracted to me as I've been to her, to hear it from her lips…it makes me want to give this woman everything she wants. I grab the condom out of my back pocket and shove my pants down. She tries to touch me, but I gently knock her hand away. If she touches my bare cock, I'll be lost. I roll on the condom then pick her up, pushing her hard against the door. She wraps her legs around me, and as soon as I get myself at her center, I meet her eyes.

Ally. My Ally.

"Logan," she breathes, and I thrust inside her, never breaking eye contact. I memorize it all, the look of pure ecstasy on her face, the hitch in her breath, the way her slick heat surrounds my cock.

"Fuck, you feel so good."

So wet. So tight. I'm so damn lost in her.

Her eyes flutter closed. "Yes."

Her pussy clenches around my cock, begging for more. I grip her tighter and fuck her with everything I have. I can't describe the sounds we make—they're too feral and loud and undistinguished. All I know is this is where I belong—inside Allyson Worthington.

"Is this what you want, Allyson? Is this how you like it?"

"Yes…more. Fuck me hard. I want you to break me. Shatter me."

Jesus. I pull all the way out of her then shove back in with so much force I wouldn't be surprised if I leave her bruised. I do this over and over. Her sexy moans get louder and louder.

"That's right. Take it like the good girl you are."

She screams out as she starts shuddering, her pussy gripping me like a vise. "Logan...I'm....I'm...."

"Yes, baby. Come for me. Let me feel that sweet cum on my cock." I fuck her with more shallow strokes, but no less hard or faster. Then I look at her right as she shatters. I feel her soak my cock as she comes so spectacularly I can't fight my own release. A hot spike of pleasure rushes through me. A guttural moan escapes me as my cum fills the condom. And I don't stop fucking her until I'm completely and utterly spent.

We slump into each other, and I bury my face into her neck. I'm done. Except I'm not. I'm nowhere near done with Ally.

I slowly remove myself from her body and let her back down to her feet as we both try to get our breathing back to normal. I pull my pants up and she adjusts her dress to cover her. Damn, we didn't even undress fully.

"I think the whole hotel heard what we just did," I say on a laugh.

Her eyes widen. "Oh God, we were pretty loud, weren't we? I've never..." she trails off and I raise my eyebrows, letting her know I'm waiting for the end of that thought. Her already flushed cheeks redden even more. "Um, I've never been quite so enthusiastic."

I laugh and give her a quick kiss. "I like your enthusiasm. There might be a standing ovation for your enthusiasm out in the hall."

A look of mortification comes over her and I can't help but laugh. "I'm joking. Hopefully." She covers her face with her hands, but I pull them down. "Hey, anyone who heard us will be crazy jealous. There's no doubt that you were thoroughly and utterly pleasured."

"Right," she says softly. She doesn't look at me so I tell her I'm going to the bathroom to give her a moment.

As soon as I'm inside though, I realize I need a moment too. My hands are shaking as I dispose of the condom. After I clean up, I splash some water on my face. That was…so damn good—too good. I want so much more that I'm not sure I'll ever get enough. When my body and mind finally stop reeling, I leave the bathroom, but she's no longer at the door. I walk fully into the room, dread filling me with each step. She's not on the bed. She's not in the room at all. It seems Ally absolutely crossed one-night stand off her list.

chapter ten

He's not in class. After all the time I spent this morning telling myself I couldn't skip class, now he's the one skipping out. I suppose I should be relieved. I got what I want, right? I don't have to face him after my cowardly exit on Saturday. Except I want to see him. I haven't been able to think about anything else.

As soon as I stepped into that hotel room and saw him standing there against the Austin skyline, something took hold of me. I knew without a shadow of doubt I wanted this. I wanted him.

And it all still feels unreal. I've never talked so boldly. I've never begged. Then again, I've never felt like that before. I didn't want the moment to end, and yet I was so crazy for a release I thought I would die if I didn't get it as soon as possible.

My God, the feel of him inside me was the best thing I've ever experienced. It felt…undeniable. Then as soon as he went to the bathroom, I started shaking. The intensity of the sex combined with the thought of all the noise we made was too much. My mind started going crazy with the thought that people would be waiting in the hallway, cameras poised and ready, for a glimpse of the sex-crazed couple. It was a ridiculous thought, but once it was planted, I couldn't shake it.

I peeked into the hall and when I saw it was empty, my relief was palpable. Then I thought of facing Logan after what happened between us and panic set in again. So, I ran for it. It was a one-night stand, after all. Wasn't I supposed to leave? At least, that's what I've been telling myself ever since.

Now, the lecture is in full swing and he's nowhere in sight. Is he pissed I left? Relieved? I don't know what to think, what to feel. I want to talk to him, I want to find out if he's as affected as I am. But is that allowed in this weird deal we've struck? Ugh, I want to roll with it and experience everything, but I also want to make sense of it all.

I glance around the room again, hoping to see him, but he's nowhere in sight. I slouch in my seat in disappointment.

My phone screen lights up and I jolt upright as soon as I see Logan's name pop up on the screen. Yes, I've already changed his name from Clark to Logan. Now that I've said it, I can't go back. I love his name. I love that it's mine now.

> Logan: How was your weekend? Anything unexpected happen?

I smile at my screen as my stomach works itself into a tangled web of knots. The teasing has to be a good sign, right?

> Me: I went on a date, actually.

Logan: Oh yeah?

Me: It was an imaginary date, but still one of the best I've been on.

Logan: This guy sounds like a very charming...wolf

I bite my lip from laughing out loud.

Me: Absolutely, very wolfish. He charmed me all the way to his hotel room.

Logan: And...?

Me: A lady never tells...

Logan: Tease

I bite my lip to keep from laughing. This is the best I've felt since I left his hotel room. It feels like us, and I was so afraid there would be an awkwardness between us.

Logan: Did he make you feel good, Allyson?

I straighten even more and glance from side to side before glancing back at my phone. He's calling me Allyson. What does that mean?

Me: Allyson?

I hold my breath as I wait for him to respond. Did I mess up the vibe? Should I not have addressed it?

Logan: That's your naughty list name. *winky face emoji*

Me: Is that so?

Logan: You're avoiding the question, Allyson.

Me: Yes. He made me feel good. Very good.

Logan: Did he press his lips to the curve of your neck?

Heat creeps up my neck as if I can feel his lips there. I can't get turned on during class. This is absurd. Yet, I type…

Me: Yes

Logan: I wish I could press my lips to that spot now. Right where your sweater has slipped from your shoulder.

I inhale sharply and start looking around again. He's here? I turn fully around this time and am shocked to see he's directly behind me, a row between us. A smile slowly forms on his lips. Gotcha smile. I turn back around quickly. I can't believe he's been right there the whole time. My face burns with embarrassment. I take a few breaths and tell myself I've done nothing embarrassing. Okay, he probably noticed me glancing around for him, but I can handle that as long as he isn't telepathic. My phone lights up again.

Logan: Do you want that, Allyson?

Me: What are you doing? We're in class.

Logan: I'm aware. You still haven't answered my question.

Me: Logan…

Logan: Say it again.

Me: You can't hear me

Logan: I remember what it sounded like on your lips. Say it again.

A shock of desire hits me right between the legs. Knowing he likes me saying his name as much as I love saying it is hot as hell. I cross my legs, but it only fuels the tingling taking over my body.

Me: Logan

At this moment, I wish he was telepathic so he can hear the way I say it in my mind—breathy and unsteady with desire for him.

Logan: Now answer my question, Allyson. You want my lips on you?

Me: Yes

Logan: After I kiss that sweet neck, I'm going to make my way down to those pretty tits of yours.

My face flames hot and I duck my head.

Me: OMG! Logan! What are you doing?

Logan: Sexting. On both our lists.

I shake my head and look over my shoulder to glance back at him. Out of the corner of my eye I can see that smug smile still on his lips.

Me: We're in class!

I close my eyes and think about the way his lips moved over my skin. The feel of his hot tongue over my nipple. The way his breath felt on my inner thighs. How I was so close to coming I knew I needed him inside me that instant.

Liquid heat fills me as I remember him inside me, hard and thick, giving me more pleasure than I've ever experienced. If he keeps talking like this, he'll send me right over the edge all over again.

I can't breathe properly, and I'm so hot I feel like I might burst into flames right here. I feel like I'm on display and have to remind myself no one knows what's on my phone, yet I glance around. The people around me are either paying attention to the lecture, that I haven't heard a word of since Logan's first text, or staring at their own phones, oblivious. The only person who knows I'm going crazy with lust is the man behind me.

I glance over my shoulder again. What does he mean after class? He's not smiling anymore, and I fully turn around so I can see all of his face. His blue eyes are practically black, and his face is drawn so tight I know he's struggling with his own desire. We lock eyes for several seconds before he looks down and starts typing on his phone. My phone vibrates in my hand again and I turn back around.

My chest tightens and this overwhelming feeling bears down on me. This is insane. It's too much. Yet…I don't think I care. I feel like I did when I stepped into his hotel room and I'm not ready to let it go. I type out my response before I can take it back.

As soon as those two letters are sent my heart slams into my chest. What did I agree to?

I can't focus through the rest of class, not that I have been so far. The bell buzzes and it shocks me right out of my seat.

We both gather our stuff and make our way down our own rows at the same time. I don't take his hand and he doesn't glance at me though I know he's aware I'm right behind him. We head out of the classroom and head up the stairs in the hallway. Almost every person we pass either gives a Logan a what's up, a fist bump or recognition registers on their face. The man is known to practically everyone. By the time we get to the third floor, I'm a bundle of nerves.

They all saw him. What if one of the girls that gave him a flirty smile turns back around in hopes of "running into him" again? To my relief, the hall we turn into is vacant, but as he closes in at the end, I notice the name on the door in front of us. I know Dr. Hardy. He's friends with my mom.

Logan stops at a utility closet a few feet from Dr. Hardy's office. I hear voices behind Dr. Hardy's door. Oh my gosh, he's doing office hours now. Shit. Logan slowly turns the knob of the utility closet. My heart is pounding, and Dr. Hardy's voice seems to be getting louder. I glance over and see a shadow moving behind the door's frosted window.

Suddenly, I'm being yanked into the closet and Logan is silently closing the door behind us. He grabs something, a step ladder, and jams it under the door handle. Then he pulls me into the far corner, mostly hidden by shelving. My backpack falls from my shoulder just as I hear two voices outside the door. I look at Logan, panicked. It's dark, but light enough to see that his gaze is excited and intense. We stand there for several silent seconds, holding our breath, as the voices linger. Logan's finger hooks on the edge of my shirt and he slowly raises it, his finger brushing the skin of my stomach. My breath comes out in a shuttering exhale then Logan grabs my face and kisses me.

Everything fades away and there's only us—his mouth on mine, kissing me like he's starved and I'm the only thing that will sate his hunger. I know he's the only thing that will sate mine. I'm hot and needy and desperate for more. My arms wrap around his neck and pull him closer. He pushes me against the wall and grinds his hips into me.

"Are you wet, Allyson?" He growls into my ear.

I shiver and fuse my mouth to his again. He presses his hand between my legs and I arch my hips into his touch. He doesn't waste any more time and unbuttons my jeans as I cup his cock. I rub my hand up and down and he groans into my mouth. I work his jeans as he slips his hand into my panties.

"Fuck, you're wet."

"For you." *Only you.*

I push his boxers aside and take him in my hand, giving his cock a long pull. He shudders and my body lights up even more with the knowledge that I turned him on.

"I need inside you. Now." He growls and tears himself away and pulls off his backpack. I almost laugh out loud. I can't believe we've been doing all that and he still had his backpack on. He stills as he goes to grab his wallet.

"Shit. I didn't replace my condom."

He stares at me. And I stare at him. I'm on the pill, but I'm not ready to take that kind of risk with him. Not when our relationship isn't going past graduation. But there's no way I'm leaving this closet without more. I pull him to me and take his cock in my hand again.

"Touch me, Logan."

A gorgeous and sexy shuttered moan escapes him as he thrusts into my hand. His hand trails down over my breast down back to where I yearn for him most. He pushes a finger inside me and a broken moan leaves me. My God. I'm crazy with need. For more. For everything. I pump my hand faster and when he pushes another finger inside me, my brain short circuits. I can only feel— him thrusting inside me, my body clenching around him, the exquisite pain of pleasure that's building higher and higher.

"Harder, Logan. Faster...I need..." My breathy plea is lost as I work him over, showing him exactly what I want.

He fucks me just how I want him to. "Is this what you need, Allyson? Is this how you want your pussy fucked?"

His hot words have my body locking up, rushing right to the edge, and then he moves fingers over my clit and I freefall right into the abyss. His other hand comes over my mouth as I scream. My climax washes over me in waves, and I feel a warmth on my hand as Logan shudders against me. I look down and watch his cum spill over my hand, my pleasure spiking even more at knowing I did this to him.

Our labored breaths mingle as we come down from our high. I don't want to move, but the reality of the mess we've made is intruding. He leans away and takes off his outer flannel shirt then his inner T-shirt. He uses his T-shirt to clean off my hand and himself before folding it in on itself and stuffing it in his backpack.

"Thank God for winter layers, right?" he says after we're both fully dressed again. I laugh softly, but the sound of a door shutting in the hallway has it dying in my throat.

We both still and wait. No other sounds come, and Logan relaxes, but I can't. My whole body starts shaking. Black dots fill my vision and it's suddenly hard to breathe.

We got each other off in a closet...with one of my mom's friends' offices fifteen feet away. And someone was just in the hallway. Did they hear us? Was it Dr. Hardy? Oh my God. What if he sees me coming out of the closet? What will he do? Will he tell my mom? What if someone else sees us? They'll immediately recognize Logan. A huge weight presses down on my chest and I can't breathe at all.

"Are you okay?" Logan takes my head in his hands. "Hey, breathe. Slowly. In and out. It's okay, I've got you."

He continues to murmur sweet words, and I slowly calm.

When my breathing finally gets close to normal, I meet his eyes for the first time. Concern furrows his brows.

"What's going on?" He softly moves his thumb over my cheek.

"What if someone heard? What if someone sees us? I know Dr. Hardy. He knows my mom. What if..." My voice trails away and I push my hand through my hair, the panic building again. I need to get out of here, but I can't. I can't leave. Someone might see me.

He tips my face up. "Look at me."

I can't focus on him this time. "We could go to jail. We could be put on academic probation or get kicked out. I can't..." Tears burn my eyes. We could have ruined our lives for three minutes of pleasure.

"Allyson." he snaps, and my gaze immediately finds his. "You're okay. I said I'll keep you safe, and I will."

You can't guarantee that. I don't say it though. Instead, I take slower, calming breaths and nod.

"I'm going to make sure it's safe to leave. I promise. I won't put you in danger. Ever." He leans in and brushes his lips across mine as if to seal the promise. I relax in his arms, his words meaning more to me than he probably realizes. And I believe him, probably foolishly, but I do.

"That was fucking awesome," he says with a grin, and I appreciate him trying to break up the tension. A light laugh bubbles out of me and his smile widens. I can't even put a label on this one. He simply looks happy. He brushes his lips with mine again. It's so gentle and tender that something cracks inside me. This man will break my heart if I let him.

When he ends the kiss we share another smile, but it lasts only for a moment because he jerks back a step, his expression now shuttered. The distance between us suddenly has nothing to do with physical space.

"So, should we call that one sex in a public place or breaking a college rule?" he asks.

The list. Right, this had all been about the list. "Um, well, I guess technically we didn't have sex, but I'm pretty sure we broke a college rule. Oh, and dirty talk. Or did we already cross that one off?"

He leans down at my ear. "That one will never be fully crossed off, that I can guarantee." He gives me a naughty smile just before he picks up our backpacks. He hands me mine and I shrug it on. "I'll go first and check it out and let you know if it's safe to come out, okay?"

I nod and he surprises me by reaching out and squeezing my hand before removing the ladder and slowly opening the door and stepping out. I stare at my hand until he opens the door a few seconds later and I quickly slip out. We walk down the hallway until we get to the restrooms and each go into our own. I wash my hands and wish I could splash some water on my face and not wreck my make-up. Instead, I put my cool hands on my neck. I look into the mirror. Nothing has changed, yet I feel different. I'm having fun. Despite my freak outs, the adrenaline hit is thrilling…but I can't let myself get sucked into it again. It's too risky. In every way.

I shake my head away from those thoughts and pull myself together until I look like I haven't been ravished in a closet. When I walk out, I'm surprised Logan is there.

"You didn't have to wait for me."

He shrugs, his expression guarded. "I wanted to make sure you were okay."

I smile at him and nod. "Thanks, I'm good. Sorry if I freaked you out. This whole public thing got to me a bit more than I expected."

His lip quirks up on one side. "Being risky means taking risks."

"Yeah, yeah. Clearly, I made a list for a reason."

He chuckles and nods his head toward the stairs, and we head out together. Still not holding hands. I really want to hold his hand. I shouldn't.

"I'm this way," I point to my left once we're outside.

"I'm this way," he gestures in the opposite direction. We stare at each other awkwardly for another beat then he tips up his chin. "See you, Ally Cat."

It shouldn't surprise me he's using my nickname again. We're not doing a sexy item so Allyson is out, and he's never called me Ally, yet it feels a bit like a slap in the face, like he's purposely putting distance between us again.

Or he's calling you by your nickname and that's it, Ally.

I'm thinking too much. And if he is trying to put distance between us, isn't that what we're supposed to be doing? We're done with our item so it should be back to Ally Cat and Clark, right?

I don't want to call him Clark, but I feel like if I don't then I'm giving away something. Something I don't want to name.

"Later, Clark."

chapter eleven

"I feel like this is cheating. It's too Halloweeney."

I bark out a laugh. "Halloweeney? Is that a real word?"

Clark shrugs, trying not to smile. "Sure it is. I just made it up. Speaking of being Halloweeney, why are you dressed up?" He softly bops the cat ears on my head, the same ones I wore last year. But that's the only evidence of a costume.

"Because I'm your Ally Cat." I meant it as a joke, but somehow it comes out sounding more seductive and sinful.

His smile slowly fades as his gaze grows hotter. Suddenly, I can't breathe and somehow, he's closer to me. Did he lean in? Did I?

"Yeah, you are." His voice brushes against my ear—low

and rough. Possessive. I have the sudden urge to jump him and rub my tingling body parts all over him. Let him possess the hell out of me.

Needing to shake off the desire rushing through me, I put a bit of distance between us as I grab his wrist and point out the woven bracelet with the Superman logo that I gave him when he picked me up. "I'm not the only one sporting Halloween gear."

He blinks as if he too needed to get out of the same trance then he rolls his eyes at me. "You gave this to me, Ally Cat."

When I'd seen the bracelet, I'd immediately thought of Clark and couldn't resist buying it as a joke. He'd thrown back his head and laughed, and to my surprise, put it on. The whole point of tonight is to laugh and be silly, which is why I changed our plans from watching horror flicks to walking through haunted houses. The place is packed with everyone trying to get in their last night of scares, but thankfully, I have VIP tickets so we get to skip most of the line, which moves, forcing us to break gazes.

"How did you get these tickets anyway?" he asks.

"Joel. He got them but hates haunted houses. Besides, he's partying at his frat."

"The guy you sometimes kiss, right? Or has the status changed?"

I shrug. "We kissed a bit more last semester, nothing serious. Then he started dating someone."

"So, you're still friends?"

"Yeah, we've always been friends. We've been hanging out recently. He just went through a break-up."

"Fuck buddies?"

"No, I still haven't slept with him. I don't know, we're just spending time with each other."

His mouth flattens. "Does he know you're here with me?"

"Yeah, he knows we're anti-Halloween buddies."

Clark makes a noise but doesn't say anything. He looks around at the crowd with a stand-offish expression that makes me think this wasn't the best idea.

I tug on his sleeve. "Hey, we don't have to do this if you don't want to."

He looks at me. "Nah, it's good. It's a lot of people, but haunted houses are like the live action version of a cheesy horror movie."

Before I can respond, this totally messed up clown face jumps in front of me, sending me squealing and stumbling back. Clark catches me before I end up on the pavement. My heart is pounding wildly as Clark busts out laughing. Once I realize I'm not really being attacked, I start laughing too.

"Damn, Ally Cat, that was awesome. Okay, I'm totally ready for this now. If you're this easy to scare this should be a riot."

I playfully punch his arm, which only makes him laugh more. Clark pulls out his phone. "Okay, if we're going to do this, we need to do it right." He holds out his arm with the camera in selfie mode so it's us and the creepy clown.

I can't help but laugh at the sight of the clown posing behind us as I hear the snap of the camera.

"Don't post the pic, please."

His brows bunch together. "Why not? Because your mom is the university president?"

"No, I'm not on social media and don't like my picture on it."

The perplexed look on his face tells me that he doesn't understand how I couldn't be on social media. It's hard, not because I want to be on it, but because so many people communicate through it and my avoidance of it makes group projects more difficult. And while I might not be on any social platforms, I know Clark is—and he's popular. He might not be a starter for the Toro football team, but he's the hot junior walk-on who made such an amazing sack a few games ago that it went viral.

"That's why I never found you. You're not on any of them? Even ReelGood?"

ReelGood is a video-based app, and I might have caught a few of the thirst videos of him. It's easy to be anonymous on that app or just be a viewer, but I still try to avoid it.

"Nope."

"Is there a reason?"

I look at him. "Yes."

He opens his mouth but closes it before asking my reason. "Okay, but I'm sending it to you, because it's an awesome photo."

A few minutes later we're at the front of the first haunted house. There are three houses to go through, each with a different theme. This one seems to be demented clown themed as a man resembling Pennywise ushers us in. My nerves are on edge as my heart kicks up. My body is ready for fight or flight.

Suddenly, my hand is enveloped in Clark's. I look up at him and he winks down at me. "I got you, Ally Cat."

I feel his words throughout my body, but they seem to settle most around my heart and in between my legs.

He's only being nice. Get a grip, Ally.

Yet the way he leaned in earlier, the rough way his voice sounded...

The room we're in suddenly opens up, and another freaking clown comes at us, sending my lust fleeing as I scramble behind Clark in a fit of screams. Clark laughs and pulls me around the clown and through the dark hallway to the next thing that will jump out at us. The haunted house is one big fucked-up carnival with all sorts of freaky people jumping out at us. We finally stumble through the exit in fits of laughter.

"Okay, it's official. I hate clowns, but that was fun though."

"Oh, really? It was fun hiding behind me and pushing me toward all the freaks?"

"Totally!"

He shakes his head at me as we head to the next house which looks to be monster themed. Lots of stalking and gross costumed monsters chasing us. We laugh our way through, and I'm no better than before and glue myself to Clark's back the whole time. I'm not going to admit how good it felt to have my arm wrapped around his torso or how I felt hints of his muscles underneath his shirt. Ugh, this attraction to him is not what I need. Joel and I have been flirting with the idea of taking things to the next level, and I never feel like this with him. But I like that. Clark…he'll consume me, and that's a feeling I don't want—or trust.

"Okay, did I hear one of those guys say you smelled good, and you thanked him?" Clark asks me after we exit.

"Yeah, I always say thank you when I'm complimented."

He barks out a laugh. "He was trying to freak you out, not compliment you."

"Oh. Well, it didn't work. He should have said I smelled like crackers or something like that. That's weird, right?"

"It's weird when a stranger sniffs you, no matter how you smell."

I scrunch my nose. "I suppose. So, do I smell good or was that guy being freaky?"

His eyes widen slightly then he shakes his head. "He was being freaky."

"Well, you're going to have to smell me, because I'm standing by the fact that he was complimenting me."

He rolls his eyes then turns me around so his front is to my back, the way the monster stalker was, and leans down so his face is near my ear. I hear him slowly inhale and my eyes flutter close. This should be weird, but it's not. It's totally hot. I probably shouldn't have asked for this. He doesn't move for another moment, and I let myself lean into him, only a little.

He jerks away and I stumble back before I gain my balance and face him again. All our earlier humor is gone from his face. Damn, do I smell bad?

"Well?"

"You smell like sex."

I suck in a breath as I meet his gaze, his sapphire eyes are so dark I can't tell for sure if they're still blue. "Oh, um, how do I...?"

"You smell like sweat and your shampoo. Sultry and sweet. Like sex."

Holy hell. I can't breathe. My body locks up as a raging heat flows through it, and if he keeps looking at me like that I'm going to melt at his feet. I don't know what to do, because my instinct is to throw myself at him and let this fire consume us both.

Shit. No. Stop.

"Um...so, you're saying I turned the freak on." I make my voice sound like I'm impressed with myself.

He cracks a smile. Back On Track smile. "Ally Cat, he had horns."

"And you clearly have never read a monster romance. Horns are totally hot."

He rolls his eyes. "This conversation is ridiculous. Come on, freak, let's do the last house."

As soon as we enter, my stomach tightens. This house feels different. It feels real, like we're stepping into a real horror story. I glance at Clark and his mouth is pulled tight.

"I don't like this one," I say. We're still in the first room, which looks like a foyer in an old Victorian era house.

"Me either."

I take his hand in mine and he grips it tightly. A woman steps out of a wall, making us jump back. Her long strawberry-blond hair hangs straight down over her shoulders. She's deathly pale and dressed all in white with blood dripping from her eyes.

"Oh fuck no," Clark says and turns back to the entrance door. He bangs on it. "Let us out. Right fucking now."

"You can't escape. You'll never escape the nightmare," the woman says in a creepy, croaky voice.

Clark starts pounding harder and faster, demanding to be let out. His voice gets more and more panicked sounding. He's hitting the door so hard I'm afraid he's going to tear it down. Suddenly the door opens, and he darts out, pulling me behind him. Once we're outside, he basically drags me all the way to his truck then comes to a sudden stop. It's then I realize he's having a full-out panic attack. He's breathing hard and pressing a hand to his chest as if he's having a heart attack. His face is beaded with sweat.

"Clark?"

He doesn't answer me. His eyes are squeezed tight as if he's in a lot of pain. Not knowing what else to do, I wrap myself around him and press my cheek to his chest, right over his pounding heart. I squeeze him tight to me and hum a soft tune. Slowly his breathing starts to calm, and his heartbeat settles. Then his arms come around me and he hugs me back. I don't know how long we stay like that, but I don't ever want to leave. He might have been the one having the panic attack, but I don't think I've felt this comforted since last Halloween.

"Thanks," he says and places a kiss on the top of my head.

I lean back and look at him. "Are you okay?"

"I am now."

"Give me your keys," I say. "Let me drive. No arguments."

Surprisingly, he hands them over without a word. I drive

us back to my condo, pull into a visitor's spot, and kill the engine. "Come in."

He stares at me for a beat then nods.

"Nice place," he says when we get inside. "Do you have a roommate?"

"Thanks. My parents bought it so I would have a place during school then plan to rent it out after I graduate. No roommate. My friend Ginny stays here sometimes, but officially still lives at home with her mom."

I go into the kitchen and grab two beers from the fridge then go back into the living room where Clark is sitting.

"Thanks," he says and takes a healthy drink.

"Want to talk about it?"

He's silent, staring straight ahead, as if caught in a trance. "She was a ghost."

It takes me a second, but I realize he's talking about the girl in the haunted house. "Yeah."

"She reminded me of my mom. Kind of looked like her. It freaked me out."

I take his hand in mine and squeeze it. She reminded me of someone, too. Myself. Of what I could have become if I'd let the darkness win.

He sets his beer down and lets go of my hand then presses both of his hands to his eyes. "Fuck. I miss her so much." Emotion clogs his voice, and I know he's fighting tears. He's so tense, and I don't think he'll let himself really feel.

I stand. "Follow me."

He drops his hands and looks at me. The hurt and grief in his eyes breaks my heart. I hold out my hand and he takes it. I lead him into my bedroom. I kick off my shoes and he does the same. I point to my bed and he looks at me warily, but he crawls on top of the covers. I scoot in next to him and pull his arm around me so we're spooning.

"It's okay. You can let it out. I'll be right here."

It feels like he's not breathing, his body tense around me. Then suddenly he relaxes into me, pulling me tight against him. He's quiet, but the slight shaking of his body tells me he allowed himself to let go. Silent tears slip down my cheeks. My heart aches for him. Through everything that has happened over the last few years, I can't imagine not having my mom. I expected her to be disappointed in me, my actions, but she only stood by me. Fought for me.

"My parents were separated," he says after a while, his voice slightly hoarse. "But that night my dad was coming to dinner. He canceled at the last minute and my mom was annoyed. It was the second time he canceled that week."

He stops, his body tenses again. I put my hand over his, and after a moment, he relaxes a little.

"My mom decided to out with some friends and I went to a party. I always had to check in with her when I came home late so I went to her room…"

My heart leaps into my throat at his pause. Oh my God, what happened to his mother? He takes a deep breath before he starts again.

"She was on her bed with a bloody cloth on her head. There was blood on the bathroom floor. They think she slipped getting out of the shower. She managed to get a towel before lying down. She was barely breathing when I found her. She made it to the hospital, but…it was too late."

I take his hand in mine and bring it up to my lips and kiss it. "I'm so sorry."

"She'd had drinks. I don't think she realized how bad it was. She never called 911. She didn't call anyone."

The pain and anger in his voice has me turning in his arms, and I bury my face in his chest and hug him tight to me. I even wrap my leg around his. I want to cocoon him as much as I can. Let him take all my comfort. He pulls me in, resting his head on top of mine. We're holding each other so tightly it's barely comfortable, yet it feels wonderful.

I close my eyes, and when I open them again light is streaming through my window and I'm all alone.

What happens on Halloween, stays on Halloween.

chapter twelve

Logan
X Skip class for ~~sex~~ hand job
X Sext someone during class
X List Add: Bang against a wall

I crank up the radio and tap my steering wheel along with the beat. I even sing at the top of my lungs, not giving a fuck who sees me. I just had one of the best training sessions I've had since before the season ended. I shaved two seconds off my forty-yard dash, yeah, it's the two seconds I gained over the last month, but at least I got it back. Everything else fell into place, too. I'm so damn excited, I can't stand it. I haven't felt like this since I stepped on the field in my first start.

I'll never admit it to my roommates, but some sex and fun is exactly what I needed. *Sex with Ally* is exactly what I needed. As soon as the thought enters my mind, I wince. Yeah, I've wanted her for years, and finally being with her is more amazing than I'd imagined, but that's it. It's good sex. Nothing more.

Such good sex that when I pulled her into that closet, the only thing on my mind was sinking inside her. I was going on pure want and desire. Then afterward I was grinning like a fool and making promises I shouldn't. I'd totally forgot about the lists.

And I still shouldn't be worrying about her panic attack, and how I wish I knew what really caused it, or how I can ease all her fears. This is strictly about the lists. We can't let emotions pop up and confuse things.

I pull into my driveway, turning down the volume so I don't get blasted next time I turn on my truck. I get out, and as I round the hood, I notice the car sitting at the curb. I watch as Jack Mackenzie gets out of the driver's seat. I should keep walking but seeing my dad at our house has me shocked still. Other than seeing him on the hike and bike trail, I haven't seen him since last Halloween. He's texted and called, but I've ignored all his attempts to reach out.

"What are you doing here?"

"I saw you the other day. On the hike and bike trail."

"So?"

My father's mouth tightens. "Son, you've ignored my texts and calls for months. I know you saw me with Miranda. I wanted to see you...talk to you."

"No thanks, I'm good."

My father sighs and yanks off his sunglasses. "Look, I've let this temper tantrum of yours go on for years. I'm done. We need to talk, Logan. Do you know how it feels to learn my son got invited to the NFL Combine through a co-worker?"

"Temper tantrum? I'm not a toddler. Actually, I've been an adult for a while. I was plenty adult enough when I came home and found my mother dying. Adult enough to get her to the hospital while you were off fucking someone else. Just two weeks after you left mom with a pinky promise and a kiss on the front porch."

Surprise comes over his face at my words. They never knew I saw them that day.

"She wouldn't have gone out if you hadn't canceled that night. You fucking *promised* to be there!"

My dad's head falls then suddenly he screams and throws his sunglasses and they hit the sidewalk, splitting into pieces. A deafening silence falls between us. I can feel my dad's anguish. An unexpected feeling of guilt and sympathy washes over me.

"Have you ever thought about how much that night kills me? How I live with the pain and guilt every day? Do you know how many times I've relived that day and wondered if I'd showed up, would she still be alive? If I hadn't turned my phone off, would I not have lost you too? Not knowing those answers kills me. Every day."

My chest tightens and tears burn my eyes.

"Logan, I left you alone because I thought it would be easier for you. I thought it was my punishment. My sentence. But I can't do it anymore."

"Yes, you can. Go and let your new girlfriend comfort you."

"I want to ask her to marry me." His words fall between us like a bomb, my ears start ringing, and this numbing feeling fills my body. He hangs his head for a moment then looks back at me. "This isn't exactly how I wanted to bring it up. But I want your blessing. I want you to meet her. She'd like to meet you, too. She has a daughter that's going to start at CTU in the fall."

My head is reeling and a pain I don't understand churns inside me.

"You don't need my blessing. Go ahead and enjoy your new family, and don't worry about me. I'm doing fine on my own." As soon as the words leave my mouth, I have the over-whelming urge to scream and punch something.

"Are you?"

No.

The word coming so quickly to the front of my mind pisses me off. I have survived these past years with the bare minimum from him. I don't need him or his broken promises. I don't need his new fucking family. I don't respond, and my dad eventually sighs and picks up the broken pieces of his sunglasses.

"Logan, I'm not going to stop trying. I'm not going to let you have your way. Not anymore. My heart might have healed some, but it'll never be complete without you. I miss you. So damn much. So, you can push me away as much as you want, but I'm just going to push back. Here's your warning." He meets my eyes as if he's sealing his vow then turns and walks away.

My throat suddenly feels tight. That scream I'm desperate to let out is stuck inside a bundle of emotions I don't know what to do with. So I go straight to the recycling bin in the kitchen and pull out an empty beer bottle and hurl it at the nearest wall. As much as I want to punch something, I refuse to hurt my hand because of him. I shatter bottle after bottle until that scream finally gets free.

My dad's visit put me in a permanent bad mood for the rest of week. The only positive thing it's done is remind me to pump the brakes with Ally and the lists. I need to focus on school and football, on the life ahead of me. I haven't spoken to her since the utility closet and have done my best to ignore her confused looks. It might be a dick move, but I need to make it clear that sex changes nothing between us. No emotional entanglements. We're strictly a list.

I walk into psychology and grab a seat in the back, knowing how much she hates it, and pull my computer out of my backpack.

"Hey," Ally plops next to me, and I jerk my gaze to her. A gorgeous smile graces her lips, immediately heating my blood.

I look away and force my voice flat. "Hey."

There's an awkward pause, and I can feel her stare, but I keep my eyes on my computer.

"So…" Her voice is hesitant. "Since our test is Monday, do you want to get together this weekend and study?"

"That's off list." I see her flinch out of the corner of my eye.

"Off list? It's studying, Logan."

I look at her then and see a mixture of anger and hurt in her expression. "Our deal is to keep things strictly to the list."

She blinks at me a few times then her face goes completely blank. She swivels in her seat, and it's as if an invisible wall has come down between us. It might be exactly what I was going for, but I kind of hate it. I shake my head at myself. I can't have it both ways.

Class starts and I'm quickly overwhelmed. The professor is throwing a whole new set of stuff at us that will be on the test. When class is dismissed, everyone is getting up slow from the weight of what's ahead of us.

"Damn, this class wasn't supposed to be this much work," I say as I pack up.

"Yeah, I bet you're wishing you took me up on my offer to study now, huh?" Ally tosses me a sardonic smile before walking out of the room.

I deserved that and she's right. She made an A on the essay we turned in last week, and I barely passed. This class requires an eighty for credit, which I need to graduate this May. That night, I text her, praying I can win her over.

Me: I have an idea. Ever had a sexy study session?

Ally Cat: What constitutes a sexy study session?

Me: Studying with a side of kissing and touching and maybe a little fucking.

Ally Cat: *rolling eyes emoji*

Ally Cat: I think you've realized what a pain in the ass our test is going to be and are looking for a reason to study with me now.

Me: No! Never! Okay, maybe…. *praying hands emoji*

Ally Cat: I thought studying was off list.

Me: Hear me out, this is a total list add opportunity. A study session that turns into hot sex is definitely something we should experience.

Ally Cat: I still have grad school ahead of me, remember? Plenty of opportunities.

The idea of her taking advantage of opportunities without me doesn't sit well, but I push that feeling aside.

Me: If you won't add it to your list then I'll add it to mine. Come on, what better motivation to study is there? It's a win-win.

Ally Cat: I'm not adding to my list. Besides, I'm not really motivated to 'list' with you right now.

Epic groveling time. Again.

Me: I'm sorry I was an ass today.

Ally Cat: Ass. Douche-bag. Rude as fuck
asshole. I could go on. Not just today. All
week.

Me: I know. I'm sorry.

Ally Cat: Sorry isn't going to cut it, Logan. I'm
not going to be treated like this. My list isn't
an excuse to be an asshole.

Her words are tough to take because she's totally right. I acted like a grade-A dick and she didn't deserve it.

Me: I'm so fucking sorry, Ally Cat. My dad
stopped by, and it put me in a bad mood all
week. But it's no excuse to be as an ass. You
didn't deserve it. It won't happen again.

When she doesn't reply, I'm not sure my apology is enough. Shit, have I've fucked everything up?

Me: Tomorrow, let's mark off #16 on your list
(look it up). If I succeed in making amends
then we add sexy study session to my list for
Sunday.

Still no response. Time for my trump card.

Me: I need help, Ally Cat. I need this class to
graduate.

Ally Cat: Fine, I'll meet you tomorrow. No
promises on Sunday.

chapter thirteen

Logan texted me to meet him in front of the stadium to do number sixteen, which is *try a new sport*. I assume it's football related, but my mind keeps envisioning some kind of athletic sex position. The idea shouldn't excite me considering how mad I was at Logan yesterday. I kind of hate the phrase *off list*, especially if he uses it to act like I'm good enough to fuck around with but not good enough for friendly conversation.

Saying he saw his dad thawed my anger some, which is the only reason I'm standing here, hoping he meant everything he said last night. Logan comes out a set of glass doors wearing a fitted tank and athletic shorts. My brain short circuits at the sight of the muscles in his arms. We haven't exactly had a chance to get fully naked during our times together, and I suddenly want to touch him…everywhere.

I meet his gaze, and he's totally guessed what I'm thinking.

"That's not what I had in mind today."

My disappointment must have shown on my face because he laughs. "Damn, woman, you're going to make me go off list."

I bristle at that word, and he grimaces before closing the distance between us. He pulls me into a hug. "I really am sorry for being a dick."

I sink into him, loving his crude apology. I know him well enough to know he's sincere, so I let go of my anger, ready to push past this awkwardness.

"I forgive you. Don't do it again."

"Deal."

I lean back and look at him with a saucy grin. "So, trying a new sport could be anything *sport-like*."

I see a spark of heat flare in his eyes before he abruptly steps back and grabs my hand. "I have a plan. Stop trying to derail me. Besides, we won't be alone for long."

"You're no fun," I tease.

"I'm tons of fun and you know it." He gives me a dark, naughty look as he leads me through the stadium to a tunnel that opens to the field.

"Whoa, we're going on the field?"

He grins. "Yeah, ever been on it?"

I shake my head, and I can't stop my smile as we step back into the sunshine. Wow, the stadium feels completely different from this vantage point. It's so immense. I can't imagine what it feels like full of screaming fans. He takes me right to the middle of the field where the Toro decal is painted.

"Fuck," I say as I take it all in, and he laughs.

"I know. Pretty great, right?"

"What does it feel like with all the fans around you?"

He inhales as he too looks up into the stands. "It's inde-scribable. There's just this intense energy that pushes down on you, fuels you. That's the only way I can describe it. It's beautiful."

"Are we allowed out here?"

He shrugs. "I pulled a few strings. We usually train on the practice field, but I thought you'd enjoy this more."

"I saw the last training video you posted. You've got some pretty good dance moves."

He looks at me. "You saw that? On ReelGood? Thought you weren't on social media."

"I got on ReelGood again. I'm user…whatever numbers and letters they gave me."

"Again? Why did you get off in the first place?"

It's my turn to shrug. "Not my thing."

His expression tells me he knows I'm lying. "Um, clearly not if you're back on it."

"Just drop it."

"Why can't you tell me? You can't keep ignoring social media, especially as a psychology major. You have to under-stand the ins and outs of the different social media platforms."

"Trust me, I know how they work."

"But things are constantly changing."

"That's what research is for."

He taps my arm. "Come on, Ally Cat. You know—"

"Off list, Logan!" I spin away from him, hating that he made me say those words.

He grabs my arm and pulls my back to his front. "Hey, I'm sorry. I shouldn't have pushed. That's not what we do."

I wish his words brought me comfort. He's right, we avoid all the hard stuff or keep it on Halloween then pretend it doesn't exist. What if we did push? What if he knew about the dark corners of my past? I probably should have told him years ago, but even though I was the victim, what happened has been my secret shame. Something I never wanted anyone to know.

I face him and he has such an open and sincere expression on his face, I decide it's time.

"The reason I have such a hard time trusting is because of something my boyfriend in high school did." I feel like I have rocks in my throat. I never talk about it, but I force myself to go on. "He filmed me. Us. Having sex…and I didn't know. Not until it was blasted all over my school."

A pained expression comes over his face. "Oh God…no wonder you were so upset about the picture. Fuck, Ally Cat. I'm so sorry." He pulls me into a tight hug and I let him hold me, let the heat of his body give me the courage to go on.

When we pull apart, we sit cross-legged facing each other, right in the middle of the football field. He takes my hands in his and waits for me to go on.

"When I was in high school, I didn't need a list to take risks. I was this out-going blond who loved pushing the limits."

"Blond?" he asks as he takes in my dark brown hair.

"Fake blond. This is more natural, though I put in lowlights to make it darker. I changed everything about me. Even my name. My real name is Allyson Shaw. I took my mom's maiden name when I moved to Austin."

He looks at me, his expression solemn.

I take a deep breath. "That Halloween, Danny and I went to a house party and started playing Truth or Dare. Things kept getting racier then Danny's best friend dared me to go to the master bedroom and christen it with Danny. I took the dare. We'd had sex before, and the thought of doing something so naughty in the middle of a party and on someone else's bed was really exciting to me."

He nods, squeezing my hand either in understanding or encouraging me to go on.

"We, um, did it doggy style, and he filmed me from behind. Thankfully, no body parts were shown, but it was clear what we were doing. I was making lots of sounds. He did it because his friend wanted evidence that we completed the dare. A few days later it was leaked on our school news program during announcements. The whole school saw it. Some kids filmed it and shared it. Some were stupid enough to post on social media. Too many people had been at that party, so it spread pretty quickly who was in the video. And of course, it made the news."

"Fuck! How did it not get flagged as pornography?"

"It was. I was still a minor so the video died a quick death, but the damage was done. Lots of kids got in trouble. It was a legal nightmare. Danny swore he didn't do it, and the fact that he reported his phone stolen a few days earlier helped him not get convicted for leaking it. He did get counseling and community service for filming it, he was seventeen too."

"Do you believe him?"

I shrug. "I didn't at first, but he was as shocked and enraged as I was, so eventually I did. I didn't trust him anymore though, so that was the end of us."

"Did they ever catch who leaked it?"

"No, it really looked like his ex-girlfriend did it. They had a messy break-up and she accused me of stealing him even though that wasn't true. Nothing could be proved though."

His expression is tight with anger but also a mixture of sympathy and guilt. "Fuck. I'm so sorry about pushing you about the social media stuff." He pulls me to him until I'm sitting in his lap. "Thanks for trusting me with your story."

I nod. "Only Ginny knows. And only because she got me drunk after I went berserk on this guy who was taking a picture up the skirt of a girl dancing on a bar."

"Ginny is really good at getting you drunk, huh?"

I laugh at that, and I'm thankful that he lightened the

mood. I smile at him, and he leans in and rubs his nose with mine. We pause just like that, and I hold my breath, wishing he'd kiss me. But he doesn't. It's off list today. Before I make a fool of myself and kiss him, I pull away and ease out of his lap.

"So, am I playing football today?"

He hesitates for a second then pops to his feet and helps me to mine. "Hmm, how'd you guess?"

"I don't know. Maybe because we're on a football field."

"The best football field in the country." He nods over to the thing that has two padded arms on it that they push to practice blocking. "Let's try the blocking sled first."

"Blocking sled. I never knew what it was called, but that makes total sense."

We get to it, and Logan gives me directions on exactly how to attack it. Then he gets on and tells me to give it a try. I do what he told me, as much as I can tell at least, but the thing doesn't budge. I try again and again, but it never moves and eventually he starts laughing at my effort.

"Hey, you added like two hundred pounds by standing on it."

He grins and raises his shirt to show off his ripped abs. "Two-fifty."

I blink and take in the skin he's showing off. He even has that V-shaped muscle that dips into his low-riding shorts with a nice little trail of hair that leads me right to where I want to be. I can't believe I've had two-hundred and fifty pounds of pure muscle around me. In me.

Suddenly, it feels like it's July not February.

A snap of fingers appear in my vision. "Eyes up, Ally Cat."

"You're the one showing off the goods."

His lips curl as his gaze makes its way down my body. He stops at the apex of my legs, and I feel his stare as strongly as if he'd touched me there. I need his touch there. I'm aching for it.

He tears his gaze away and mutters a curse before turning away from me completely.

"You sure you don't want my new sport to be crazy, hot sex on a football field?"

"Fuck. Don't tempt me."

He jumps off the sled and gestures for me to try again, and this time I actually move it. Only a few yards, but still. I look at him with a smug smile. He gestures for me to get on it then he rams it, moving it about fifteen yards with perfect ease.

I roll my eyes. "Show off."

From there, he goes on to show me several different drills and maneuvers. Then he explains one of the biggest things is to make sure the offense can't get their hands on you, so they practice hand fighting drills. He shows me a few things then challenges me to try to touch his chest.

"Wouldn't it be better if I play defense?"

He grins. "You want me to try to grab your chest?"

Oh. Would it be horrible of me if I said yes? He must see the indecision on my face because he laughs.

"Okay, okay. I see your point." I get into the crouched stance he showed me earlier. "You're going down, Mackenzie."

"I'll go down anywhere, Ally Cat. But not on the football field."

My face flushes. "Oh my God, just stop. Are we doing this or not?"

He laughs and crouches in front of me. "Give me your best shot."

It's on the tip of my tongue to say that should be my line, but if I do, I'm not sure we'll ever get away from the sexual innuendos. So, I wait a few seconds then lunge forward, and he easily knocks my hands away. I try again, and again and it's like child's play for him. I get nowhere near any part of his body. Any trick I think might get him is immediately thwarted. I try one last time, then all of a sudden he lunges forward, scoops me up, and has me flat on my back. It happened so fast I didn't even register that he cradled my head with his hand, but he totally protected me. The fall didn't even hurt, and I don't know how that's possible.

I stare up at him. "Um, whoa."

He grins. "I didn't hurt you, did I?"

"No. How in the world? That was so fast."

His grin takes on this cocky lilt. "Because I'm good, baby."

I want to roll my eyes at him, but I'm too impressed. Suddenly, I'm very aware of his big body on top of mine. My breasts are flattened against his chest, his knee is nestled between my legs and it's taking all my willpower not to grind into it. His eyes fall to my lips, and I lick them. He makes a rough sound as his hand sinks into my hair and pulls my face closer.

Suddenly, he stops.

Off list. He doesn't say it, but I see the moment he thinks it.

"What the fuck is wrong with you? When you got a woman underneath you, you're supposed to kiss her!" A voice calls out.

Logan and I both jerk and I see Nate and Wes walking toward us. Logan grumbles but pushes off the ground and holds a hand to help me to stand. I want to take it and pull him right back down on top of me. I don't even give a damn who sees us. But I don't. I let him help me stand.

"Are you okay? That was quite a tackle," Nate says, his gaze running over my body in a way that tells me he's checking for injuries. It strikes me then how good-looking he is. His hair is sandy blond, and he's sporting a light beard that gives him this sexy, rugged look. His eyes are such a unique color you could stare at them all day trying to figure out what to call them. Hazel is probably what his driver's license says, but they could arguably be brown, green, or gray. There's no way nothing happened between him and Ginny.

Wes steps forward, with his gorgeous jet-black hair, light tan skin and brightest pair of blue eyes I've ever seen. Add in that easy, flirtatious smile, and it's easy to see how very few women can resist him. "If you need a man who can seal the deal then you need to not look any further."

He winks at me and I laugh. "Are you really still using cheesy lines like that to get laid?"

Nate and Logan burst out laughing and shout, *burn*! But Wes isn't fazed.

"Works like a charm." He winks again. "And the only burn I saw is the missed kiss opportunity in the middle of this field."

Logan punches Wes' arm.

"Logan is showing me how to be a great edge," I say to get us past the almost kiss.

Nate and Wes share a look with Logan I don't quite understand before Nate turns his attention back to me. "How'd it go?"

"Tragic. I'd rather watch all of you in action."

The three of them smile, and I can practically feel the excitement and adrenaline radiating from them.

"That was the plan," Logan says and nods toward the end zone, and I turn to see several more players entering the field. I instantly recognize a few of them. Sam Strickland the quarterback; Wade Williams, a wide receiver; and Tanner Adams, the center.

This is insane. I can't believe I'm in Toro Stadium, surrounded by Toro players. As they approach, I suddenly feel very short. And at five-eight, I'm above average for a woman. While Logan's six-foot-three towers over me, some of these guys tower over him.

Logan introduces me to everyone, and I try not to look like I have stars in my eyes.

"So, you're our new teammate today? Ever played center?" Sam asks with a mischievous grin.

"Fuck no, you perv," Logan says and pulls me closer to him.

Sam gives him an innocent look. "What? I'd take the ball from shotgun."

"Yeah, right."

"No, Ally needs to be on defense," Wade says. "I'll let her cover me all day."

"Seriously? What the hell has happened to you all?" Logan says and they all laugh.

Wade taps my arm. "Just kidding, girl. We love razzing Lo."

"Well, it's clear you all want to impress me. So, I'll just head over to the sideline and brush up on my cheerleading skills."

"You were a cheerleader?" Logan asks, a dazzled expression on his face.

"Yep. You should have seen my toe touch." I give him a saucy smile and he groans. The guys tease him some more, but Tanner gets them all to stop joking around and they start talking about what drills they want to run. Watching them all in action this close is beyond impressive, and they aren't even going full-out. There are so many things you catch that you can't see from the nosebleed section, or even your television set.

After running certain drills, they start to play for fun. My God, they're all hot. Every single one of them. They keep using their shirts to wipe sweat from their faces, showing off their defined abs. It's impossible not to stare. Yet, the only one I truly want to look at is Logan. I've never really seen him like this. Competitive. Focused. Fierce. His intensity is so much of a turn on, I'm surprised I'm not emitting pheromones.

Sam throws a beautiful pass while Wade and Wes battle it

out down field. Wade catches it right before Wes gives him a push out of bounds. They're only seven yards from the end zone. They line up for the next play, and Sam is in the shotgun position. A nervous knot fills my stomach. As soon as the ball is snapped, Logan is off. He easily knocks the offensive lineman out of the way and guns right for Sam. Sam rolls to his left to avoid the sack, but Logan is too fast. He wraps Sam up, indicating a sack without the actual tackle, but he also swats at the ball, causing it to slip out of Sam's hands. As the ball falls to the field, Nate is there to snap it up and starts running in the other direction.

The defensive players go wild, chasing after Nate in celebration. I'm jumping up and down, screaming, and as they reach the end zone, I'm running toward them. Logan turns and faces me right as I throw myself at him. He catches me and swings me around, and when he sets me down his hands dive into my hair and pull my face close, but he stops himself short of kissing me. I want to yell at him not to stop. I'm so out of breath and turned on, I want this. I want him. Instead, he presses his forehead to mine.

"That was fucking impressive, Logan," I say when I can breathe properly.

"You think?"

"Total turn on."

He groans. "You can't tell me that right now."

"It's only fair after what you just did to me."

"All—" His fingers grip my head tighter, but he doesn't say more. His gaze is intense, almost pained.

A throat clears, and Logan eases his grip. I glance over to see the entire defense looking at us with huge grins and curious expressions. Now would be a good time for the field to open up and take me with it.

"Do we all get a hug like that?" Wes asks with another flirty grin.

I smile at him then hold up my fist for him to bump. "How about this?"

"Not nearly as fun. But I'll take it." He bumps my fist, and I do the same with all the players, even the offense who has joined us now. They all say their good-byes and start heading off the field leaving just me, Logan, Wes, and Nate.

"That was a beauty of a play. Thanks for the TD," Nate says and fist bumps Logan.

"It was awesome. Looks like someone has their head screwed back on," Wes says and gives Logan a fist bump.

Then the guys swing their gaze toward me, and it hits me that they're the ones that suggested Logan get laid to get out of his football slump. And now they're looking at me like I have a magical va-jay-jay or something. My face heats. Never in my life would I think I'd be some sort of muse or groupie or whatever I am.

"I, um, should go. Y'all are amazing to watch. Really."

They all puff up with pride before Logan tells me he'll walk me out. I can't believe everything that's happened today. I confessed my biggest and darkest secret in the middle of the Toro football field then had one of the most fun days I've had in a long time. And Logan was...perfect. As soon as we're in the tunnel, I take his hand and squeeze it. "Thanks for today. For everything. This was really fun."

He stops and watches me for a moment. I wish I could read what was going on in his mind. "Thanks for telling me. For trusting me."

Emotion clogs my throat. I do trust him. More than I ever thought I would. But I can't tell him that. It reveals too much. So, I nod and squeeze his hand again.

He looks like he wants to say something else, but instead he closes in on me until I'm caged between the tunnel wall and him. "So, did I earn some sexy study time?"

I roll my eyes at him. "Yeah, yeah. You earned your study

time. But we're adding it to my list. My rules."

A flirty smirk forms on his lips. "I'm good with that. And it's a *sexy* study session. Don't forget that part. It's very important."

"More important than earning an A on the exam?"

"Right now, the only thing I care about is getting my hands on you again." He dips his head until our lips are a breath away. "Anything else you want to add to your list right now? Like a 'you're an amazing football player' kiss?"

He's kind of adorable when he's horny.

"I'll give that for free." A fire lights in his eyes as I lean in, but I shift and kiss his cheek.

What can only be described as a growl comes from him. "That's not exactly what I had in mind."

"I know." I pat his chest and ease my way around him. "See you tomorrow."

chapter fourteen

I watch her leave, still reeling from everything that happened today, and I know she barely scratched the surface of what she went through after that video came out. I can only imagine how horrible it was for her. I really fucking hate that taking the picture of her list scared her so much. I wish I'd never done it. Yet, if I hadn't, would we be here right now? I'm not sure I can regret that. What I do know is I'm going to make damn sure she gets to do every item on her list without a single worry. I want her to take back that piece of her life.

I return to the field, and my friends are still there and staring at me with huge shit-eating grins. I guess the cat is out of the bag that Ally and I are sleeping together. They knew I was stopping her from going out with Ben at the frat party, but

I never told them what happened afterward. I'm never going to hear the end of this from them now.

"Nate and I were just discussing if we should say I told you so or if we should let it go since you already know we were right. What do you think?" Wes attempts to look contemplative.

"Isn't this you already saying it?"

Wes makes a mock surprised face. "Oh no, look what I did there."

I roll my eyes. "You're a jackass."

"A jackass that was *right*."

I flip him off.

"Explain something to me though, Lo. If Ally is your fuck buddy, then why did you waste at least two opportunities to kiss her?"

"We're not fuck buddies."

Both of them look at me like I just said the dumbest thing in the world.

"She called you Logan," Nate says. "You told us that Halloween girl only called you Clark. I'm guessing things have gotten more personal."

I shrug. While I love her nickname for me, I love that she only calls me Logan now. I still haven't called her only Ally. I almost did earlier. Fuck, I wanted her so much. I still do. My body is practically throwing a tantrum at being withheld from its favorite plaything.

"And you were a beast out there," Wes chimes in. "Are you dating her then?"

"No, not dating."

Wes looks at me skeptically. "Listen, be careful with that one. I knew the moment I met her she wasn't the fuck buddy type. Even if I did try."

"Maybe she just didn't want to fuck the man-whore football player."

Nate crosses his arms and studies me. That's never a good sign. It means he's going to hit me with a question I probably don't want to answer. "You sure you know what you're doing with her? I hate to say this again…I really hate to, but Wes has a point."

"Hey!" Wes puts his hands on his hips as if he's truly offended.

"Ally and I are good. We know what we're doing," I say.

"Are you sure?" Wes asks. "Because it looked like you had too many opportunities to kiss the girl and you didn't. Maybe y'all aren't doing it right?"

I flip him off again and head toward the blocking sled to grab my stuff and put everything back where I got it. It's bad enough I'm all hot and bothered by not being able to touch Ally, now I have these morons with their third degree. Unfortunately, Wes and Nate follow me like a couple of teenage girls.

"Oh, I know, she's *Pretty Womaning* you, isn't she?" Wes says as he catches up to me.

"What?"

"You know, the no kissing rule. Just fucking. Like that old movie with a smokin' hot Julia Roberts in it."

"Why have you seen that?"

"Did you not hear me? Young, hot Julia Roberts."

I shake my head. "No, she's not *Pretty Womaning* me."

"Then what the fuck, man?"

"Why is this an issue for you? It's none of your business." I point to the other side of the sled, indicating for him to help me push. He and Nate line up, and we push the sled back toward the end zone tunnel.

"Because it makes no fucking sense! You wanted to kiss her. She wanted to kiss you. Why the hell aren't you kissing?"

"Because it's off list!" Shit. As soon as the words come out of my mouth, I realize my mistake. I just vowed to protect her no matter what, then I go and blurt out her secret. Fuck! Wes and Nate stop pushing and look at me with renewed interest.

"Off list? What does that mean?" Nate asks.

"Forget it." I start pushing again and they help, but Wes doesn't let it go.

"Oh no, you're explaining this."

A grunt is my response as we get the sled back in place. Then they both look at me expectantly. Shit, how do I explain without breaking Ally's confidence? Then it comes to me.

"I have a college bucket list and she's helping me cross things off."

The guys stare at me for a beat then they start laughing.

"No, you fucking don't!" Wes says.

I shrug. "I made it freshman year."

"Prove it."

I roll my eyes, but I head back on the field. When we get to my backpack, I pull out my wallet and pull out the folded piece of paper and hand it over. I started keeping it on me so I could pick an item whenever I wanted.

"This is definitely a freshman's bucket list," Wes says with a snicker.

"Yeah, pretty standard stuff. But you said I needed to have some fun and I haven't done some of those things so…"

Wes is snickering at the list. "There's no way Ally is going to have a threesome with you."

"Don't worry about what we are and aren't going to do."

Nate looks up from the list, confusion on his face. "Which number were you doing today?"

Uh, shit.

At my pause, Wes points. "You're fucking lying!"

I snatch the list from them before either one of them can analyze it further. "I have the list, don't I?"

"But so does she," Nate says with a knowing grin. Why does he have to be so fucking smart?

"That's it!" Wes says with an excited gleam in his eyes. "What's on her list?"

"I'm not telling you." Ugh, so much for trying to keep the focus off Ally and her list.

"Why not?"

"Because it's her list and I'd be a dick if I told people about it. I didn't mean to tell you this much so you two better keep your big mouths shut. I'm serious about that."

"Who are we going to tell? Besides, a college bucket list is no big deal," Nate says. "Lots of students do it. Look at you."

"Right," I agree and pray that's the end of it.

"So, playing football with her was an item?" Nate asks and I nod. "And you're only doing list things with her and nothing else?"

"Right. We're done when we graduate or when the lists run out."

"You're list buddies!" Wes exclaims, and I shrug. His grin widens. "She's got some kinky shit on her list, doesn't she?"

I give him a warning look. "Watch it."

"Whatever, I know I'm right. So, why is kissing off list?"

"They only kiss when they're doing an item that requires it. Today's item didn't. Am I understanding this right?" Nate asks.

I nod.

"What's the fun in that?" Wes asks with a scrunched-up face.

There's no fun in it. I totally wanted to kiss her today. I wanted to tell her to forget the whole off list thing, but we need it. We're already having trouble finding the balance between sleeping together and acting normal.

"We're keeping things no-strings. She's going to grad school, and hopefully I'll be in the NFL. But if I'm not, I'm still not staying here," I say finally.

"Why not?"

"Because I don't want to be here. Come on, you know I've been dying to get out of this town." As far away from my dad, and all the memories I'd rather forget, as I can get. "Besides, the PR firm I've been interning for has offices in Dallas and San Francisco. My boss mentioned them having some entry positions available." I shrug. "If football doesn't work out then I'll probably interview."

"Whoa, that's awesome. Maybe I'll hire you to keep me out of trouble when I go to the big show," Wes says.

"Well, I'd certainly stay busy," I say and Wes flips me off then he says he has to run, and we all fist bump him again before he takes off.

I grab my stuff to head toward the locker room, but when I look at Nate, he's watching me closely. "You look way too serious, man."

"You wanted to kiss Ally today. You like her."

I shrug. "She's a good kisser, and shouldn't I like the woman I'm having sex with?"

He shakes his head at me. "Be careful, man. Or I don't think it's going to be as easy to leave as you think."

"Trust me, we both have our own agendas. Neither one of us has a desire to take this further." I bring my water bottle to my mouth and take a big drink. Maybe it will wash away the sour taste my words leave in my mouth.

"This isn't exactly what I had in mind."

Ally looks up at me from the blanket she has spread out on the grass in front of the main tower on campus. "Oh, what did you have in mind?" A sinister smile plays on her lips.

"Someplace more private. Much more private."

"And you expected us to actually study if we were somewhere more private?"

I drop my backpack on the ground and sit next to her. "Honestly, I wasn't thinking about studying."

"Exactly."

"This is supposed to be a *sexy* study session, Allyson."

"I know." She gestures toward the blanket. "And don't Allyson me yet."

"A blanket doesn't equal sexy." I glance around and while campus is mostly vacant, there are other people hanging out and taking advantage of the gorgeous weather. In a couple days, it'll be cold again, but today is spring-like. So much so that Ally is wearing a dress. It's long-sleeved, but thin, with tiny buttons going down the center of her chest to her waist where a sash style belt is tied. "But the dress helps." I rub a finger along her leg, slowly bringing up the hem of her dress.

She bats my hand away. "I think you're dwelling on the sexy part too much."

"And I think you're dwelling on the study part too much."

She gives me a pointed look, like she's trying to scold me, but there's too much amusement dancing in her eyes to take her seriously. Fuck, she's cute.

"Okay, okay. I'll be good. So, tell me why you picked this spot?"

She lifts her shoulders and looks away, which only proves there's a reason. "Thought it was a nice day."

"No, there's a reason, and it's not just so I would behave. Come on, it's hard not to believe you haven't studied here before, so tell me."

She sighs and I swear she's blushing. "Okay, but it's going to sound silly to you."

"Maybe not."

She looks at me doubtfully. "Don't say I didn't warn you. One of my favorite things to do is sit here on a beautiful day like this and people watch. I love seeing all the couples. Some lie next to each other and read, some study together, some talk and kiss and touch and…I wanted that."

I look out at the various people on the grass. The couples do look awfully cozy, the kind of cozy I'd like to be with Ally. I've never done this before either. Yeah, I've sat here with friends to pass time between classes, but never in this way. It was always too relationship-y. My roommates' warnings ring in my head. Is this too far into relationship territory? Shit, it doesn't matter. It's a list item now, and I vowed to give her whatever she wants. But it has to stay strictly list-only.

At that thought, I notice two people walking down the path along the grassy mall hand-in-hand. It's two guys, but that's not what caught my attention, it's because one of them is Ally's ex.

"Isn't that Joel?" I nod toward the couple.

Ally glances over and she flinches as she sees him with the other guy. "Yeah, with Matthew."

She doesn't sound surprised. "He cheated on you with a guy? Was that a surprise?"

"No, I always knew he was bi," she says as she watches them settle on the grass at the very bottom of the hill. A small bitter laugh comes out of her.

I nudge her knee and she looks at me then. I can't quite make out her expression. It seems to be a bundle of emotions. "What's going on in that head of yours?"

Why the hell did I ask that? I just told myself to keep things on the surface.

She blinks a few times and looks completely bewildered. Like she doesn't know where to start. I start to tell her to forget it then she speaks.

"The one time I tried studying here with him, he complained how he couldn't see his screen because it was too bright and was generally put out the whole time. We left after ten minutes."

And now he's doing exactly that with his boyfriend.

"Why did you stay with him so long?" I shouldn't ask, but I want to understand why she stayed in a relationship lacking all the passion she clearly wants.

"He was safe."

"What do you mean?"

"After what Danny did...I didn't want to date again. I hated the idea of having a boyfriend. But with Joel, things were easy. Uncomplicated. I didn't have to worry about him hurting me."

"But he did."

"Yeah. Him moving on before breaking up with me brought up all my trust issues again."

I notice she only talks about the trust he broke. Nothing about a broken heart.

I pull her to me and lay us down so her head is resting against my chest. "Ally, I promise you're safe with me."

Her breathing changes, becomes a little more erratic. I shut my eyes, realizing what I just said. Why can't I keep that word out of my mouth when it comes to her?

"Am I?" She pauses and I can feel her heartbeat pick up against my body. "Sometimes with you, I've never felt so defenseless. You make me forget to be scared."

My chest tightens. Her words fill me with so many emotions, I don't know how to begin to sort them out. What I do know is Ally letting go of her fears is exactly what I wanted for her.

"That's the point of the lists, Ally. To push your limits without worry." I tip her head up so she's meeting my gaze. "I take on your fear and let you enjoy the thrill. Let me give you that. You deserve it."

You deserve more than I can ever give you.

Her beautiful green eyes drink me in, and I understand what she means about feeling defenseless. Because right now it feels like I'm caught in the lineman's sight and there's nothing to do except take the hit.

"I don't know what I deserve, but I'm learning not to ignore the things I want."

"What do you want?"

"For you to kiss me on this blanket in the middle of campus."

"I'll kiss you anywhere." I brush my lips against hers. "Everywhere." I seal my mouth to hers and give her a kiss that leaves no question of how much I want her. I move so half my body is over hers. I pull up her leg and let my hand explore her smooth skin and practice more restraint than I truly have to keep my hand from going where I want to feel her most. Our kiss is frantic now, messy and demanding.

I pump my hips into her once, letting her feel exactly how much I need her. She turns her head, and my kiss moves to her cheek, then I trail it down her neck.

"Okay, you have to stop." She's gasping for breath and holding me tightly, her actions belying her words.

I don't want to stop. I want to sink into her so badly I don't care if all of campus sees. She grabs my head and pulls it up so I'm forced to meet her dilated and lust-glazed eyes. "We've got to stop."

I'm so fucking high on her I never want to come down. "I need to be inside you again. It's been too long, Allyson."

She gives a small nod and looks as drugged as I feel. I move off her so we can both compose ourselves. After a few moments, she turns to me. "Time to study."

I groan. "You're killing me."

"Believe it or not, I hate studying. Half the time I spend at least an hour staring into space so I started making deals with myself to get through it. Like work for an hour then I get to buy myself a cupcake, stuff like that. It motivates and rewards me."

"So, study first then…dessert?"

She smiles, her eyes dancing. "Exactly."

"Okay, let's get this done."

She laughs at how quickly I sit up and drag my book out of my backpack. My hard-on is painful to work around at first, but it slowly figures out it isn't seeing any action anytime soon. We fall into a groove and get through the material with ease, and I realize how great Ally is to study with. We laugh and kiss and touch, and it's by far the best time I've ever had studying. We're on the last page of the study guide, and my gaze keeps going to the tiny buttons I plan to rip open soon. I shift away from her in an effort to keep myself under control.

"Ally?"

I look up to see a woman on the sidewalk to our right looking at us. Ally makes a shocked, panicked sound. "Um, hey, Mom."

Oh shit! I suddenly recognize President Worthington. She's not in her usual professional attire but still looks business-like now that I look at her closely. Ally jumps up, and I do too. I'm so glad I wasn't in the middle of mauling Ally and sporting a raging boner to meet her mom.

"What are you doing here?" Ally asks her mom as she makes her way toward us. Her voice sounds way too guilty. I look over at her and she looks guilty too. Damn, you would think her mom caught us going at it.

"I work here. Remember?" Mrs. Worthington looks like she's trying not to laugh.

"It's Sunday, Mom."

"I know what day it is." Her mother smiles then looks at me, a very curious gleam in her eyes.

"Hello, President Worthington, I'm Logan Mackenzie." I hold out my hand for her to shake and she takes it. I met her during football season, but I have no idea if she remembers me.

"Yes, Logan, I remember you. Very nice to see you again. How do you know my daughter?"

"We actually met when I was her RA at Nichols Dormitory."

Her eyebrows shoot up and she glances at Ally. "Oh yes, that's right. I didn't realize you were friends."

"We have a class together this semester and have only run into each other over the years."

She nods and looks at her daughter and the blanket. "Studying? Or...?"

"Yes, we have a test tomorrow," Ally says, her tone completely annoyed now. "What are you doing here? *On a Sunday.*"

"Unfortunately, there was an incident in the chemistry building yesterday and I need to assess the damage."

"What happened?"

"Drunk college students, I suspect. Unfortunately, I have to make sure it's nothing more sinister since chemicals are involved. I'm heading that way now." Her mother looks at me again, absolutely assessing me. "Are you a psychology major as well, Logan?"

"Sociology."

She smiles at me then. "I guess I'll let you two get back to studying. Maybe I'll see you again, Logan."

I don't know how to respond, so I nod and smile.

"Oh, Mom," Ally says before her mother walks away. "We're finishing up and I was pointing out your office to Logan earlier. Think we can run up so he can see the view?"

I try my best not to let my shock show. What the hell is Ally doing? Does she want to show me the view or does she want dessert? Sweat beads on my forehead.

"I suppose so." Mrs. Worthington digs in her purse and pulls out a set of keys. She takes a key off her ring and hands it to Ally. "Put the key in my center desk drawer and leave the door unlocked. I'm dropping back by before I leave."

"Okay, thanks."

I wait until Ally's mom is at the other end of the mall before I look at Ally. "You were telling me about the view, huh?"

She gives me a naughty grin. "Ready for dessert?"

chapter fifteen

I laugh as Logan's jaw drops. I grab the blanket and stuff it back in my bag.

"Logan, snap out of it. Time's a-wasting."

He blinks a couple of times then shoots into motion, gathering all his things. I laugh again. This is crazy. I probably should be panicking, but instead, I feel free. As soon as I realized my mom's office would be clear, I knew exactly how I wanted our sexy study session to end even if it's crazy and reckless. But I'm going to let Logan take my fear so I can enjoy the thrill.

I grab his hand and pull him toward the main building. My heart is thundering in my ears. I can't believe we're going to do this.

"Hey," he nudges my shoulder. "Are you sure about this?"

I meet his gaze. "I'm sure."

He blows out a breath and pushes a hand through his hair looking nervous as hell.

I giggle as I punch a code for us to get in the elevator. "There are cameras until we get in my mom's office," I mutter under my breath.

"Shit. Okay."

I look at him and smile. "You're kinda adorable when you're nervous."

He looks at me and puffs out his chest a little more. "I'm not nervous."

"Sure, you're not."

He gives me a side-eye look but says nothing. We don't touch during the elevator ride, doing our best to look super casual. But as soon as the door shuts to my mom's office and the lock clicks, he pushes me up against it and takes my mouth. Our bags hit the floor and I wrap my legs around him as he grinds his hips into me.

"You're fucking crazy. You really want to do this?" he says in between kisses.

I kiss him back, pulling him further into me. "I see your nerves have left you."

He trails his mouth down my neck, and I arch it to give him better access. "If you want this, I want this." Then he stops and meets my gaze. "But I want you to be sure."

"I'm sure." I lean in and place a soft kiss on his lips. "Let me feel the thrill, Logan."

He grins. "Baby, I'm going to thrill you so good you're not going to remember your name."

He pulls me further into the room and all the way to the windows that look out to the Capitol and downtown. His mouth brushes my ear, his warm breath sending a hot tingle down my body.

"I want to fuck you right here." God, his mouth. I love it when talks to me like this. "From behind, looking at this view."

My heart drops as soon as I hear his last words. I spin around before he can press himself into me and panic like I almost did in the hotel room. "No. Not from behind."

He blinks before he realizes why. "Ally, I'd never—"

I put my finger over his lips before he can say anything else. "I know. But I know what I want, Logan. My list item, remember?"

His gaze turns molten and his voice dips low. "What do you want, Allyson?"

I slowly let out a breath of relief and pull him away from the windows to another set of doors. I open them to reveal another room with a long conference table in it. The table is made of dark polished wood with a Toro decal right in the middle.

I look at him. "I want you to fuck me on the table."

His eyes are wide as he takes it in, then he looks at me. "You've thought of this before, haven't you?"

"From the first moment I saw it."

A sexy smile forms on his lips. "I love the way you think, Allyson."

He examines the room, and I realize he's looking for cameras. I love how he's taking this precaution; it makes me trust him even more. He pulls the doors shut behind us then leads me to the end of the table. "Sit."

I hop on and spread my legs. He takes off his glasses, but there's no mistaking the heat in his gaze as he watches my dress hitch up. "You wore that dress to torture me, didn't you?"

I only smile.

"I've been dying to rip those tiny buttons off for hours. Unbutton them. Let me see your tits."

Jesus, he's killing me. Slowly, I release them one by one, loving the way his breath becomes more erratic as my fingers move. I part my dress and unsnap the front clasping bra I bought especially for today. He inhales sharply as he touches me, his thumb stroking over one of my aching nipples.

"So pretty and pink," he mumbles before leaning down and replacing his thumb with his tongue. I weave my fingers into his hair, loving that with only one touch from him, my whole body is on fire. He licks, gently bites, and kisses me until I feel like I'm going to burst right out of my skin. He yanks me to the edge of the table, pushes up my dress, and rips my panties off. He falls to his knees.

"Logan, we don't have time…"

"Yes, we do. You didn't let me taste you, and I'm not passing it up this time." He kisses my inner thigh then right at my center and my hips jerk off the table. Oh fuck. My head falls back as he slowly licks me before slipping his tongue inside me, tasting me fully. Oh my God, this has never felt so good. I'm out of my mind.

"More. Logan, you have to make me come. Right now."

He growls, and the vibration sends another shock of pleasure through me right before he hits the perfect spot and I come apart. No, I rip apart. My orgasm spikes through me so suddenly I have to bite my lip to stop myself from screaming out. It feels so damn good, I never want it to end.

"More."

He stands. "Oh, I'm going to give you more." I've never seen anyone undo their pants and put on a condom faster than Logan does now. God, he's beautiful. So hard and thick. He gently pushes me down so I lie down on the table and he pulls me to the edge and enters me in one quick thrust, a loud groan escapes both of us.

"You're so fucking wet. Always so greedy for my cock, aren't you, baby?" He puts my feet on his shoulders. "Hold on tight because I'm about to take you on the ride of your life."

He slams into me again in a powerful thrust that has me arching my back as a sweet pain fills my body. Then he starts fucking me hard and fast, his pace punishing and frenzied, and this time I'm going to truly rip apart. The pleasure is sharp and intense. I don't know if I can handle it, yet I don't want it to stop. I need more. I need to know how far I can go before I lose it all.

"Come for me, Ally. I need to feel you come again. I need to feel you cream on my cock right here on this big table. Give it to me, baby. Right now."

He presses a finger to my clit and immediately sends me over the edge. I'm falling into pure, hot bliss. He lets out an animalistic sound as his fingers dig into my hips.

"That's it, Ally. Fuck...your pussy feels so good." His thrusts come quicker and faster as his own release chases mine until he eventually collapses on top of me.

I'm not sure how long we stay like that, floating back to Earth, our breath slowly steadying. We look at each other, goofy smiles on both of our lips.

"Was it everything you wanted it to be?"

"Everything and more."

I wonder if he realizes he said my name. He said it earlier then again while fucked me. Not Allyson. Not Ally Cat. Only Ally.

A look passes over his face that I can't quite interpret, but I wonder if he's thinking about how that felt like much more than a list item. As soon as the thought crosses my mind, I push it away. I can't start getting all romantic.

He pulls me up and gives me a quick kiss. "That was fucking hot."

"The hottest." I run my tongue along his bottom lip, and he moans.

"You gotta stop or we'll never get out of here."

The reality of where we are hits me. I glance at the clock on the wall. Thirty minutes have passed since we left my mom. "We have to go. No, we have to clean. Oh no, what are we going to do with the condom? You can't leave it here. What if it doesn't flush? What if..." The thought of my mom knowing I had sex in a daring situation again makes my chest tighten.

"Hey." Logan tips my chin so I'll look at him. "We can do this. We'll get it all done one thing at a time, okay? Look, she didn't walk into us mid-fuck so the worst is over, right?"

I blow out a laugh and nod. The tightness eases. We quickly put ourselves back together, then I run to the private bathroom and get the cleaning supplies from the cabinet. The table is super shiny when I'm done, and Logan said he tied off the condom, wrapped in a handful of toilet tissue and put it in his backpack so no evidence was left behind. Once we're back in the elevator, I breathe easy.

He looks at me. "You okay?"

My stomach is in knots, and I feel a little dizzy as the adrenaline wears off, but I don't feel panicked. That's a definite improvement. "I'm okay. I think I'm getting a little less afraid of my list."

His eyes roam over my face. "Your list looks good on you, Ally Cat."

"It feels good. Thanks. For grounding me, but also letting me fly."

The corners of his eyes crinkle in a smile that doesn't touch his lips. One of his fingers grazes mine and I move my own into his touch, letting my pinky hook around his. Suddenly, he pulls it away. I look at him and he's frowning at his hand before he clenches it in a fist then releases it. What does that mean? As soon as we get outside, I see my mom walking up the steps. Heat fills my cheeks as my stomach tightens. Will she be able to tell I just had sex?

"Oh, you're still here, good! You didn't answer my text. Dad is on his way with lunch."

"Uh…my phone is on silent." I glance at Logan and his eyes have an edge of panic to them.

My mom looks at Logan. "You'll join us, Logan."

He opens and closes his mouth a couple times then gives a nod. "Yes, ma'am."

I would burst out laughing if I wasn't so petrified. I can't go back into her office. Not *now*. "We can do a picnic," I say.

"Your dad is picking up Torchy's Tacos. It's too messy for a picnic. We'll eat at the conference table in my office."

Logan lets out a choking cough and my stomach knots painfully. If I walk back into that conference room, there's no way I won't give myself away or go into a full-blown panic attack.

"Come on." My mom gestures as she climbs the steps. I look at Logan, silently asking him how we're going to get out of this. He must sense my panic, because his own uncertainty fades as he reaches out and grabs my hand.

"Hey, it's fine. We cleaned the hell out of that room. We're just having lunch with your parents."

I nod. "Oh my God, you're meeting my parents." A nervous giggle comes out of me. What else is there to do but laugh?

"Yeah, right where I just defiled their daughter," he whispers. "I'm so screwed."

"No, that was me, remember?"

He shakes his head and laughs. "See, this is funny. We'll get through it." He squeezes my hand before letting it go.

When we get up to the office, the conversation is going well, then Dad gets there and goes straight for the conference room. He plops the bags of food on the table and my gaze goes directly to the end where I was laid out twenty minutes ago. I glance at Logan and he's looking at the same spot. When he meets my eyes, I see the heat in his. Shit, he can't look at me like that. Not now.

"Logan, this is my dad, Tom Shaw," I say, and my father holds out his hand to Logan.

Logan looks like he's swallowed an apple whole before he snaps out of it and shakes my father's hand. "Logan Mackenzie, nice to meet you, sir."

My dad looks from Logan to me then back to him. "You dating my daughter?"

"Daddy!"

Dad looks at me with faux innocent eyes. "What?"

"Nosy much?"

"I'm your father, I'm allowed." He folds his arms across his chest and gives Logan a hard stare.

I roll my eyes. "We're friends, Dad."

I look over at Logan and surprisingly he's holding his own as my father stares him down. "I've known Ally since her freshman year, and she's been a pretty great friend to me over the years."

My heart beats a little faster at the note of affection in his voice. My dad's expression doesn't soften, but I can tell he liked what Logan said.

"Tell me, Logan, do you like Torchy's?"

"I'm an Austinite, sir. Tacos are my favorite food group. Did you get any trashy style?" A Torchy's taco served trashy style is smothered in their famous queso.

My dad cracks a smile. "Is there any other way?"

And just like that Logan and my dad are friends. They start unloading the bags, and I notice Logan stands closest to 'our spot' and keeps sneaking glances at it. I'm not sure how we're going to get through this lunch without burning a hole in the table.

My mom enters and peers over my dad's and Logan's

shoulders. "Wow, the cleaning crew did a stand-up job last time they were here."

Logan jerks and suddenly the soda sitting near his hand falls and spills all over the table. "Fuck!" As soon as the word is out of his mouth, he grimaces. "Shit, I didn't mean to say that."

Then he realizes he's cursed again and rolls his eyes. "Damn it."

At that point, he throws his hand over his mouth.

My mother has her hand over her mouth to stop herself from laughing. My father doesn't bother trying; he throws his head back and releases a hearty laugh. Logan looks at me with a mortified expression, and I can't help it, I join my parents. He narrows his gaze at me then relaxes and starts laughing at himself.

"Well, son, I think you hit all the basics. Now you need to mix it up. Let's get this motherfucking table cleaned off."

After a moment of shocked silence, Logan and I burst into laughter once again. From there, our lunch goes much more smoothly. We mostly talk football since Logan leaves for the NFL Combine soon. But he's also joking around with my dad and handling all my mom's questions with ease. My parents and Joel never got along this well. Not that Logan is my boyfriend.

I glance at him and let myself wonder…what if? What if we were more than our lists?

"So, do you have any plans on what you might do if football isn't in your future?" my father asks.

"I'm hoping it will be in one form or another. I'm interning at a PR firm, and I enjoy working with contracts and such. Their Dallas and San Francisco offices have sports departments and are hiring entry level positions." He shrugs.

"Wow. You never told me that," I say before I can stop myself. He's really leaving. Okay, I knew that. If he gets drafted or picked up by the NFL, he could be moving across the country. But it's really sinking in that he's leaving no matter what.

He glances at me then away. "I haven't given it too much thought yet. We'll see after the draft." He looks back at me. "You'll be in grad school."

His words are meant as a reminder: don't get attached.

"Yeah, I know. Just didn't realize you had other plans. It sounds really great, Logan." I pray my voice sounds light and genuine as I turn my attention back to my taco. Not that I'm hungry anymore.

In a few short months I might never see Logan again, and I need to get used to that now. We're a list and that's it. I just need to enjoy the ride, and when I graduate, I'll get off and move on.

chapter sixteen

Logan

Last Halloween

The last person I want to see today is my dad, but he insisted I meet him. It seems my mom being dead five years is much more special than any other year she's been dead. It requires a reunion. I don't even know why I agreed, but since I visit her grave every Halloween anyway, I decided I could tolerate a few minutes being here with my dad as well.

"Hey son."

I turn away from my mom's headstone and see my dad approach with a bouquet of lilies that look like the ones I brought.

"Hey," I say and turn back to her grave. My father sets his bouquet on the other side of the headstone from where I laid mine.

We stand there together in silence for a long time. Sadness and grief surrounding us like a thick fog.

"I miss her," I say, not really sure why I confessed my feelings to the man I've barely spoken to in the past five years.

"Me too," my dad says, and I want to come back with a mean retort. After everything that happened, it doesn't feel like he should be allowed to miss her. But she was his wife for almost nineteen years, and I know he loved her, even if he wasn't in love with her anymore.

"The other day 'Sitting on the Dock of the Bay' came on," my dad says. "Remember how much she loved that song? How terribly she sang it, and we'd give her such crap. But she didn't care."

A smile immediately creeps on my lips, and I can hear her and her cracking singing voice.

"She'd crank up the volume and start singing and dancing. Gah, she did that once during school carpool. I was so mortified." I smile at the memory as tears prick my eyes. I'd give anything to have her embarrass the shit out of me now.

Suddenly, tears are spilling down my cheeks. My dad closes in and pulls me into a hug, and for the first time since she died, I let him comfort me. His body starts to shudder too, and it feels good to share my grief. I didn't realize how isolating it's been for me until this moment. It's only been my Halloweens with Ally that have come somewhat close to comfort.

When we finally part, I feel surprisingly lighter. Usually when I leave the cemetery, I'm back where I was when she first died—angry and sad.

My dad gives me a gentle smile. "Would you like to get dinner? I'd love to spend some time with you."

"I can't. I have plans." I'm not feeling soft enough toward my dad to cancel plans with Ally. This is our one day together and there's no way I'm missing it.

My dad's mouth flattens. He probably doesn't believe me, and usually I wouldn't give a fuck, but I guess my crying jag has softened me.

"Maybe tomorrow? I have practice until seven, but I'm free after that."

His eyes light up. "Really?"

I shrug. "Sure."

His eyes get glossy, but he clears his throat and quickly blinks. "Great. Want to go to Matt's El Rancho? You still like that place?"

"Yeah, that works."

"Great." He nods and I'm pretty sure he wants to hug me again, but instead we turn back toward our cars. I notice there's another car parked in front of his with a woman sitting in the driver's seat. She's looking at us, and I glance at my dad to see him subtly make a hand gesture towards her. She gives him a small smile then glances at me before quickly looking away.

"Do you know her?"

My dad doesn't say anything, and there's a hesitation in his step. We stop at my truck and his expression is uncomfortable. "Um, yeah. That's my girlfriend, Miranda."

"You brought your girlfriend to your wife's grave? Are you fucking kidding me?"

"Look, I didn't know if you would show up or if you would even speak to me. She came for support, that's it."

"And were we all going to go to dinner together? You thought it would be a great idea to introduce your son to your girlfriend on the anniversary of his mother's death?"

"Logan, no, it's not—"

"What the fuck is wrong with you?"

"Logan, please—"

"No. I knew this was a terrible idea. I should have never

agreed to see you. Not today of all days. You disappointed me five years ago, and nothing's fucking changed. Just leave me alone, okay?"

He doesn't stop me this time, and I get in my truck and drive off, refusing to look in the rearview mirror. I drive straight to Ally's place. The need to see her is overwhelming. When she opens her door with those adorable cat ears on her head like every other Halloween we've been together, it takes all my willpower not to grab her and kiss the ever living fuck out of her.

I want her.

Yeah, I've always wanted her, but right now…it's so damn hard to deny how much I want to fuck her. How I want to fuck her over and over again. Fuck her until I can't feel anymore.

"Clark? Are you okay?'

I realize I've been standing here staring at her like some starved animal.

"Yeah."

She blinks, her expression concerned. She steps back so I can come inside. Our plan was to get back to the cheesy horror movie marathon, like our first Halloween.

"So, are you ready to *Scream*? Again?" She presents the television screen like some model on a game show where *Scream 2* is queued up and ready to play.

"Sure."

Her shoulders slump at my lack of enthusiasm. "What's wrong?"

"Nothing.

"Are you sure? You seem—"

"I'm fine," I snap and plop onto the sofa.

She folds her arms across her chest, and I can't help but to stare at how amazing her tits look in that shirt. "Yeah, sure, you sound fine."

I glare at her. "Are you going to start the movie or what?"

"No, not until you tell me what crawled up your ass and died."

I bite back a smile. And she raises her brows in question.

I run a hand through my hair. "I visited my mom's grave and saw my dad. Things didn't go well."

Everything about her softens, and she immediately comes over and sits next to me on the sofa. She takes my hand in hers and I latch onto it like a lifeline.

"What happened?"

I never told her how the rest of that Halloween played out with my dad. Not that I have any desire to talk about all that now.

"He brought his girlfriend to my mom's grave."

Her brows snap together. "That's, um…a little indelicate."

"You think?"

"I'm sorry, Clark. I've got a pantry full of junk food and a fridge full of beer, if that makes you feel better."

"How do you always have beer? You're not even twenty-one yet."

"I got a cool neighbor that checks with me every time he goes on a beer run, plus I give him an extra five bucks."

"Man, he's going to hate it when you turn twenty-one."

"Six more weeks." She does this little cheeky dance.

I smile at her. Fuck, she's beautiful. Beautiful in so many ways.

She snuggles into me, wrapping her arms around my middle. We stay like that for several minutes. It's just like our first Halloween. But the want I felt for her then is nothing to what I feel now. My hand is practically shaking to touch her. To cup the soft breast that's pressing into me. To bare it and suck it and bite it. I want to give her tits so much attention that I make her come just from that.

"Is this okay?"

No, it's not okay. It's fucking fantastic. And that's the problem right there.

"Where's your boyfriend tonight? Frat party again?" I learned that she and Joel started dating not long after last Halloween.

She stiffens. "I don't know. We're not together anymore."

Oh fuck. She's single. She's single and in my arms feeling like heaven. Tonight could be different. Tonight, we could cross the line we've been toying with for three years.

She looks up at me, and I see a lot in that one look. Vulnerability. Want. Heat.

I know in that moment that tonight things will change. I'll kiss her. Touch her. Fuck her. I'll fuck her just like I wanted to earlier. Furiously. Selfishly.

Her hand curls into my shirt and she leans in. My heart thunders in my chest. This is it. Her lips are a breath away from mine. And I jerk away.

She blinks, and the mixture of hurt and confusion in her eyes kills me.

"I have to go." I jump off the couch before I pull her into my lap and do all the things I want to do to her.

"What? You're leaving?" She wraps her arms around her middle, as if trying to protect herself.

"Yeah. Got a team meeting tonight."

"On Halloween? You didn't think to mention that before now?"

"I was distracted by my dad stuff."

She turns her face away, but not before I saw her eyes turn glassy. It feels like a knife has been thrust into my gut.

"See you, Ally Cat." I leave, refusing to look back again. If I do, I'll stay. And that's the last thing I should do.

I'm starting for the Toros and having a remarkable season.

My name's on everyone's lips. The walk-on leading the nation in sacks—it's unheard of. I actually have a possible future in the NFL now. Even if I don't, my future isn't here—where my mother doesn't live, but my dad lives on. As soon as my diploma is in hand, I'm gone. I have no business making promises I can't keep.

chapter seventeen

When my dad said he wasn't going to give up, he really meant it. I've gotten a text from him almost every other day. At first, they were just one-liners with most of them trying to get me to meet up with him to talk. I ignored them all.

So, when his text came through today, I was ready to swipe it away, but the first line catches my attention. I click on it and what I find reads more like a book than a text.

I think I fell in love with your mother the moment I saw her. She came into my history class, new to my school, and I couldn't look away. She was so beautiful. But it was her laugh that won me over. The teacher said something that made her laugh, and it hit me like cupid's arrow. I knew I had to do whatever I could to keep that laugh in my life. We became inseparable. It was scary when we got preg-

I don't know what to think of his text. A part of me wants to tell him to stop, that I'm not interested. But I don't. Instead, I wait for the next one.

It's like I'm reading about a completely different family. How could they never tell me about any of this? How did I not realize she'd been pregnant? I could have had a sister, and no one ever said anything.

I want to respond. But what do I say? I'm still pissed. But now I feel guilty too. I should have known. I should have figured it out.

I don't text him. I wait for the next one.

Losing your mother was devastating. But losing you too, it kills me every day. What happened, what you had to deal with and how you had to tell me…honestly, I felt I deserved your hate. I wasn't there. For her. For you. I needed to be punished. That's why I let this rift between us last all this time, why I waited so long to see a therapist again. I wanted to suffer. But by doing so, I've allowed you to suffer too. By failing to set things right, I've just caused both of us more pain. Please forgive me for that.

Each lengthy text is harder to read, and yet I find myself anxiously awaiting the next one.

I didn't plan on falling in love again. It just didn't feel right anymore. I met Miranda about six months after your mother died. We became friends. Dating each other wasn't on our minds at all. Slowly, we became closer. She encouraged me to go to therapy, to find a way to make amends with you. It was only after I started healing that I allowed myself to see that sometime over the years, I'd started falling for her. One day I kissed her, thinking I've either ruined everything or have a chance at everything again. Kissing her turned out to be the right thing to do. But I don't have everything, not without you in my life.

chapter eighteen

Me: I'm at the library and thinking #19 would
be a great treat for all my studying.

It usually doesn't take Logan long to text me back when I'm talking about a list item so it surprises me when twenty minutes pass and I don't hear from him. We haven't spoken much since our sexy study session. Meeting my parents was definitely off list. It couldn't be helped though, and we just need to get back on track with focusing strictly on the list.

A body sits in the chair next to me and I jump as a feeling of excitement bubbles inside me. I look up and all the excitement instantly pops. It isn't Logan, but Joel.

I pull my earbuds out. "You scared me."

"Sorry, I said your name, but you didn't hear me."

I nod. Other than seeing him the other day across the mall, I haven't seen him since we broke up. "Hey. What's up?"

He looks away, unsure. "I saw you and wanted to say hi. Was hoping we could talk. All I've gotten from you is a couple of texts about getting your stuff from my place since we've broken up. I think we deserve better closure."

I sigh. "Okay, yeah, you're right."

He gives me a relieved smile and after a few silent moments, he says, "I'm sorry things ended the way they did."

"Me too." My stomach clenches, and I ask the one question that's been bothering me this whole time. "Why didn't you break up with me?

He closes his eyes and dips his head. He takes a breath before meeting my eyes again. "Honestly, Ally, I kind of forgot we were dating."

"What?"

He sighs. "When you walked in on me and Matthew…that was the second time we'd ever fooled around. Yeah, I had started having feelings for him, but I didn't think he liked me back then things just happened. Me and you, we hadn't seen or talked to each other in a while and hadn't slept together in a lot longer than that." He shrugs. "You weren't on my mind." He looks at me, his expression guilty. "Sorry."

Well, damn. That stung. Yet he's not wrong. It had been a long time since we'd been together in any way, which is why I'd stopped by.

"If you were having feelings for someone, you should have said something. We could have called it quits."

He stares at me before he gives me a curious look. "Ally, were you hurt at all or are you just upset I didn't break up with you first?"

I open my mouth to say he should have broken up with me when I realize how it must sound. We were friends. Lovers. I should have been heartbroken.

"You were the one person I knew I could trust. And when I saw you and Matthew…it was like Danny all over again, in a way."

He takes my hand in his. "I'm so damn sorry, Ally. I didn't mean to. I promise."

I nod. "I believe you." I sigh. "Were you heartbroken over me?"

"Not in the way I should have been. I've missed you as a friend."

"Me too. I don't know, Joel, should we never have gotten together?"

He shrugs. "I think we needed each other for our own reasons. I'd gone through a bad break-up, and you were there, and with you I always felt good. Felt—"

"Safe. I was safe."

He nods. "Yeah. And I was safe for you too."

I nod. "And Matt? Do you feel safe with him?"

He smiles. "I do. But it's different. He allows me to be myself in the best possible way, in the ways I was hiding from by being with you."

My breath catches in my throat, and he winces. "That probably sounds awful."

"No…no, I get it."

"It's the way you feel with Logan, right?"

"What? Logan and I are just friends."

He lets out a quick, quiet laugh. "Ally, I saw y'all the other day. On the main mall. You two couldn't keep your hands off each other."

"Oh." I look down at my hands.

"I didn't remember what your Halloween guy looked like, and then when I saw him, I realized it was Logan Mackenzie. You always called him Clark."

"It's a nickname."

"Ally, I know you like him. You always have. If you aren't dating, then what are you doing?"

"It's…um, hard to explain. But it's good. We're hanging out until we graduate."

"Ally, you aren't the kind of girl to fuck around."

"Sure I am. Just ask anyone we went to high school with." I let out a humorless laugh. Yeah, it's a deflection. I don't want to talk about Logan. I don't want to admit to myself that I'm struggling to keep my feelings for him at bay. Or how Joel explaining his feelings for Matthew reminded me of mine for Logan.

Joel watches me, and I'm pretty sure he's about to call me out on my bullshit, but he just shakes his head. "Speaking of high school, did you know Trish goes here now?"

I straighten and meet his gaze. A pain twists in my stomach at the mention of Trish McFee. The person who was suspect number one on who leaked the video of me and Danny.

"What? I thought she went to school out of state?"

"She did but transferred here last semester. We ran into each other, and she was totally fake-nice. I told her to fuck off and walked away. Just be careful and turn around if you see her."

"Oh, I will. I have no desire to face her."

"There's my girl." He squeezes my hand again then gives me a look I know well, the one that says he wants to say something, but doesn't want to hurt my feelings. "Listen, I know I have no right to say this, but this thing with Logan…don't settle for less than you deserve. It was scary with Matthew at first. I even tried to break-up with him. But it's been amazing. I wish I'd let all my stupid shit go sooner. I want that for you too, Ally. I want you to be happy."

Tears burn my eyes. "I'm trying. Really. Things with Logan…they're good for me. I know what I'm doing."

My heart twists at my last words, but I smile through it,

reassuring Joel. It's the truth. I'm just not sure if it's the whole truth or white lies I'm telling myself.

He returns my smile. "Good." He lets my hand go and glances at his watch. "I gotta run, but let's not be strangers."

"Okay, I'd like that." We hug and it really does feel good to feel friendly toward him again.

After he leaves, I zone out, processing everything that just happened and doing my best not to dwell on the fact that Trish is on the same campus as me. The buzz of my phone breaks me out of wanderings.

Logan: Which library?

Me: EGM 5th floor. Table in northeast corner

Logan: omw

Logan: btw, it's sexy when you talk directions

A giddy feeling fills me. It's not like I haven't seen or talked to him over the past week, but it's been short and sweet and lacking our teasing banter. I've missed it. I really like having Logan as my friend on more than Halloween. I like having...I stop myself from letting my thoughts go any further. This is good. This is what I want.

Someone's backpack jangles nearby and I look up, shocked it's Logan.

"Did you run here?"

"Hell, yeah." He drops his backpack and yanks me out of my seat then takes my place and pulls me into his lap. I barely realize what he's doing before his mouth is on me. We both groan as our tongues meet. Every time I kiss him it's like kissing him for the first time, but it's also like coming home. I'm reintroduced to his taste, the feel of him, then I immediately remember how amazing it is to be in his arms, how natural and familiar it is. I know exactly how I like to kiss him.

How he likes to kiss me. Each slide of our tongues brings me a new pleasure. The fact that maybe he's as excited to see me as I am him makes it even better.

"Allyson," he breathes against my mouth and my body lights up. I love when his voice is all rough and desperate. I grind my hips against him, and he moans taking our kiss deeper—more urgent—until we're so hot we need to slow down. Except slowing down does nothing to stop the fire burning between us. He breaks the kiss and we're both panting.

He digs his fingers into my hips. "Okay, we've made out. Now let's do my library item." His voice is tight, urgent.

If I remember correctly, his item is sex in a library.

"We can sneak into one of the private rooms." He kisses me again, his mouth leaving a hot trail from my lips to my neck. "I need to be inside you."

I moan. "You can't say things like that."

"Yes, I can. C'mon, Allyson, let's tackle the naughty side of my list." His tongue touches that sensitive spot in between my neck and collarbone and I shiver. He's not making this easy on me.

"You keep Allyson-ing me. Your horny is showing, Logan."

"Fuck, yeah, it is." He lifts his hips into me. "You know you like it."

"I do, but that doesn't mean I'm going to give in. Those rooms probably have cameras in them, because horny college students like you are always trying to have sex in them."

His hands grip my hips. "Allyson, please."

There's an urgency in his voice. A desperation in his eyes. There's more to this than his list.

"Hey," I say, taking his face in my hands. "What's going on?"

He flinches, surprise flashing in his eyes. "Nothing. It's been a hell of a week and I want to do my list, that's all."

"Come on, something's been bothering you all week." His expression starts to close off and I know he's about to scream off list. "Tell me and I promise we'll do an item on your list." I wiggle down into his lap and give him a saucy smile.

His nostrils flare. "You don't fight fair."

I give him a big smile and he shakes his head. "Fine. My dad keeps texting me. He's started telling me things about his life. About things with my mom. He's telling me things I never knew about. He keeps asking to meet up."

"And you still don't want to?"

He shrugs. "Anytime I talk to him, it all goes to shit. And I'm still angry. I don't think I'll ever be not angry."

My heart aches for him. I cup his face, give his cheek a soft caress. "Maybe not. But you'll always be angry if you don't try to get past it. Maybe talking to him will be a step in lessening the anger. Maybe it's a way you both can heal."

His expression is wary, but it seems like he's considering my words. "Okay, that's solid advice. Thanks, Dr. Worthington. I can pay in the form of one list item."

His hands grip my hips again and grinds them against his. I feel the fact that a certain part of him is very rigid. "You're incorrigible." I grip his face a little tighter so our gazes are locked. "You know, if you haven't yet, you really should talk to a professional. Maybe even with your dad."

I can tell he doesn't want to talk about this anymore, but he gives me a sincere look. "I know."

I lean in to give him a soft kiss, but he immediately takes over and kisses me until I'm breathless. "I want you." His voice is rough and intense as his gaze falls to my breasts while his hands slip beneath my shirt and slowly make their way to the same place. "If not the library, then let's go back to your place. We can take on a different item."

He pauses as his fingers get to the underside of my breasts and my body is on fire. He meets my gaze. He knows I want to give in and smiles before he kisses me again. Convincing me. Breaking me down.

"Now who's not fighting fair?"

I can feel his smile as he sprinkles kisses along my jaw.

"Ugh, I'm working on my thesis. I need to get more done before I have to get to my internship."

"What's your thesis on?"

He's not kissing me anymore, but his fingers continue to brush my skin so it takes me a second to comprehend his question. "Impacts of social media on mental health."

Logan raises his eyebrows at me in surprise, his slow torturing touch stops.

"Yeah, you might have given me a push on the football field. I want to help others deal with the emotions that come with the fallout of social media. Things could have gone so differently for me if…if I hadn't asked for help."

His brows bunch together, and I keep going before he can ask me more. I'm not ready to tell him about that part of my life yet. "Anyway, it's time I stop hiding from social media, in a sense. I'm really happy with the direction this is going."

He smiles at me, his hands come out from under my shirt and he gives the hair at my shoulder a little tug. "That's awesome, Ally."

My cheeks heat. "Thanks."

"How much do you have left to do? And when do you have to leave?"

I glance at my computer. "Maybe another hour, then I have another hour before I have to be at work."

Motivated Grin flashes on his lips. He gives my lips a quick kiss then lifts me off his lap, puts me back in the chair and takes the one next to me. "Setting a timer for an hour. I can knock out my homework too."

I kind of love that he didn't press me to leave, because honestly, one more kiss and I would have caved, and I really need to get this done. He sets his phone in the middle of the table and hits start on the timer. I look at him and he winks at me before he pulls out his laptop.

Other than taking glances to admire how sexy he looks with his glasses and serious study face on, I'm almost done for the day. He shuts his laptop and mouths "be back" at me and leaves the table. Right as I finish up, he returns with an I've Done Something Naughty grin on his lips. He holds up a card shaped paper.

"I got us a study room. No cameras. What do you say?"

It's official. I'm completely addicted to Logan and our lists.

chapter nineteen

I drain the last sip of my third cup of coffee and contemplate a fourth since I still have one more assignment to finish. Cafe Jolt might have to cut me off if I start bouncing off the walls from caffeine overload.

I've let Logan and our lists distract me away from homework too many times. Speaking of, he's meeting me here soon so we can head to my place to Netflix and chill. There's no way I'm missing that. Not with Logan leaving in a few days for the NFL Combine. I already have a very revealing nightie picked out for the occasion.

About halfway through my assignment, a backpack is dropped on my table then Ginny plops down in the chair next to me.

"What'cha doing?" Her voice is beyond cheerful.

"Homework."

"Awesome." Ginny is practically bouncing in her seat, and homework is never awesome.

"Okay, what's up? You look like you're about to burst."

"What are you doing for spring break?" Her wide eyes are practically dancing as she asks.

"I don't know."

"You and Logan don't have plans?"

Spring break is still a few weeks away so I haven't given it much thought. I certainly can't assume that Logan and I will spend time together. Things have been great, but we've definitely stuck strictly to the lists.

"We haven't talked about it."

This news seems to thrill Ginny. "Good. Because we're going on a road trip. It's on your list." She says this as if it being on my list seals the deal.

I did promise Logan I would be exclusive, not only to him, but to our lists. Would he share with Ginny?

"Okay, want to tell me where we're going and why? I have a feeling this really doesn't have anything to do with my list."

"No, the list is just how I'm convincing you. I was thinking New Orleans and maybe somewhere else. I want to avoid the typical beach spring breakers. And why? Because you're graduating and I can actually afford to go." She shifts in her chair so she's facing me more. "I've hit up three sorority houses since getting my toys in and have made serious bank in only a few weeks. The company noticed and gave me this kind of newbie bonus."

"Oh my God, Ginny, that's awesome!" I pull her in for a hug.

"Allyson?"

Everything inside me stills as a sick feeling creeps up my throat. I haven't heard my name uttered from that voice in four years. I can't move. I can't breathe. Ginny glances at me with a worried expression before she looks toward the voice.

"It is you!" I take a deep breath and look Trish McFee—the girl that probably ruined my life—in the eyes. She looks the same, more filled out in all the right places. She was always the all-around popular girl in a total Regina George from *Mean Girls* way.

"Hey Trish," I say. "I didn't know you went here."

She laughs. "Oh yeah? I started last semester. It's so good to be back in Texas. CTU is so much better for my major. I'm pre-med."

"You want to be a doctor?" There's no way I'm hiding my shock from her. Lord, help us all if Trish becomes a doctor. She's more likely to tell her patients to get over themselves than diagnose them.

"A surgeon."

That makes sense. I could totally see her cutting people open. "Well, good luck." I turn back to my computer hoping she'll take the hint and leave. She doesn't.

"How's college going? Play any more games of Truth or Dare?"

I look at her, unable to believe she just said that. She's doing a really poor job of hiding a smile.

"Wow. You really are a piece of work," Ginny says. "I mean, you're like a villain straight out of a teen drama series. I didn't think people like you really existed."

Trish looks at her, seeming to notice her for the first time. "Who the hell are you?"

"Her best friend. And I've heard all about you."

Trish lets out this bitter laugh. "Are you still blaming me for your little slut video? You took the dare so you should be responsible for your actions."

"I never agreed to be filmed. Or to have it blasted all over the school."

I swear a look of pride flashes over her face. "Karma's a bitch, Allyson. Maybe you shouldn't steal other people's boyfriends."

"I didn't steal Danny and you know it. You two broke up."

She narrows her eyes and leans in. "I saw you two at the Fourth of July bonfire. The way you were flirting with him. I know exactly what you were doing."

I roll my eyes. "And like I told you then, we were just talking and joking around. With a group of people. I had nothing to do with your break-up. I didn't even know you'd broken up until school started. I hadn't seen Danny since the bonfire."

"Whatever you need to tell yourself, Allyson. He broke up with me and you two started following each other on all the socials. I'm not stupid."

"I'm so done with this conversation. If Karma's a bitch then I can't wait to see what happens when it comes for you."

"Fuck you."

Out of nowhere, Ben steps up to our group. We'd chatted a few minutes when I first arrived, and I was relieved to find he had no hard feelings about our failed date. "You need to leave," he says to Trish. "You're being disruptive and disrespectful."

"Oh, give me a break," Trish says. "She is too. Why isn't she being kicked out?"

Ben smiles at her. "Because I like her. Now leave." He crowds her so she has to move toward the exit.

She flashes him a hard look before she storms out. Logan walks up from the other direction and looks from Ben to Trish's retreating back. He pauses then frowns and exchanges some words with Ben. Logan looks at me then back to where Trish disappeared.

"Are you okay?" Ginny asks, bringing my attention back to her.

My heart is pounding, and I could probably throw up. I feel like that was pretty much a confession. It's nothing that would hold up in court, but I know now, deep down in my bones, that Trish leaked the video.

My hands are shaking as I run them through my hair. "I'm okay. But I could really go my whole life without seeing her face again."

Ben and Logan reach our table. I give Ben a grateful smile. "Thanks for that."

"No problem. She was a lot."

"You have no idea."

"I gotta get back. Let me know if y'all need anything." He gives me a polite smile and taps Logan on the shoulder as he leaves. I'm pretty sure Ben assumes Logan and I are a couple now.

Logan takes a seat and looks at me with a concerned expression. "What was all that about?"

"Remember how I said I think Danny's ex released that video? Well, that was her."

His eyes widen and he straightens as he looks where Trish disappeared. "The blond?"

"Yeah. Trish. She's terrible and hasn't gotten any better with time. I know she did it. I can just feel it."

"Shit." Logan runs a hand through his hair. He looks like he's going to be sick.

"Are you okay?"

He looks at me then. "Yeah...I'm so sorry." He takes my hand and gives it a squeeze. "Did she confess or something?"

"No, she's too smart for that. But she said enough to make my doubts disappear. Thank God I'm graduating early."

"No joke," Ginny says. "She's worse than I imagined, and what I imagined was pretty bad."

"I want to forget the last five minutes happened."

"Absolutely. Let's talk about our road trip," Ginny says.

"What road trip?" Logan asks.

"I was just telling Ally that we need a BFF spring break trip before she graduates." She looks at me. "I never thought I could afford to go on spring break. Please…" She bats puppy dog eyes at me.

I melt a little. I glance at Logan and he's smiling at me. "Sounds fun. Y'all should go." I know I didn't need his permission, but it makes my heart happy that he recognized that we needed this.

"Do you have plans for spring break?"

"I think the guys are planning a trip to South Padre. It's on my…" He stops and I know it's because he was going to say it's on his list. He did have spring break at South Padre on it now that I think about it. "I've never been," he says instead.

"It'll be your own BFF spring break trip," Ginny says with a little too much enthusiasm.

Logan gives her an amused smile. "Yeah, wouldn't really call it that, but sure."

I laugh at that then face Ginny. "Okay, I'm in."

Ginny throws her arms around me and bounces me up and down. "I'm so freaking excited!" She gives me one last tight squeeze. "I gotta run but talk to you soon so we can start planning."

After Ginny leaves, I turn to Logan. "I need ten more minutes and I'll be ready to go."

He nods. "We don't have to, you know? We can Netflix and chill some other time."

"Why? Do you not want to anymore?"

He stares at me for a moment then shakes his head. "No, of course, I do. Didn't know if you were too busy."

"No, I just need to submit my homework and I'm free. Are you okay? Getting nervous about the combine?"

He shrugs. "A little, but I'm okay."

He doesn't seem okay though. He seems distracted. Maybe

I can distract him in a different way, "I'll need to show you my new comfy clothes when we get to my place."

"Comfy clothes?"

"Yeah, have to have comfy clothes when you Netflix, right?"

"What about the 'chilling' part?"

"Oh, it's good for that too, but I don't want to *reveal* too much."

His eyes flare with heat. "You gonna press that send button or what?"

chapter twenty

Logan
X Sex in the library
X Win at beer pong
X Quickie between classes
X Sex in my truck bed

I drop my bags on the floor of my hotel room and plop on the bed, taking in a deep breath. I'm in Indianapolis, and tomorrow I take a big step toward a career in the NFL. This seems so unreal. When I was a junior in high school and recruiters were clamoring for me, I really started letting myself believe I could have a shot at a professional career. Then mom died, and the dream died too. Even after Nate and Wes encouraged me to try out and I made the team, I didn't think being a pro was realistic. I'd accepted it.

But now, now there's hope...and I don't know how I feel about it. I've gotten so used to not considering football as a career, I can't seem to get my frame of mind back to it. I'm definitely excited, but also afraid to get too excited.

I dig out my phone and text Ally that I made it. She asked me to when she dropped me off at the airport, and then she got all flushed and quickly told me I didn't have to. Yeah, it's kind of an off list move, but we're friends too so it's no big deal.

While we've been tackling our lists like crazy lately, I hate that I didn't tell her about my history with Trish. I don't know what good would come of it though I did consult the guys. I only told them that Trish was her former bully, not the details of their past, and they agreed telling her would only hurt her.

Ally texts back telling me to have fun and good luck. It shouldn't disappoint me that that's all she says, but it does. Today at the drop-off, I wanted to kiss her good-bye. I should have, because not kissing her only made things weirder. We did this awkward hug and kiss on the cheek that left me wanting.

My phone buzzes again, and I glance at it hoping to see another text from Ally. But it's from my dad.

Dad: Good luck this week! I'll be watching.

I stare at the screen for a good long while. I still haven't responded to any of his texts. I don't know what to say. I don't know what I want to say. Not thinking about it too much, I text back a thanks. I can handle that much.

A few minutes later, he texts again.

Dad: You texted back. I'm trying not to make a big deal out of it. But you texted back.

Dad: Thanks

I find myself smiling.

Me: Don't make it weird. I just got to my hotel room. Going to grab dinner with some of the other guys soon.

Dad: Okay. You can text again if you want. If you want to talk to someone about your day. No pressure.

Me: You're making it weird again

Dad: I know

Over the week, I text my dad every day. We mostly talk football, which is fine with me. I'm exhausted—mentally and physically. I miss Ally. We've texted some, but not nearly enough. At night I think of things I can add to my list so we'll have plenty of opportunities to see each other when I get back.

This week has been good. I had some really strong days, and my stats are promising. The interviews I went to went pretty well too. There are definitely some teams I didn't jive with though. Overall, I'm feeling positive that the NFL could be in my future. But I'm ready to get back to Austin tomorrow, something I never thought I'd feel. And I have no desire to analyze it.

When Dad texts, this time he asks if he can pick me up at the airport. I want to tell him he made it weird again, but at this point, I think it would be me making it weird. Maybe this would be a good way for us to ease our way into seeing each other again. It's just a thirty-minute car ride. I agree and text Ally that he'll be picking me up. She sends gifs and texts that clearly show her excitement and support.

When I get into Austin, I open my texting app to see my dad said he'd be there about twenty minutes after I land. But it's been twenty minutes and he's not here. I wait another twenty before I text him. Another ten minutes roll by and there's no response. Fuck this. I knew I shouldn't have agreed.

I pull up a ride-share app to order a ride then my phone starts ringing and the ID says Miranda Ward. This has to be his Miranda. My stomach immediately tightens, and a cold dread suddenly fills me as I quickly swipe to answer. "Hello?"

"Um, Logan? This is Miranda. Your father and I…"

My heart is pounding in my ears. "Yeah, I know who you are. What's wrong? What's happened? He's supposed to be here."

"I know. Um, he was in a car accident."

Oh fuck fuck fuck fuck.

"Is he…" I can't say the words. There's a huge knot in my throat.

"He's stable. He's pretty banged up and has a badly broken leg. He'll need surgery soon."

"What hospital?"

"North Memorial."

I close my eyes. The same hospital they took my mother to. Where she died.

"I'll be right there."

I order a ride, which is thankfully just waiting in the cell phone lot. On my way to the hospital, I text Ally and the guys all on the same thread. They ask if I want them to be there, but I tell them no. I feel like I might throw up on the whole ride. I can't trust Miranda's report, not until I see that he's okay for myself.

When I'm finally shown to the curtained area where my dad is, I stop outside it, too afraid to go in. Afraid of what I might see. It takes me several seconds to work up the courage. Then, with a pounding heart, I force myself to step around it.

My dad is strapped to a bunch of machines, his face is bruised, his shoulder and arm are wrapped, and his leg is stabilized and elevated. He looks horrible. But he's alive. This strangled sound fills the area, and he turns his head in my direction. It's then I realize the sound came from me.

"Son." His voice is low and weak as he slightly raises one of his hands to gesture toward him.

I go to his bedside and sit in the chair next to it. I put my head on his bed and all the emotions I'd kept a tight rein on lets loose. I feel his hand rest on my head, comforting me.

"I'm okay. I'll be okay. I'm sorry. I'm sorry I scared you."

I can't seem to stop crying. He could have died. Because of me. Before we had a chance to make things right.

Finally, I raise up and wipe my hands down my face as I take a shuddering breath. "What happened?"

"Got T-boned. Fucking idiot ran a red light. I need surgery on my leg. Just waiting on the surgeon." His words are slurry, and he closes his eyes. I can't tell if he's falling asleep or trying not to.

"On lots of pain meds, huh?"

My dad gives a weak smile. "A tad. I'm...I'm glad you're here."

"I won't leave." He takes my hand and gives it a gentle squeeze as he drifts off.

"Um, hi." I look up to see a woman at the curtained entrance. I recognize her from the cemetery and hike and bike trail. "You must be Logan. I'm Miranda."

I smile. "It's nice to meet you."

She slowly enters and stands at the end of the bed. She tells me he broke his tibia and that he should be going into surgery within the hour. He might need surgery on his shoulder too, but that's the worst of it with the rest just being some bad bruising. Though it sounds like he's going to have to go through some intensive physical therapy.

"I'm glad you're here," she says after a pause in the conversation.

"I was going to say where else would I be, but...I guess considering everything...you probably wouldn't expect me to be here."

She gives me a kind smile. "Actually, I did. Your dad has been so happy this week talking to you."

I look back at my dad, my throat thick with tears. "Are you okay with me staying with you during the surgery?"

Her eyes fill with tears. "I would like that very much. Your father would too."

Once my dad is in surgery, I text the thread to give Ally and the guys an update. Miranda is easy to talk to while we wait. She's not like my mom, but I have a feeling my mom would have liked her. I could see them being friends. It's a weird thought that I don't know what to do with. Miranda's daughter, Brianna, joins us after a while. We talk a bit about her going to CTU in the fall.

She's worried about my dad, and it sounds like they have a good relationship, which makes me irrationally jealous. It's my fault I don't have a relationship with my dad. I shouldn't begrudge her for having one.

I learn Miranda and my dad have only been officially dating for less than a year. She tells me how they became friends, and how she was glad they found their way to becoming a couple.

I can't help but to notice the similarities between my dad's relationships with Miranda and my mom to mine with Ally. How I was immediately captivated by Ally's laugh that first day, then we became friends, and now more. Yet, are we really more?

No, I can't let my mind go down that road. Especially now. As my dad's surgery enters the second hour, I start feeling even more antsy. When is it going to be over? I can't remember how long I waited when they took my mom. It felt like hours at the time, but I don't think it really was.

"Hey."

I look up and see Ally standing in front of me. I stand, unable to believe that she's here.

"Um, I know you said you didn't want company, but—"

I pull her into a hug, not letting her finish. "Thanks for not listening to me."

She squeezes me. "You're welcome."

This is off list but maybe for today we get a pass. I look past her to see Nate and Wes are here too. I've never been so glad to be ignored. I introduce them all to Miranda and Brianna, and then we sit. My arm brushes Ally's on the armrest then I feel her pinky graze mine. I touch hers back then lock our pinkies together. I glance down, not sure how I feel about what I just did. All I know is my heart is now racing and my chest feels tight. I don't know if I can handle this gesture right now. Ally shifts our hands until all our fingers are intertwined and everything calms.

We stay like that until Miranda, Brianna, and Ally leave to get coffee. I notice Wes' gaze seems to zero in on Brianna's behind. I slug his arm. "That's my future stepsister, and she's still in high school. Stop staring at her ass." I don't tell him she's already eighteen.

"Relax, I'm not going to hit on her. You're awfully protective over someone you just met."

"She's nice. Not for a guy like you."

"Like me? Um, charming and hot and nice and good in bed?"

"Exactly."

Wes rolls his eyes. "Don't worry, I'm not interested in jailbait."

When they get back, Ally and Brianna keep us distracted by talking about CTU. Then the guys talk to me about the combine. Finally, the doctor comes out and tells us that everything went well, and my dad is in recovery. Logically, I knew this would be the case, but the reality of it has me excusing myself from the waiting room. I make it to the hallway before the surge of emotions erupts. I'm shaking. My chest burns.

Suddenly, arms are pulling me into a hug. Though my eyes are closed, I instantly recognize it as Ally. I wrap her into me and breathe her in. Let her touch soothe me.

"The last time I was here it was for my mom. And when the doctor came out…" A broken breath comes out of me.

"He's okay. This time it's okay."

I nod and crush her to me. We stay like that until I feel like I can breathe easier again. We lean back and look at each other. She is so fucking beautiful. I want to kiss her. But I'm afraid if I do, I won't want to stop. That I'll never let her go. And I have to.

"Thanks. For today. For coming." I slowly untangle myself from her. "You don't have to stay. I'm good now."

She smiles, but I can see the hurt in her eyes. "Okay, if you're sure. I…I wanted to be here for you, Logan."

I mutter a thanks and use every ounce of willpower I possess to pull away from her.

Over the next few days, I'm in and out of the hospital checking in with my dad and overwhelmed with catching up with classes. The day he gets discharged from the hospital, Miranda texts and asks me if I will come have dinner with him and stay while she has an obligation with Brianna. I'm surprised to learn that they don't live together, but she plans to stay with him while he recovers.

Dinner goes well. But now that he's out of the hospital, the fact that we haven't talked about all his texts feels like the elephant in the room until he finally addresses it as we sit at the dining table and asks me if I read them.

"I did."

"Good. I mean, I hope they were okay. I didn't know what to do anymore."

"No, it was fine. Good, I guess. I'm… It really pisses me off that y'all kept so much from me."

My dad holds my gaze. "I know. I'm sorry. Parenting…isn't

the easiest thing to navigate. We were trying not to hurt you, but…in the end, it just made it worse." He shakes his head and runs his good hand over his face. "I feel like I've fucked up every part of being a father."

"Not every part. You refused to let me go. Isn't that sort of the first rule of parenting?"

I can see the relief my words give him. "I could never."

I sigh, all my resentment seems so petty now. "I'm sorry I was so mad. That I didn't consider all you lost too."

"Thanks." He shifts. "Logan, I don't want to lose any more time with you. I want to be part of your life. I want you to be part of mine too. Do…do you think we can have that?"

I nod. "Yeah. I'd like that."

"Really?" Tears fill his eyes.

"I've already lost one parent, and all this made me realize I really don't want to lose another one. Mom would hate how I've treated you."

A sad smile forms on his lips as a few tears streak down his face. He swipes them away. "She wouldn't be happy with me either. I can just hear her calling me a stubborn ass."

She'd absolutely say the same of me. "I like Miranda," I say. "I think Mom would have too."

"She did. Or at least Miranda liked her. Miranda was a temp in Simone's office once, and Miranda said they really got along. They only knew each other for that week. Miranda and I met at a bereavement meeting. She lost her husband. She put two and two together and realized Simone was your mom."

It's odd, but the fact that my mom liked Miranda brings me this feeling of peace.

"So, um," I clear my throat. "If you want to marry her…it's okay."

I can tell my dad is trying not to get emotional again, but his eyes well up. "Um, you don't have to yet. You can get to know her more and—"

I hold up my hand stopping him. "Dad, you have my blessing. I don't think any more time needs to be wasted."

He swallows and nods and eventually gets out a choked-up thanks. We sit quietly for a few minutes, letting the heaviness of everything settle.

"So, Miranda told me you have a girlfriend," my dad says breaking the silence.

"Um, no."

He tilts his head with a curious expression. "She said there was a girl at the hospital with you. That you held hands."

"She's a friend." I glance down and fiddle with my phone.

"A friend you want to be your girlfriend?" Amusement lilts my dad's voice.

"Dad, I don't really do girlfriends. Besides, we're graduating. I'm moving and she's going to grad school."

"Why don't you do girlfriends?"

I look at him. "I haven't been interested in getting into a relationship."

His mouth flattens. "I'm guessing that has to do with me. With me and your mom."

I shrug. "Just not interested. I could be in the NFL in a few months. Why would I want to tie myself down?"

He nods. I feel like he wants to say more, but he doesn't. My phone dings with a text message. I glance at it on the table and see it's from Ally.

Ally Cat: List add: Bullshit!

What? She's adding to the list without me? I pick up my phone and fire off a text.

Me: What's going on?

Ally Cat: Bullshit!

What the fuck?

"Who's Ally Cat?"

My dad's question surprises me, and I snap my head up to see he's leaning in and eyeing where my phone is on the table. He winces. "Sorry, didn't mean to snoop. The name caught my eye. Is that the girl that's just a friend?"

"Yeah." Gah, I'm such a fucking liar.

"Cute nickname," my dad teases. "You look pretty concerned about her text. Is everything okay?"

"Not concerned. Confused. It doesn't make a whole lot of sense."

I pick up my phone then right as rapid-fire texts come through, this time from my roommate thread.

> Wes: Better get your ass home soon. Your girl and tequila are a cute combination.

What the fuck!

> Nate: One tequila. Two tequila. Three tequila. More!

Another one comes in from Ally and it's a picture of a lime in between two sultry lips I know very well.

> Ally Cat: Come play with me, Logan.

My dick jumps to attention at Ally's text. I can practically hear the erotic purr in her voice. This girl. I'm really curious what she's doing getting drunk with my roommates.

"You should go."

I look up at my dad. "What? No, I need to stay."

"Your girl wants to see you. I'm fine. Miranda will be home soon. She just texted me," he says as he holds up his phone.

"She's not my girl."

My dad chuckles. "Tell that to the look you had on your face."

I ignore that. "If you're sure?"

"I'm sure."

"Okay, um, I guess I'll see you later." Now it's all awkward between us again.

"Maybe this weekend? You can get to know Miranda and Brianna better."

"Yeah, that works."

I gather my stuff and start heading out the door. "Logan," my dad calls and I turn back. "How's her laugh?"

Fuck. I should say nothing and walk away. Instead I say, "One of my favorite things."

Logan
Take a body shot
List Add: See Ally drunk
Off List: Ally in my bed

I walk through the door of my house and immediately Ally, Wes, and Nate turn to look at me from the kitchen table. They raise their drink-laden hands and shout in greeting, "Bullshit!"

It's then I notice the pile of cards on the table. They're playing the drinking game, Bullshit, and now it all clicks in place. Ally's smiling widely, a little intoxicated glint to her eyes.

I mentally check *See Ally Drunk* off my list. Somewhere in all this, I started adding little things about Ally to my list. Things just for me like, *Distract Ally During Class* and *"Accidentally" Touch Ally.*

I realized the other day that though Ginny has succeeded

in getting Ally drunk, I've never seen her remotely tipsy. She's as adorable as I thought she'd be.

"What's up?" I ask as I walk into the kitchen.

Wes turns toward me. "Ally showed up, demanding we do something fun tonight. So, I told her she could join us for a threesome, and she said she was all in. Sorry, bro, your dick isn't invited."

"Bullshit!" Ally shouts and throws her cards at him as he and Nate almost falls over laughing.

I stare at my roommates. "Y'all are wasted."

Nate immediately sits upright. "Am not." He keeps a straight face for about two seconds then bursts into laughter. Whoa, he really is drunk, and Nate doesn't get drunk. A few drinks here and there, but I've only seen him drunk maybe twice.

As if he realized he's not sober, he points a finger at me. "It's your fault! You were supposed to come home."

"I had dinner with my dad. Miranda had to do things tonight and needed someone to stay with him."

"Oh no," Ally says, suddenly sounding sober. "Do you need to be with him? I'm sorry, I didn't—"

I wave off her concern. "No, it's fine. Miranda is home now."

"Well, since Ally is such a prude about threesomes, we decided to get some tequila and play drinking games," Wes says. "We waited an hour for you, man, but once we found out Ally had never played Bullshit before, we had to start. We started out playing for tequila shots, but after we had two shots to her none we realized shots were going to land us in the hospital and switched to beer."

I look at Ally, and she's now smiling proudly. She's definitely not as sloshed as my roommates.

"I think she's hustling us," Nate says with a bit of a slur, and Ally giggles.

She did this for me, I know it. She wanted to distract me from how hard my dad's accident has been on me. I take the seat next to her and fight the overwhelming need to pull her into my lap and kiss her. I really like seeing her in my house surrounded by my friends. Too much. What is she doing to me?

"You in?"

I look at her, her eyes sparking with challenge. "Bring it on, Ally Cat."

She smiles and, fuck, if it doesn't send my heartbeat up several notches.

Wes sets the tequila bottle on the table. "You need to catch up. Take three shots."

I shake my head but pour a shot then quickly pound three back. My head immediately feels the hit as my body warms. "Okay, let's do this."

After a few rounds, it's clear Ally has a gift for this. Wes and Nate, already being inebriated, are a little easier to call out, but she's calling me out too. I thought I'd be able to easily tell when she was bullshitting, but she changes her tactics every time. The best part though, is how she's flirting with me under the table. Her foot keeps tangling with mine or making its way up my leg. She's making me so hot, I can't think straight, which is probably on purpose. Ally has a competitive side to her and it's sexy as hell.

After Nate gets caught bullshitting again, he throws his cards on the table. "Okay, I'm out. I need to go pass out before I get sick."

He stumbles to his feet and Wes laughs at him then almost falls out of his seat. "Shit, I think I need to, too."

Nate hauls him up. "It's official, bro. We've been bested by the Bullshit Queen." He and Wes bow unsteadily, and Ally stands and bows back then they all share a fist bump.

Nate and Wes stumble their way to their rooms, and it's only me and Ally. She looks at me all smug and cute.

"Look, at you. Your ego is about to burst it's so huge."

She gives me a winning smile. "Hey, it's not every day you take down boys twice your size at a drinking game."

"You did good, Ally Cat." I put out my fist for her to bump, but she only stares at it.

"I don't want to fist bump you."

My body instantly comes to attention at the hot intensity of her voice. "Oh? What did you have in mind?"

She bites that luscious bottom lip of hers in concentration. Then she leans across the table and grabs the tequila bottle. She pours a shot then stands and pulls her shirt over her head.

"What the hell, Ally?" I look over toward the guys' rooms.

"I think the loser needs to take one final shot." She works the shot glass in between her breasts. "I believe body shots are on both of our lists."

My mind blanks. Tequila and tits—two of my favorites. Shit, this girl. Last month she never would have done something like this and now she looks so confident and sexy I can't help but smile. I take off my glasses, grab a lime from a plate on the table, stand and take a step closer. Her breath hitches and her breasts heave. As sure as she is, I love seeing how I affect her.

"Open your mouth, Allyson."

She does and I place the lime between her teeth. I lean down and brush my lips against her breasts. I dart my tongue out to touch the skin near the glass. She makes a low sound in her throat. I meet her lust-filled eyes right before I take the shot glass between my lips and shoot it back. As the tequila slides down, I drop the glass in my hand and take the lime from her lips. I bite it to get a quick squirt of sourness before I drop it and take her sweet lips.

Her tongue meets mine. She tastes of beer and lime and

Ally. She moans into my mouth and I pick her up and put her on the table. I yank down her bra and pick up the tequila bottle. I cover part of the spout and lightly pour the tequila over her breasts then immediately lap it up. She arches against my mouth, letting out a loud moan.

"No sounds." I stand and pull my shirt off. I twist it until it resembles a rope. I wrap it around her wrists. "You can't move either."

Her eyes are heavy-lidded as she looks at me. "This is supposed to be my show."

"Now it's mine. I'm going to get drunk off your body, Allyson." I lightly push her so she's flat on the table. I hook my fingers in the waistband of her leggings and pull them down along with her panties. Fuck, I love her body. I grab the tequila and pour a line from her breasts to her pretty pussy. I slowly kiss my way down her body, licking up the tequila as I go. I spread her legs and dribble tequila right over her clit and taste her.

Her body bucks against my mouth. "Fuck," she yells out.

"No sounds." I slowly bring my tongue over her again and a loud groan escapes her as she shakes her head.

"I'm not being quiet. Get over it. Now, give me more, Logan."

Fuck. This woman is constantly surprising me. I just hope to hell that my roommates have passed out. I give her exactly what she wants and soon she's shaking underneath me as her orgasm rips through her. She's fucking loud. The sexy, feral sounds coming from her only make me harder. Only makes me want her more. When she finally goes slack beneath me, I look up to see her pleasure-shattered face.

"You look awfully satisfied, but I'm not done with you yet."

"Oh, yes, you are." She starts to pull herself up, so I help her the rest of the way. She immediately starts undoing my pants. Seeing her bound hands working my zipper… goddamn…it's fucking hot.

She presses one of my shoulders so I sit back in the chair then she sinks to her knees. I sit up straighter. "Whoa, what are you doing?"

She looks at me with a raised eyebrow. "Really?"

"I want to fuck you."

"Not tonight. Tonight, I'm fucking you." She takes my cock in one of her hands and slowly moves it up then back down. "I know you've been dying for me to have your cock in my mouth."

"Fuck, Ally, you can't talk like that."

"Oh, Ally doesn't talk like that. But Allyson does. And you know you like it."

She's making me crazy.

"Grab the tequila," she orders. I do and wait for further instruction. "Pour." She nods her head toward my dick. This is going to be a mess and I don't care. I circle the open bottle around the head of my cock and she immediately puts her mouth over me and sucks hard. Fuck, it's so good. So damn intense. Then she lightens her movements. Licking, kissing, sucking, and moving her bound hands over me. My climax is building so fast I don't think I can hold off.

"Fuck, I'm about to come."

She moans around me, and I climb closer to the edge.

"You want my cum in your mouth, Allyson. Ready to take me all in, baby?"

She groans loudly and that's all it takes. A sharp spike of pleasure rips through me, and I'm coming in her sweet mouth. She swallows me down while continuing to work me over, making it the most intense, amazing blow job I've ever had.

When she releases me, I grab her hands and remove my shirt from her wrists then pull her into my lap and kiss her. I shouldn't, but how can I not after what she did to me? "Okay, your idea was better."

She laughs. "I'm glad you agree."

"Oh, I agree. I would agree again. And again."

She gives me a playful swat on the shoulder before standing. She adjusts her bra so she's covered up again then turns around to pick up her panties. I burst out laughing at the cards stuck to her back and butt.

She looks over her shoulder at me. "I have cards all over me, don't I?"

I nod and help her peel them off then dress myself. I glance at the table; it's a mess of crumpled cards and spilled tequila. "I think I need to replace the cards now."

She looks at the table and laughs. "Yeah, I would say so. It was a big list day. Three items in one day. At this rate, we'll be done way before graduation."

My stomach lurches at her words and I don't really want to analyze why. "Three?"

"Bullshit, body shots, and tied up."

Right. She turns to me, now fully dressed. She gives me a small smile then lifts up and places a light kiss to my lips. Is it off list? Or are we in an off list gray area since we're finishing up an item? The thing is, I don't care. I'm only glad she kissed me.

She pulls away. "I should go."

"You can't drive, Ally."

"I'll order a ride and get my car tomorrow."

"Stay." The word is out of my mouth before I even realized I thought it. I should take it back. It's off list. Way off list, whether we recognize it or not. Except I don't want to.

She looks unsure. Like she knows she should say no but doesn't want to either.

"It's late. It's just sleep, Ally."

"Are you sure?"

This is my chance to change my mind. To tell her this is a terrible idea. I don't.

"Yeah, I don't want you getting a ride this late alone. Plus, you reek of tequila. Stay."

"Okay."

I take her hand and lead her to my bedroom, ignoring the fact that my heart practically jumped for joy when she agreed. Once inside, we stand there awkwardly for moment, staring at my bed. Shit, my room is a mess. Clothes are all over the floor, along with textbooks, notebooks, and a bunch of random crap. I grab a shirt out of my dresser and hand it to her.

"Bathroom is in the hall. There should be an extra toothbrush in the cabinet."

"Thanks," she mumbles before she ducks out of the room.

I quickly straighten my room. Not only have I never had a girl spend the night before, I've never had a girl in my bed before, period. When I've hooked-up in the past I always went to their place so I could leave without false excuses. Not that we're having sex tonight. I told her only sleeping—stupidly.

When she comes back into the room, I immediately still. We might have just licked tequila all over each other, but I'm struck dumb by the sight of her in only my 'Block, Tackle, Sack, Repeat' T-shirt. Her dusky nipples are straining against the worn white cotton that is now almost translucent because her damp hair has wet the material. She smells like my shampoo, and having my scent on her pleases this primal part inside of me I didn't even realize I had. How the hell am I supposed to survive tonight without touching her?

I rush into the bathroom so I don't throw her on the bed and fuck her brains out. I take a quick, and very cold, shower. I pull on boxer briefs and a pair of gray sweatpants. Normally, I don't do underwear, but I need as many layers as I can get between me and Ally.

When I get back to my room, Ally's looking at the bulletin

board I have on my wall. There are class syllabi on it, some football accolades, and random pictures. She's looking at a pic of me and my roommates at last year's spring game then her gaze shifts to the one below it. Her hand reaches out and touches it. It's of us and that psycho clown from our second Halloween. I'm not a print pictures kind of guy, but I had to print something for a class project shortly after that Halloween, so I decided to print it as well.

She glances at me and blinks a few times when she notices I'm half naked. Her eyes fall to my crotch, and it immediately starts to stir.

"Eyes up, Ally."

She smirks at me. "Like your eyes weren't wandering earlier."

My gaze dips then I immediately raise them to see her laughing softly. She points to the picture. "I made your board."

I shrug. "I happened to be printing pictures and thought it was a good one."

"Mmm-hmm." She approaches me and takes my hand in hers and lifts it up. Her finger grazes the Superman bracelet I'm wearing. "I noticed this the other day when I took you to the airport. I don't think I've seen you wear it since that night."

"I wear it." I swallow then confess, "I usually wear it when I'm having a bad day. Or if I need a little encouragement." What I don't tell her is that I also wear it anytime I think of her. Anytime I want to see her.

Her expression has a dreamy look to it, and I can't believe I confessed so much. Her gaze dips to my mouth and mine instantly does the same to hers. The pull to her is undeniable.

Suddenly, she pulls back and clears her throat. "So, which side do you sleep on?" Her gaze goes to the bed.

It takes me a moment to process her words. "Um, the right."

"Me too. Am I going to have to fight you for it?"

I cross my arms across my chest. "No, it's my bed. I get my side."

"But I'm your guest. You should give it to me as a courtesy."

I snort a laugh at that, and a mischievous look comes over her face before she darts for my bed. Before I know it, she's slipped under the covers on my side of the bed.

"Well, that does it. Looks like we have to share."

I turn the light off then pull back the covers, scooting over to her side of the bed. I wrap my arm around her waist and pull her tightly into my body. She lets out a surprised squeak before relaxing in my arms. "My mom did always tell me sharing is caring," she says.

"Then we have to do it."

She giggles and it's fucking cute. I tighten my grip, loving the way she feels against me. For the first time since we started the list, I'm seriously contemplating going off list and staying off list. The thought sends this hectic feeling through my chest that I don't fully understand. What I do understand is that I can't have these thoughts with the amount of tequila and beer I've had tonight.

I nuzzle my face into her neck, inhaling her scent. "Ally?"

"Yeah?"

"Thanks for tonight."

She turns a little toward me. "I know the last few days have been hard. I was just hoping…"

"It was perfect."

"How's everything going with your dad?"

"Good. He's doing pretty well considering his injuries."

"That's not what I meant."

"I know." I sigh. "Things are good, actually. We're going to work on…reconnecting, I guess. I'm going to have dinner with him and Miranda this weekend,"

Her hand on top of mine, squeezes. "That's really good, Logan. I liked her. And Brianna is really nice too."

"I had this thought at the hospital that she and my mom would probably have been friends if they'd ever met. Turns out they knew each other briefly and liked each other. I like that. Is that weird?"

"Not really. Your dad is moving on and so are you, in a way. I imagine it feels a little bit like you have her blessing."

I nod. "I miss her."

She burrows into me. "I know you do."

"What if I forget about her? I'm scared that I'll get used to Miranda and it'll be like my mom never existed."

"Logan, you know that's not going to happen. Miranda isn't replacing your mom. No one can. Miranda will fill a different role for you. Even for your dad. That space your mom has in both of your hearts, that's never going away."

It feels like Ally is making her own space in my heart too, and I don't know if I can stop it. Or if I want to. I pull her into me until she's flush against me and let the tequila lull me to sleep.

I startle awake and it takes me a moment to remember the warm body wrapped around me is Ally. Ally is in my bed. I lean over and kiss her shoulder, and she stirs, her body moving a little more over mine. I tip her head up and gently kiss her lips. With the little light filtering in, I see her eyes blink sleepily before she kisses me back. When we stop, I can see that she's fully awake, though her eyes are heavy-lidded. I want to be inside her right now more than I want my next breath.

As if she read my mind, she moves on top of me and grinds on my already hard cock. I grip her hips and press her even further on me. She moves again, slowly dry-fucking me. And even though we're not skin to skin, I know I could come like this. But I want to feel her. I want to feel her juices over me.

I reach down and pull my cock out of my boxer briefs then pull aside her panties, she presses back down on me, letting my cock slip through her wet folds. She adjusts her hips so she's rubbing her clit on my cock.

That's right. Use it to get you off.

I can't explain it, but I know we can't talk. Words mean we'd have to acknowledge that this is off list. Even our moans are mostly silent, heavy breaths. She's so fucking slick that our motions are making the sexiest, messiest sound I've ever heard. She leans forward and grinds hard against my cock then I feel her start to shudder. She groans softly and I watch her take her pleasure, and it's fucking beautiful.

As her shudders ease, her pussy slips over the head of my cock, she moves over me a few times and that's all it takes. I grab her and flip her onto her back and push up her shirt. I grip my cock, and only pump it twice before my orgasm washes over me in a silent groan. I watch as my cum spills over her tits in long ropes. She arches up, taking every bit, and it's fucking hot. When I'm done, I take my hand and spread my cum all over her. Covering every inch of her tits and stomach.

Mine.

She's breathing hard, and I know she's looking at me, but I can't bring myself to look into her eyes. I feel too primal. Too out of control. I can't believe I just painted her with my cum. I've never done anything like that. She probably thinks I'm crazy.

She reaches down and draws a finger from her belly button to her breasts then she puts her cum-covered finger in her mouth and sucks it dry. I meet her gaze then and see that she liked it. I slip a finger in between her still drenched folds, give her clit a quick graze, then bring my finger to my mouth and suck off her sultry taste.

She gives me a sated and pleased smile. I reach over and

take her shirt the rest of the way off and use it to clean her off. Then I pull the blanket up so she's covered again. She curls into a ball, her expression relaxed and content as she closes her eyes.

I slip out of bed and go to the bathroom to clean up then head to the kitchen to grab us some water. The mixture of beer and tequila is already cotton in my mouth, so it's going to be worse in a couple of hours. When I round the corner, I see Wes standing in front of the open fridge, a bottle of water in his hand, staring at the table. It's still a mess of cards and tequila.

He glances at me then nods toward the table. "You're cleaning that up. You also owe us a few new decks of cards and a bottle of tequila."

"Fair. In the morning." I grab a water from the fridge and down more than half.

"And disinfect the table, for fuck's sake. Whatever y'all did sounded freaking kinky."

"You didn't have to listen."

"I put on my headphones, but it didn't quite drown out everything."

"You need better headphones."

He shrugs. "She stayed?"

I nod as I take another drink of water.

"Isn't that off list?"

"We didn't really discuss it. It was late."

I can feel Wes looking at me, but I don't meet his gaze. I know it'll reveal too much, especially after what just happened in my room. I finish my water and grab more for me and Ally.

"Hope you know what you're doing," he says as I leave the room.

The words are spoken quietly, but I hear him loud and clear. I slip back in bed and wrap myself around Ally again.

I hope so too because I'm not sure I do anymore.

chapter twenty-two

I love Texas. I hate Texas weather. After two solid weeks of budding spring weather, the arrival of March is met with a cold snap. Just when I started packing away my coat and scarves and pulled out my sandals, too. I burrow further into my scarf as the biting wind slaps my face. My eyes are watering, my nose is freezing, and my hands are going numb. This is pure misery and as I walk across campus, every student I pass looking as miserable as I feel. Why couldn't this come on the weekend when I could stay home under a blanket instead of my busiest school day of the week?

What I wouldn't give to be curled up on the couch with some hot chocolate…and having Logan curled up next to me would be pretty nice, too. Now that I know what it's like to sleep next to him, it's hard not to long for it again. We haven't spoken about how what we did in his room was off list. How it was hot and filthy and one of the most intimate things we've done. The next morning, we got out of bed and pretended it didn't happen. It's like our Halloween mantra all over again, what happens off list...

When we emerged from Logan's room, Wes looked from the still-wrecked kitchen table to me with a knowing smirk. Nate was sprawled on the couch, an ice pack on his forehead. He opened one eye, looked at me, and started to smile then groaned in pain. My face had gotten so hot I hightailed it out there as quickly as possible. I expected Logan to be weird since then, but we've been really good. There's an intimacy between us that wasn't there before. It's a little uncertain, and yet, somehow easy. I want to go off list again. I only want to be off list.

Of course, I would fuck all this up by catching feelings. There's no way he wants to stay off list with me, not after how well the combine went. He's going to the NFL, I can feel it. I've always known how he felt about relationships, and I can't see him changing his mind with this huge future in front of him. If I say something, things could end. And I'm not ready for that.

I push all my confusing feelings away and cut between buildings, quickening my pace. I want to get into a heated building as soon as possible. When I round the corner, I immediately notice Logan and his bright blue beanie standing outside the business building. And he's not alone. A girl in a puffy coat is closing in on him, her arms snaking up his shoulders and around his neck. My stomach lurches and time seems to slow—as if it goes in slow motion so I can fully contemplate what I'm witnessing. She smiles up at him, and recognition slams into my chest like a wrecking ball. Trish. Trish has her arms around Logan. I press a hand to my mouth, seriously afraid I might throw up.

Logan takes her arms, unwrapping them from his neck, then he suddenly stiffens. He turns, as if he can feel me, and as soon as our gazes collide, his expression fills with dread—and guilt.

I turn and start running back in the direction I came. Tears that have nothing to do with the frigid wind cloud my eyes.

"Ally! Wait!"

I don't. I pick up my pace and duck into the building to my right. I blindly race up the set of stairs, not knowing where I'm going, just wanting to disappear. I hear the door open and slam shut behind me. Shit. When I get to the second floor, I slip into the nearest classroom that's thankfully empty and press myself against the wall, covering my mouth to quiet the sobs that I hadn't even noticed until now. I hear him come into the hallway then silence. A moment later, he enters the room and I lose it.

"Shit. Ally, I'm so sorry. Please listen. It looked worse than it was, I swear."

I bury my face in my hands and I can feel the heat of him close in on me, his hands touch my hips. My first reaction is to sink into his touch, to take his comfort, but then I remember he's the reason for my pain. I jerk away from him.

"Ally, please, let me explain."

Over and over, I see Trish with her arms around him, looking at him with a knowing smile. He touches my hands, urging me to drop them from my face. I do and his thumb slowly swipes across my cheek, clearing the tears. I finally raise my gaze to his and he looks almost as pained as I feel.

"You know her," I say.

He gives me a grim nod. "I hooked up with her last summer."

Oh God. No, I'm not hearing him right.

"It was only once. I met her at a party, and it was a drunken one-night stand. She knew I didn't want any more than that, but she DM'ed me a few times afterward. I ended up blocking her when she didn't take the hint. That's it, I swear. She totally caught me off guard today. I didn't want her to touch me."

He slept with Trish. The realization cracks something inside me, and I crumble into more tears. He pulls me into a hug, and I let him. It hurts so badly that I can't bear to turn his comfort away.

"Of all people. Why her?" I mumble into his chest.

"I know. I'm so sorry. I wish things were different. I swear I haven't seen her since."

I jerk back, his words jarring me like a wake-up call. "No, you saw her at Cafe Jolt. You knew then."

He grimaces, and I push him away. "You lied to me."

He runs a hand through his hair. "I didn't lie, exactly. I didn't know how to tell you. I didn't want to hurt you."

"Too fucking late!"

"Come on, Ally, look at this from my point of view. What happened with her was way before we happened. Do you really want me to tell you about all my past hook-ups?"

"This is different, and you know it."

He dips his head. "I knew telling you would only hurt you. I couldn't change what happened, so I thought it best to ignore it."

"It hurts, Logan."

"I know, baby." He steps closer, and I put out my arms to stop him.

"No, you don't get it. What happened between you and her hurts, but the fact that you kept it from me rips me apart. I keep getting surprised in the worst ways by the people I care for most. And you promised not to hurt me again."

"Ally." His voice is pained, and he tries to come closer again, but stops himself before I can. "That wasn't my intention... I'm so fucking sorry."

I start crying all over again. I want to sink in his arms

again, because I can hear the sincerity in his voice and know this is hurting him too. Instead, I ease further away from him. "I need to go. I can't…can't do this right now. I need some space."

I don't wait for a response as I slip out of the dark room.

<hr>

I forced myself to go to my classes though all I wanted to do was go home. When I finally get home, I send Ginny an SOS text for booze then bury myself under the covers of my bed. I don't know how much time passes before I hear my front door open and close. I pull the blanket off my head right as Ginny walks into my room with a brown paper sack in her hands. She takes one look at my face, drops the bag and rushes toward me.

"Oh my God, what happened? Did you run into that bitch Trish again?"

At the sound of her name, I start sobbing all over again.

"I'm going to fucking kill her. What did she do?"

"She…she…she slept with Logan."

Ginny rears back and her face goes red. "That motherfucker! Where is that piece of shit? I'm going to tear him limb from limb. How fucking dare he cheat on you!" She jumps up and starts looking around my room frantically. "Where are your keys? What's his address?"

"Ginny—"

"And don't tell me you weren't really going out or some bullshit like that. You said you two were exclusive. He's going to wish he was never born. I'm going to football his ass so hard."

I burst into a mixture of laughter and tears. "What does that even mean?"

"I don't know, but it's going to hurt. How dare he sleep

with that bitch?!" She finally notices my backpack where my keys are. Oh my gosh, she's really going to go kill him.

"Last summer. He slept with her last summer."

Ginny stops all her flailing about and stares at me. "What?"

"He slept with her last summer. Once."

"So, he hasn't cheated?"

"No."

"And he was with her one time before y'all ever got together?"

"Yes."

She tilts her head at me in an 'are you serious' kind of way. "Ally."

My tears come flooding back. "I know. I'm being ridiculous. My rational brain is telling me I'm overreacting. He didn't know her. Didn't know I knew her. He did nothing wrong. Yet…it hurts. It hurts so fucking much. I feel betrayed even though I have no right to feel that way." I bury my face in my hands.

"Ah, sweetie." Ginny joins me on the bed, pulling me into a hug.

"He didn't tell me. He knew who she was that day at Cafe Jolt and he said nothing. That hurts most of all."

"But can you blame him? What good would have come of him telling you?"

I rear back and look at her. "Ginny!"

"Don't get me wrong, I get why you're hurt and, yeah, he should have told you. But I can also see why he didn't. It's in the past and look how much it's hurt you."

I start crying all over again and she hugs me to her again. She's not supposed to be so logical.

"She knows him. She knows him like I know him…and I hate that."

"No." Ginny pulls back so she's facing me. "Look at me." I lift my gaze, and she's looking at me intently. "That's not true.

I don't think anyone knows him like you do. She was a one-night stand he never saw again. But you, he wants."

"Does he though? We're just a list."

"Oh, honey, you two are so much more than a list. He pursued you, you realize that, right? He's wanted you for years, and you've wanted him. Trust me, I know what it's like when a guy doesn't want you, and that's not Logan."

I think of how sorry and miserable he was earlier. Would he really care so much if we were only a list?

"Listen, for the rest of the night, I want you to let it hurt. Be pissed. Cry your eyes out. I'll even help you get drunk or sick on ice cream, whatever you want. But tomorrow, you need to let it go. It's in the past and I'm guessing he feels as horrible as you do right now."

"You make it sound so easy. It isn't."

"Who said adulting is easy?"

I laugh at that and pull her back into a hug. I feel better, but I still want to cry and yell at the unfairness of it all. Just the thought brings tears back to my eyes. I'm so ridiculous, and I can't seem to stop it.

Ginny hugs me tighter and smooths my hair. "She was a blip, Ally. You're the beacon."

chapter twenty-three

Ally

14. Karaoke night

36. Go to bowling alley on campus

I wake up feeling like I'd been run over by a Mack truck, but all the hurt and sadness has ebbed. Ginny was right, I needed to have my moment, and now it's time to let the past go and forgive Logan for not telling me. I don't like that he decided not to, but I do understand his reasoning. We have class together today, so I text him to meet me early. When I enter the hall, I see him waiting for me on a bench with two coffee cups next to him. When he sees me, he picks them up and stands, a hesitant look on his face.

"Hey," I say as I approach him.

"Hey." His eyes search my face before he looks down at the coffees in his hands. "Got you a salted caramel latte. Figured you'd want something to warm you up."

He's nervous and it's pretty adorable.

I take it. "Thanks, it's my favorite."

"I know."

I smile at him, and he smiles back. Relieved But Unsure smile. "Ally, I'm really sorry. I—"

I hold up my hand up to stop him. "I know. It's okay. I mean, the past is the past, and there's nothing that can be done about it. I really don't want Trish to ruin anything else in my life, so I'd like to move on from it."

"Really?"

"Really."

His whole demeanor relaxes, and he takes the coffee out of my hand and sets them both back down then tugs me into a hug. "Thanks. I know this isn't easy for you."

"It still stings a bit, but I mean it. Letting it go feels good. There's just one more thing." He pulls back a little so he can see my face. "I don't want you to keep things from me, even if it might be hard to hear. I've had the rug pulled out from under me too many times, and it chips away my trust."

"Ally, please know I would never intentionally hurt you."

"I know that wasn't your intention, but all those feelings of betrayal I've felt in the past came rushing back. Just promise me that from now on, we're honest with each other."

His gaze roams over my face and it doesn't feel necessarily like he's hesitating, but maybe that he's thinking carefully about his next words. Then he takes my face in his hands, his eyes meeting mine. "I promise."

I feel the sincerity in his voice. I see it in his eyes. Then he leans in, brushes his lips across mine, and I feel it throughout my body. He's kissing me. Right here in the hall where anyone can see. Completely off list. The kiss ends far too quickly, it was barely even a kiss, and yet it was perfect. The seal of a promise.

He smiles at me, and it's so sweet and trusting, my heart feels like it's about to burst.

He picks up our coffees again and hands me mine then takes my free hand with his own and leads me into class. I look down at our linked hands, not sure what it means, but not going to question it.

The next week goes by in a blur. School is nuts as it wraps up before spring break, and Logan and I are back to circling the outskirts of deeper intimacy. We're touching more. Holding hands. Quick kisses, mostly on the cheek, but a few on the lips. Yet, we're still not talking about these subtle changes or that they're off list. We seem to be in some sort of off list gray area. While we've tackled a couple of regular list items, we haven't had any sexy times since that night at his house, and all these small touches are starting to drive me crazy with need.

I get home after classes, officially on spring break now, and I should be hitting up happy hour or making plans to go out, but I just want to be with Logan. I leave in two days for my road trip, and he's going to the beach with his roommates. If I don't try to see him now, I won't see him for almost a week. I'm not sure I can wait that long to get my hands on him again.

I pick up my phone and bring up the picture of my list. Surely, I can find an item to entice him with. As I scroll through, a text pops up on my screen.

Logan: What r u doing?

Me: Looking at my list.

Logan: Oh really? Find anything interesting?

Me: I was trying to…

Logan: Where r u?

I smile then jump off the couch and run into my bathroom to freshen up. I decide to go with the comfortable but sexy look. When there's a knock at my door thirty minutes later, I'm wearing an off-the-shoulder cropped sweater and a pair of shorts that hug my hips perfectly. I open the door and find Logan on the other side holding an armful of amazing smelling Chinese take-out.

His gaze dips to my belly, and I watch as his pupils dilate. My stomach growls, breaking the heated moment, and I realize I haven't eaten since breakfast.

"I could kiss you. I'm starving."

He laughs and steps inside. "Is that so?"

"Yes." I don't think. I go on my tiptoes and brush my lips over his. Once. Twice. And the third time, he kisses me back. It's a total swoon-worthy Hollywood kind of kiss. It's sweet… until it isn't. A sexy guttural groan sounds from his throat as he drops the bags and brings his arms around my waist as the kiss turns passionate and full of promise.

I don't know how long we stand there, only kissing, but it's perfect. It's everything I need. He's everything I need. With a jerk, he breaks away from me. We stare at each other, breathing heavily.

"Shit, the soup." He bends and inspects the bag, and I start laughing.

"Did it spill?"

"We're good," he says as he picks up the bags and heads into my kitchen. "Come on, let's get you fed. I wasn't sure what you liked, so I got a variety of things."

I watch as he pulls out one Styrofoam container after another, telling me everything he got. He looks over at me and smiles and leans in and brushes a kiss on my cheek before making me a plate. As I stare at him in awe, my heart suddenly speeds up and it feels like I'm standing on the edge of a cliff with something huge on the horizon waiting for me to take the next step.

"You okay?"

"Uh, yeah. Good. Ready to eat."

Half an hour later, we're groaning on the couch from our full bellies. "We ate almost everything. How did we do that?"

He looks at the carnage on my coffee table. "I have no idea, but I'm not moving any time soon."

"Wanna watch a movie?"

"Sure."

I fire up a streaming service and start scrolling through the newly added movies. "Oh! They added *When Harry Met Sally*. Have you seen it?"

"No, isn't it like over thirty years old?"

I swat his arm. "So? It's a classic and we're watching it. You need to see it if only for the Katz Deli scene."

"Fine. Meg Ryan's hot."

I swat his arm again then settle against him. We don't talk much, but Logan's laughter tells me he's enjoying the movie. After the Katz's Deli scene my eyes start getting heavier and heavier. The next thing I know, a weight shifts next to me just before I feel a brush of a touch on my cheek then another on my lips. My sleepy brain slowly wakes up to realize I was just kissed. I open my eyes to see the room is now dark and Logan is looking at me, his glasses gone from his face, with a sleepy but heated gaze.

My hands go to his face, and I pull him back for another kiss. It's soft and sweet, but still hot and sexy. He feathers kisses all over me; he brings up my hand, kissing my palm and trailing down to my wrist where my tattoo is. I jerk my wrist slightly, but he holds on tighter. He meets my gaze. I know he has questions, but he's never voiced them. I've seen him looking at it before, but he's never touched it again. Not since that first Halloween.

He doesn't say anything now either. Instead, he leans down and softly kisses it. It's gentle and sweet, but it sears me straight to the bone. A strangled sound comes out of my throat, and his gaze comes up to mine. This is the last part of myself that I haven't shared with him. My lowest point. The place I'm so scared of falling into again. Him touching this part of me…it's almost too much, and yet it feels right.

He doesn't take his eyes off me as he kisses my wrist again then slowly moves his tongue across it.

"Logan." His name is part sob, part plea, and he immediately covers my mouth with his own again. There's nothing gentle or sweet about his kiss anymore. It's pure heat and need.

"I need you. Now."

He nods against my mouth, and I start tugging at his clothes.

"Not here," he says, breaking our kiss. "Bedroom."

He pulls me off the couch and leads me into my room. He undresses me and himself as quickly as possible before gently pushing me onto the bed, his body covering mine. His skin, warm and completely bare against mine, feels so damn good. We've rarely been skin to skin, and I'm relishing every moment.

He runs his hands all over my body, as if he wants to memorize every little dip and curve. He pulls my breast into his mouth, sucking and nipping until I'm squirming beneath him. He moves down over my torso until he's in between my legs. He kisses my inner thigh softly, tenderly, then he kisses me between my legs and it's like a fire is ignited. I'm already frantic with need, desperate for more.

"Logan. Now. I need…"

His tongue swipes over my clit, and I jackknife at the intense pleasure that zaps through me. I'm not going to last long, I can feel it. He grips my thighs, spreading me even more and pushes his tongue inside me. He fucks and licks me until I shatter in a million fiery pieces. Then he gentles his kisses until I'm completely spent. He kisses his way back up my body, taking my lips in a searing kiss before pulling away. I wrap my legs around him, urging him forward, but he moves out from between my legs.

"What are you…"

"I want to try a different position." He looks almost nervous. "From behind."

I pull back. "You know I don't want to do that."

"I know, but I think you need to. That position is all about trust, and he took that from you. You need to take it back."

"He used that position to control me, to get what he wanted from me."

His thumb brushes my cheek then he slowly trails his hand down my neck, over my shoulder and along my torso. "He manipulated you. I won't. I can't control you unless you trust me enough to give over the control. That's what makes the position so fucking hot. Because you're trusting me in your most vulnerable position. Trusting me to make it good. To take care of you."

His words send a flare of heat all through my body. He pulls me closer until we're skin to skin again. "Let me be the one who gives you back the power, Ally. You won't regret it, I promise."

Oh God. There's no way I can resist him now; he's melted away all my resolve. "Okay. Yes."

He smiles, his deep blue eyes the most open I've ever seen them. "I want you to be sure."

"I'm sure." And I really am. I wouldn't want this with anyone else.

He takes my face in his hands and kisses me. It's soft and slowly disarming me with each sweet taste. He untangles from me and gets a condom out of his discarded pants. He holds out the unwrapped condom to me. I sit up and take it and slowly roll it on. He groans, his eyes heavy with lust as he takes my hand in his.

"Come here."

My certainty transforms into nervousness. Everything feels so good right now, and I don't want it to go away. He looks so damn sexy, standing there, waiting for me, his trust laid bare. I scoot down toward him, and he surprises me by stepping back and pulling me to stand too. Instead of turning me around at the edge of the bed, he takes me away from it.

"What are we doing?"

"Something different."

He takes me to my dresser until we're both standing in front of the mirror. I catch my nude reflection and immediately turn around. Logan catches me before I can move away.

"Logan, no."

He tips my chin up so I'm forced to look at him. "Yes. I need you to see that you can trust me. I need you to see what it does to me to be inside you. I need you to see how connected we are even if we aren't face to face."

What is he doing to me? My body is begging me to listen to him, to let him do what he will to me, but my head is screaming for me to run. "It's...I'm...I'm embarrassed."

He smiles at me. "It might be a little awkward for a moment or two, but then it's going to be hot. It's going to turn you on. It sure as hell is going to turn me on."

I shake my head. "You're asking a lot, Logan."

He's asking more from me than he ever has. Does he realize exactly how beyond the list we are? This is more. This means so much more.

"I know." He runs a finger across my forehead, pulling my

bangs aside. "I'm asking you to trust me to make this good for you. I promise I will." He brushes my lips with his own. The kiss is light, almost sweet, but with enough seduction to tear down my defenses. He sips and tastes until I'm putty in his hands.

He gently nudges me, so I turn around. As soon as I catch a glimpse of myself in the mirror, I turn my gaze away.

"Look at me, Ally."

My heart thuds hard against my chest. I love that he's calling me Ally not Allyson. This isn't a list seduction. This is us. I slowly turn to the mirror and find his gaze in the reflection.

"Watch me. Watch me please you. See what pleasing you does to me. If you don't like it, just say the word and we'll stop."

I nod then watch him kiss my shoulder. My neck. When I feel his hand touch my stomach and slowly make its way to my breast, I lock eyes with him. I can't look at what he's doing to me, but I watch him look. His thumb brushes my nipple then he pinches it. I gasp and look at his hand. Now I can't look away. He gently kneads my breast and groans as he presses his cock against my ass, his face tight with pleasure.

"Watching you watch me is driving me fucking crazy. It's so hot. The way your lips part. The way your eyes darken with lust. Do you know your eyes go from bright green to deep emerald every time you're turned on?"

His hand slips down my stomach. I can't see the bottom half of my body in the mirror, but watching his hand travel down, knowing where he's going, has me nearly crying out. Then he touches me, his fingers easily sliding over me.

"Fuck, you're wet."

I am. I'm so turned on it hurts.

"Always so wet for me. Only me."

"Yes," I moan and arch my hips into his hand as he strokes

me again. I'm already close. He just gave me an orgasm, but this next one feels like it's going to be even more intense. He strokes me again, and I feel the beginnings of the orgasm sparking to life. My head falls back and he stops. I groan from the loss of his touch.

"I need to be inside you when you come again." He grips my hips and locks gazes with me in the mirror. He's waiting for my consent, and my heart tumbles over in my chest. I give him a nod.

"Place your hands on the dresser." His voice is rougher, more authoritative, and I feel its power between my legs.

I put my hands on the dresser, and he pulls my hips back, maneuvering his cock to my entrance. "Look at me. I want you to see what you do to do me. How good this feels to me."

I watch as he slowly pushes inside me. His face shudders with pleasure, and I can see going this slow is killing him, but he loves it too. He relishes every slow stroke in and out of me. It's sweet torture. It feels so damn good, I need more. I need to see him lose control.

"Harder, Logan."

His eyes meet mine as he slowly slides out of me then he slams back in. His hands tighten on my hips as he starts to fuck me. His neck and shoulders are tense, his face lost to pleasure, but his eyes stay on mine.

"You like this, Ally? Like how my cock fills you up?"

"You know I do. Now fuck me like you mean it. Make me come all around that big, beautiful cock."

He groans as he pulls my hips further back, his fingers digging into me so hard I bet it leaves a mark. I hope it does. He fucks me with abandon and seeing how turned on he is, how out of control I make him, has my orgasm crashing through me, washing over me in waves, pushing and pulling me further into this pool of pleasure he's created inside me.

"Fuck, Ally."

His fingers bite into my skin even harder, and I watch as he's taken under too. Seeing him in this vulnerable moment as he lets the pleasure take over is one of the sexiest things I've ever seen. This man has officially ruined me for anyone else.

His head falls to my shoulder, his breath slowly evening out. I should be relaxing into the moment, but my heart is still pounding away, my breath caught in my throat. He looks up at me, a sated and sexy grin on his lips, his eyes bright and happy, and it hits me. I just pushed off the edge of that cliff.

I'm in love with him. Utterly. Completely. No turning back.

He turns me around and pulls me tight in his arms. "You okay? You're shaking."

I can't control the emotions welling up inside me. The urge to cry is so strong I have to fight to stop myself from giving in. It's scary as hell, but it feels so good. I love him.

"I'm amazing." I press a kiss to his chest. "Thank you."

He takes my face in his hands and tips it up and places a light but potent kiss on my lips.

"Stay," I say, holding my breath. I'm not sure what I'm going to do if he leaves me now. I'm too vulnerable, too raw.

"I'm not going anywhere."

I burrow into his chest and suppress the urge to cry with happiness. I don't know what this means, if he feels the same, if we have a future despite going in different directions. I'm just going to take this and enjoy every moment of it and not think about how easily he can obliterate my heart.

I blink a few times as I wake and find myself wrapped around the warm and solid body of Logan. He stayed. After everything that happened last night, I didn't expect him to leave, but I didn't know if he'd change his mind in the light of day when he realized how far off list we went. But he's still here.

His hand moves and covers mine that's on his chest. He turns it so the inside of my wrist is facing us. He rubs his thumb over my tattoo softly. I shift to look up at him. His gaze flits to mine, his blue eyes soft and sleepy and sated.

"Morning," he says with a rough sleepy voice.

"Morning."

He leans his head down to kiss my lips; it's quick and sweet, the kind of kiss I'd love to wake up to every morning.

Before he can see my heart in my eyes, I lay my head back on his chest and watch him continue to caress my tattoo.

"I got it just before I graduated high school."

After a few moments of silence, he says, "You don't have to tell me if you don't want to. It seems…private to you."

"I want to." I swallow. Only my parents know the significance of my tattoo. Not even Ginny knows why I got it. "Before that Halloween, I was that girl that didn't understand deep depression or even why people would contemplate suicide."

He tenses beneath me, and I feel his heart speed up. He weaves his fingers through mine so we're now holding hands.

"I didn't understand being in a place so dark that you didn't want to live anymore. Then all these things were happening to me, and I had no idea how to handle it. My world became really bleak and narrow, and I never wanted to leave it."

His lips brush the top of my head.

"My parents took me to the beach in the spring, an attempt to make me feel better. It was a choppy day, and the waves were strong. They kept beating me down while I tried to boogie board, and I realized that was exactly how I felt all the time. Like wave after wave had been crashing over me. Then I had this thought: What if I let the waves just take me? Let them beat me until there's nothing left. So, I stopped fighting them. I let them push me under over and over. I thought I'd finally feel free, but I felt more trapped. Even more scared. Somewhere in all that it occurred to me that my life would be defined by this one thing that happened to me. And I couldn't let that happen. I started fighting again and was able to grab a hold of my boogie board and get myself above the water. My dad was already running toward me and helped me back to shore. I immediately burst into tears and told my parents I needed help."

"Ally…" He pulls me into him, pressing me tightly into his body.

"For my graduation present I told my parents I wanted a tattoo. I read that waves could represent hope and joy in the deepest of troubles. And I felt that. The waves were my darkest moment, but that experience was also what allowed me to turn things around. I added the sun to show that there's always a new day. A new chance."

He brings my wrist to his lips. "It's beautiful, Ally." Then he takes his finger to lift my chin so I'll look at him. "Do you know how incredibly strong it was of you to fight your way out of that darkness? You fucking blow me away."

I shake my head. "It wasn't easy, and it took lots of therapy. And I still have days where I don't feel very strong."

"Do any of us? What matters is that day, you were. That day you didn't let it win. God, I can't imagine not knowing you. You…you've always made my dark days lighter. Even on those days that I didn't see you, I'd think of you. Your smile. Your laugh. It always eased the pain."

"Logan."

His words break something inside me, and a flood of emotions overwhelm me. I surge forward and press my lips to his, unable to contain them. Our kiss is frantic and sloppy, but it's perfect. Always fucking perfect.

He moves over me, and I open my legs to him. His cock, hot and hard, presses into me. I sink my fingers into his hair, pulling his head away so we lock gazes, our breaths heavy and heady. "Our Halloweens together have been the best things about my college years. You've always been there for me. You always brought me peace. You calmed the waters."

He growls and takes my mouth roughly right as he thrusts inside me. Oh God, it feels so amazing. So, silky and hard. Filling me like he hasn't before. He thrusts hard. Fucking me in several full, punishing strokes before stopping, his cock inside me to the hilt.

"Fuck, Ally…I'm not wearing a condom. I gotta stop." His expression is pained, his breathing unsteady. We already had a safety talk, so we know we'll be good if he doesn't wear a condom.

"I don't want you to," I say.

He looks at me, his expression a mixture of elated and unsure.

"But if we do this, then we're off list. We stay off list."

His eyes search mine. "Ally…I can't promise what will happen after graduation."

"I know, and that's okay. But it's no longer a deadline. It's no longer a definite end. I want to be more than a list. I want to be with you, Logan. All the way."

He presses his forehead to mine. "You're more than a list, Ally. You always have been."

I press my hand to his cheek. "Fuck me, Logan. Make me yours."

He takes my lips before pulling out of me then slamming back in. We both moan as we revel in the feel of each other. Then he slams into me again. Over and over. He presses my leg down, opening me even more to him as he grinds against me, hitting my clit in the most delicious way.

"Oh God, Logan…it's so good. You feel so good."

"Fuck, Ally…your pussy is so fucking sweet. And it's mine. All mine."

The quicker he moves, the more frantic my moans get, then suddenly, I'm falling apart.

He groans. "Yes, baby. Let that sweet cum coat my cock. Fuck, the feel of you coming on my bare cock is the best fucking thing I've ever felt."

His dirty mouth keeps my orgasm going, my body demanding more. Demanding all of him.

"I need you to come. Please Logan, I want to feel you come inside me. Fill me up."

He groans at my words as his pace slows. He pulls almost completely out then slowly pushes back in. Then he switches up and thrusts into me shallowly, his thick cock torturing me in a whole new way. There's a tense mix of pleasure and pain on his face.

I grab his head and bring his lips to mine. "Let go. Shatter into me."

He kisses me deeply, his cock now like iron inside me right as he shudders and starts fucking me relentlessly, his cum filling me.

"Ally…" he says against my lips. "You're mine…promise me."

"I promise."

chapter twenty-four

Another girl's top goes off. I look over to Nate and Wes, and we raise our beers then take another drink.

"We'll be passed out drunk in an hour," Nate says.

"They're getting started early today. We might have to leave the beach before boob hour," Wes says.

I chuckle. We noticed in our previous few days on South Padre that around four o'clock there tended be an outbreak of girls hoisted on shoulders flashing their boobs, so we nicknamed it boob hour. We decided to make a drinking game out of the fun, a drink for every set of tits and a whole beer for every guy who drops trou. Needless to say, we've been pretty toasted by the time we head back to our condo at the end of the day.

It's been a good time so far, even if a little crazy at times. We headed down with a group from the football team and other school athletes. Each day we've put up a Toro flag and buried a keg in the sand, and the crowds have come. All the other guys are enjoying the bikini-clad attention. A few girls have flirted with me, but any time they hinted at more, I told them I have a girlfriend. It was weird when it first came out of my mouth. Is Ally my girlfriend? We didn't exactly label things. With our future after graduation a big question mark, do we even want a label other than off list?

"Hey, did I overhear you tell that girl earlier that you have a girlfriend?" Wes leans forward in his beach chair.

Damn, I've tried my best to keep that on the down low. Mostly because I don't even know what I'm doing. Though I'm surprised it took this long for my roommates to notice.

"Yeah."

"Have you and Ally gone off list?"

"Hey, knock that shit off," I say looking around, but no one around is paying us any attention. We're lounging on beach chairs while most people are congregated around the keg.

"No one knows what I'm talking about. What's the deal?"

I shrug and lean forward. "You know where I was before we left. A weekend together is off list," I say the last word soft though no one else is around.

"So, now y'all are girlfriend-boyfriend?"

"I don't know. We didn't put a label on it. I was just trying to get the girls off me," I shrug. "Seemed easier to say that."

"Do you want to put a label on it?" Nate asks.

I shrug again and Nate laughs as he takes a drink of his beer. "What's so funny?"

"You. Denying what's clear as day and has been from day one. What exactly is holding you back? You like her. You've liked her for years. And you're exclusive with her with all this list business when you totally don't have to be. Just commit."

"It's not that easy. We're graduating. She's staying in Austin for grad school, and who knows where I'll end up. None of the pro Texas teams need an edge rusher. If I go pro, I'll likely be across the country."

"So, you do some long-distance for a while. Grad school is only a couple of years. And she could always transfer. You're just making excuses."

I sigh. "I've never been in a relationship in my life, and you think the first one I'm in should be long-distance and full of complications? That I should ask her to potentially change her plans to fit mine? I can't keep promising her things will work out. What if I'm wrong? I've already broken and tested Ally's trust and finally earned it back. I can't do that to her again."

"Just because your parents' marriage didn't work out, doesn't mean that your relationship with Ally is doomed," Nate says.

"How can it not when it starts with so many things going against us?"

Nate gives me a look that says he thinks I'm still making excuses. Wes leans back into his chair, looking out at the water as he takes a drink of beer.

"You're being awfully quiet about all this."

Wes shrugs. "You know me, commitment isn't exactly my thing. I have no reason to talk. Besides, I get what you're saying."

Except he's holding something back. I should leave it alone, but instead I call him out on it.

Wes sighs. "Bro, I've watched you plow through offensive linemen with a hundred pounds on you like it was nothing. You've taken hits then gotten up and made a tackle when most guys would still be flat on their back. You fucking walked-on to one of the most competitive college football teams in the country and worked your way to starting."

"Yeah, so?"

"You weren't afraid to do any of that, but you're afraid of a long-distance relationship? You take all these risks with football, so why not with your love life? No risk, no reward."

Shit. Isn't that exactly why I started this whole list business with Ally in the first place? To live my life more fully. To help her live hers. I've been encouraging Ally to take more risks and yet, here I am, holding back.

I lean back in my chair. "Damn. You're right."

Wes gives me a look that says, of course, I'm right.

"Shit. Who knew Wes would have the best relationship advice of the day?" Nate says.

Wes kicks sand in his direction. "Fuck you. But seriously, it doesn't take a brain surgeon to figure out Logan's shit. Who's the dumb one here?"

"Shut up," I say then take a drink from my beer as they laugh at me. A shadow enters our little circle, and I look up to see the last person I expected—or wanted—to see.

"Hey Logan." Trish gives me a flirty smile that sends a cold shudder down my spine.

"Trish."

I notice Nate and Wes shift at the mention of her name. They haven't met her, but they know enough. She turns her attention to them. "Hey boys."

They nod, but their fuck off vibes are strong. Not getting anywhere with them, she turns her attention back to me. "We never got to finish our conversation the other day."

"There was nothing to continue."

"How do you know? We barely got started before you ran after Allyson. What are you doing with her anyway?"

"She's my girlfriend." Saying the words this time, with all my bullshit pushed away, feels fucking amazing.

Her body tenses, but it's hard to read her expression with her sunglasses on. "I thought you didn't do girlfriends."

"Just hadn't found the right girl, I guess."

She scoffs at that. "Trust me, you don't know the true Allyson."

I stand then. "Actually, I do know her. I know everything. I even know about you and what you've done, so why don't you move along. This is a private party."

She puts her hands on her hips. "It's a public beach, Logan."

Wes and Nate stand, flanking me. "Then find another part of it to stalk," Wes says, and I bite back a smile. Wes has never been one to filter his thoughts.

Not wanting to deal with Trish for another second, I walk away and head toward the keg, Wes and Nate join me and when I look around a little later, I see she is nowhere to be found. Thank God.

We spend the next hour making sure we tap the keg, and by the time we're packing up, we're buzzing hard. I'm feeling the lightest I've felt since we've gotten here, and I know it's not all the beer. The guys are right. As uncertain as my future is, I want Ally in it. We have to give it a try. I'll regret it if we don't.

I dig around in the backpack I brought to hold all our stuff for my phone. I've already talked to Ally today, but I'm dying to break our once-a-day rule. There should be a plastic bag with all our phones stuffed into it, but it's nowhere to be found. I dump the bag on the sand and it's not there at all.

Oh fuck.

chapter twenty-five

As Ginny and I pass a sign welcoming us into Arkansas, I find myself wishing I could snap my fingers and be back home in Austin. Logan is coming home today too, and I'm dying to see him. It wasn't easy to go days without seeing him after going off list and the amazing weekend we spent together. We even made a deal to only talk or text to each other once a day while on our trips so we could focus on having fun with our friends. And honestly, as much as I've missed Logan, I've had a blast with Ginny and am so glad we did this.

We hit up New Orleans and Bourbon Street for a couple of days then headed to Nashville. We took a day trip into the Smoky Mountains and came across a place to bungee jump. It was always something I wanted to do but never considered again after my life went sideways. Then yesterday, I let go of my fear and leapt. And it was amazing. I even allowed Ginny to post pictures of me on social media. I might not be ready for my own accounts again, but I'd like to be part of my friend's memories that she'd like to share.

I check my messages again and see Logan hasn't responded to my text this morning telling him we were on our way home. I'm trying not to think anything of it. I've avoided ReelGood these past few days, not wanting to be distracted by anything Logan might post, but with more hours in the car ahead of me and his lack of response starting to bother me, I open the app. I click on my following and come across a video of Logan and a bunch of other guys playing football on the beach. They're all beautiful, with their muscular torsos and hip hugging swim-suits, but it's Logan I can't stop looking at. I know how he feels, I've run my hands over the dips and hills of his abs.

God, I wish we were home already. I blow out a hot breath and keep scrolling. Another video pops up of Logan riding some waves. There are some videos from Wes and Nate's accounts too that show up for me.

One is of Wes talking to the camera with a bunch of screams in the background. He says, "Cheers to boob-hour from South Padre!" He takes a huge sip of his beer. There are no actual boobs in the video.

Boob hour? I don't exactly like the sound of that, but this is Wes we're talking about, so who knows? I move on to browsing through random videos. I come across one that's a picture slideshow and immediately recognize it as the same group of people. Wes, Nate, and Logan are tagged too. One of the pictures is of the three of them, arms around each other's shoulders. It's a great picture, and they all look really happy— and maybe a little drunk. I start to scroll past, but there's a blond in a bikini in the background that has my stomach twisting, so I enlarge the picture and discover why. It's Trish. And she's not some random person in the background; she's looking right at Logan and the guys.

My whole body starts to ache. "Oh my God."

"What?" Ginny's hands jerk on the steering wheel then looks from the road to me then back.

"Trish was at the beach with the guys."

"What? Are you serious?"

I tell her what I'm seeing.

"Logan didn't mention that he saw her?"

"I talked to him yesterday morning and this was posted yesterday afternoon. I haven't heard from him today."

"Call him. Don't jump to conclusions until you talk to him. Half the college is in South Padre."

I nod. We promised each other we'd be honest with each other, and I need to give him the chance to do so. I call, but it immediately goes to voicemail. That's weird. Does he have his phone off?

"Voicemail."

"Maybe his phone's dead. Text him again."

I do, asking him to call me when he sees it. I try to push it out of my mind as we continue on, but I feel as if a knife is slowly being twisted in my gut with each hour that passes and I don't hear from him.

"Okay, it's been three hours. I know he's heading home today too, but it seems odd he wouldn't respond."

"Maybe he's driving. Text Wes or Nate."

I text the thread that Logan started when his dad was in his accident. Hopefully, I'm not coming off as a crazy girlfriend. I'm not even sure if I am Logan's girlfriend. We didn't exactly label things, though as far as I'm concerned, that's what I am to him. No one responds back, and after another couple of hours, I call their numbers and it goes directly to voicemail.

"Okay, this is weird. I'm truly worried now."

Ginny gives me a grim look. "It's a bit odd. We'll be home in about five and half hours. Hopefully, there's a simple explanation."

I hope there is, because my mind is going in a thousand different directions and none of them are good.

chapter twenty-six

It's been the longest fucking day and I've never been happier to be back in Austin in my life. We spent the whole morning running around trying to figure out what happened to our phones, and in the end, we had to admit they were stolen off the beach while we were getting plastered. We reported the theft to the police, knowing it's a lost cause, but we did it on the off chance that someone gets arrested in possession of a bunch of phones. Finally, we packed it up for the long drive back. It felt like it took twelve hours and not six.

I pull into the driveway and we're all sluggish to get out, exhausted after all the late nights and heavy drinking, and yet we're anxious to get on our computers and get connected again. I've been kicking myself all day for not memorizing numbers. The only number I knew was my dad's, and I got a hold of him to let him know what was going on, but I hate that I haven't been able to contact Ally. Has she tried to get a hold of me? Is she worried? I know if I had tried to get a hold of her for a day and her phone went straight to voicemail, I'd be going out of my mind.

I pull down my tailgate and start pulling our luggage out. The sound of a car pulling up has me looking over my shoulder, it's Ally's car. I can see the relief coming over her face as she throws the car into park. My heart hammers at the sight of her, and I feel like I just sacked the quarterback on fourth down.

Fuck. I'm in love with her. I'm so fucking head over heels crazy about her that there's no way I'm letting her go. I don't even understand how I thought I could.

She jumps out of the driver's side, and I head straight for her. She jumps into my arms, and I pull her in close, taking in her sweet smell and warm body.

"I was so worried," she mutters into the crook of my neck.

I hug her tighter. "I'm so sorry. My phone was stolen. All of ours were."

She relaxes against me, and I pull her face back and brush my lips over hers. It's not nearly as much as I want to do, but if I delve any deeper we probably won't make it out of the driveway. "I'm memorizing your number before the night is over."

She laughs. "I didn't think about that. I should do the same. All your phones were stolen?"

"Yes." I give her lips another quick kiss and reluctantly untangle myself from her. "I guess that's what happens when you leave your phones unattended while you get drunk on the beach. We've been pretty pissed off at ourselves."

"I'm going fucking crazy," Wes says. "Let's get our shit in the house so I can check my phone on the computer."

I look at her. "Wanna stay?"

Her smile is quick and so fucking bright, I swear it lights me all the way through. "Absolutely."

Who knew that word could turn me on so much? I grip her hips and put my mouth at her ear. "Good answer."

She makes this sexy humming sound before saying, "Let me get my stuff."

I nod and look over her shoulder to see Ginny leaning on the car, her arms crossed over her chest, her gaze averted. I glance back at Nate and he's watching her with a schooled expression.

"Hey, Ginny," I call out. "You wanna come in?"

Out of the corner of my eye, I notice Nate jerk in surprise. Ginny glances at Nate then bounces her eyes back to me. "I'd rather get bikini waxed while laying on hot coals."

Wes winces. "Damn, dude. That's harsh."

Ginny gives Nate a parting *fuck you* smirk as she goes to the driver's side and pops the trunk. Nate makes some sort of frustrated sound before grabbing his luggage.

Ally approaches her. "You don't mind taking my car?"

"Are you kidding? Not having to take public transportation or ride-share for the next few days sounds like a tropical vacation for me."

Ally laughs and pulls her into a hug. "I had so much fun." They say a few more things that I can't make out but doing the whole girly BFF thing.

When they separate, I hear Ginny say, "Now go fuck your man."

She winks at me, and Ally swats her arm. I laugh, all in for that plan.

We get all our stuff in the house, and the first thing we agree on is we need food. Since Ally is the only one with a phone, she orders pizza for us all. I crash into our overstuffed chair and pull her into my lap.

"Kiss me like you missed me."

I see her eyes blaze right before she touches her lips to mine. This time I don't hold back and sink everything I have into the kiss. I could live here forever. How in the world did I ever think I could walk away from her after graduation?

"Ugh, you know you have a room, right?"

Wes' voice breaks our kiss, and I look at him as he plops on the couch with his laptop in hand. Nate is right behind him doing the same thing.

"You know you have rooms too?"

"We're not the ones wanting to get naked."

As much as I want to get Ally naked, I need to feed her first. When I do get her naked, I don't want any interruptions. I ignore him and kiss Ally again. She giggles but kisses me back. "You're terrible."

"Ugh," Wes says. "Last known place my phone was South Padre, though it looks like it's in a different area of the beach." He squints at the screen and makes a movement on it. "Hey, looks like it was near Waves Condominiums." He makes a few more strokes on the screen. "About a mile from our condo."

"Same for me," Nate says.

I should probably be doing the same thing, but the only thing I cared about was getting a hold of Ally and she's right here. There's nothing I can do about my phone until I can go to the phone store tomorrow.

There's a knock at the door, and Ally jumps up to get our pizza. A few minutes later, we're all back in our spots, slices of pizza in our hands.

"So, besides your phones getting stolen, how was the beach? Run into people you know?"

"Yeah, saw lots of people. We buried a keg every day and put a Toro flag up. Tons of people stopped by."

Ally makes a humming sound, and when I glance at her, her brows are furrowed. I look up to see Nate giving me a look. What? I'm not going to lie; she knows we were partying like that.

"Tell me about your trip."

She gives me a hesitant smile. "Yeah, it was fun. Really good. Oh, I bungee jumped!"

"What?"

"Yeah, it was on the last day, so haven't had a chance to tell you. I have a video."

"Show me."

She grabs her phone and pulls it up. "Holy shit, that's awesome, Ally. Looks so fun."

"It really was. I haven't felt like that…it felt really good. I want to do it again."

"With me, next time."

"That would be fun," she says and kisses me, and I don't waste time deepening it.

"Ugh, you two off list are cheesy as hell."

At Wes' words, Ally stiffens in my arms. Our kiss stops and suddenly what he said sinks in. Oh shit.

She jerks back. "What did he just say?" Before I can even form a word, she looks at Wes. "What did you say?"

Wes' eyes are wide with panic as he looks between Ally and me.

"Ally, it's not what you think," I say.

She turns to me. "Did you tell them about my list?"

Ally's phone starts ringing, and we both look at it on the coffee table. Ginny's calling. Ally grabs it and swipes the call away and looks at me. "Did you?"

"No, not the way you're thinking,"

"Don't lie to me." She scrambles off me, and I hate the hurt looking back at me.

"Please let me explain. Wes was giving me shit about not kissing you when we played football that day, and I acciden-tally said it was off list. I only explained that we were doing a bucket list. I didn't tell them what's on it."

"It's true, Ally," Wes says. "He barely said anything and swore us to silence. We haven't said a word."

Wes is trying to help, and I appreciate it, but his words only seem to make Ally more upset. I get up, and she steps away from me before I can get closer to her. Her phone rings again and she sighs, swiping it away again.

"You promised. You promised you wouldn't say a word." Tears cloud her eyes, and they're killing me.

Every time she says that word, reminding how I've broken my word—how I've let her down—it feels like I'm reliving my worst hit over and over again.

"I'm so sorry, it was an accident and it's just the guys. They're my inner circle, like Ginny is to you."

"He's right," Nate says. "You're part of us now."

Ally glances at him, and her stance relaxes some at that, but her arms are folded across herself, and I know that even if she understands, I've broken a small piece of trust I earned back. Fuck, why can't I stop screwing up?

I take a step toward her, and thankfully she doesn't move away. "Everything that's important and private is still just between us. I promise." Even though I have no right to say it, I can't seem to stop myself.

Her phone starts blowing up with all sorts of sounds. She glances at it. "What the hell?"

"Oh fuck!"

We all glance at Wes, whose gaze is on his computer screen, a pained expression on his face.

"What's going on?"

He looks up at Ally, and he looks like he's about to tell her her puppy just died. My stomach plummets. "Wes."

His gaze jumps to me. "Apparently, you posted to Reel-Good a few minutes ago."

"No, I didn't."

"Obviously. It's…it's a picture of Ally's list. And a filtered voice, um…"

"What?!" Ally and I shout at the same time.

He swivels his computer, and we all crowd around it. He plays the video. It's screenshots of Ally's list with an altered voice saying, *CTU President's daughter has a naughty side…I should know.*

The hashtags attached are *#kinkyally #sexlist #rycliffhighschoolsexscandal*

Ally makes an anguished sound and steps away. "Oh my God."

"What the fuck?!"

"Oh no," she says then makes a beeline for the bathroom. She slams the door behind her, but there's no mistaking the sound of her throwing up.

"Log into your account and delete it," Nate says.

I grab Wes' computer and log him out and log myself in and delete it, but it's too late. It's already been saved hundreds of times. I might be sick myself.

"Who the hell would do this?" Nate asks.

"Trish."

We all swing our gazes toward the bathroom where Ally is standing. She looks like hell, her face pale with mascara smeared all over her eyes. Her eyes narrow at me. "You were with her at the beach."

Oh fuck, I totally forgot out about our encounter at the beach. And our phones went missing that afternoon. Damn it!

"Shit, she showed up that last day. How did you know?"

As soon as the words are out of my mouth, I know they're the wrong ones. She completely closes up, though her gaze shoots daggers at me.

"I saw her in the background of a ReelGood you were all tagged in. You purposely didn't say anything when I asked."

"I forgot! She stopped by for like two minutes and I told her to get lost. That's it."

She shakes her head, not believing me. I'm not sure I blame her. "You deleted it. You said you deleted it."

"I did. You saw me delete it."

"Did you delete it off all your apps? The cloud?" Nate asks.

"Yeah, I…oh shit." I look back at Ally. "I texted you the list. I don't think I deleted it from my texting app."

Ally crumbles, and I rush to her before she falls over. She cries into my chest and every sob is slowly ripping apart.

"This is all your fault," she mutters into my chest then raises her gaze to mine. This look finishes me off. I've shattered all the broken pieces she'd put back together. I've lost her.

"Ally," I plead, my heart pounding.

"If you hadn't taken the picture in the first place none of this would have happened."

"By none, you mean us."

She flinches and looks away. "There is no us."

I knew it, but her words still cut me to the core. This can't be the end. Not when we've just begun. Not when I've realized how much she means to me.

"I deleted the video. We can fight this. We have to—"

"No!" She pushes away from me. "My life is fucking ruined, Logan! I'm part of two internet sex scandals now. I was protected before because I was a minor, but people are going to put two and two together with that hashtag. I can't come back from that. No one is going to take me seriously now. I'm done for."

"No. You can't let her win, Ally. You can't let them all win."

A pounding on the door stops me and we all turn to look at it, afraid of what's on the other side. Nate jumps up and looks through the peephole then immediately opens the door. Ginny rushes in. "Where is—" She stops when she sees Ally. "Oh Ally."

They move toward each other, and Ginny wraps Ally in her arms. Ally breaks down all over again. "Take me home."

Ginny nods and ushers her out the door. Nate grabs Ally's things and follows them out. I sink onto the couch, cradling my head in my hands. "Fuck. What do I do now?"

I feel a hand on my shoulder. "I don't know, man. This is bad."

It's bad, but it's not hopeless. I refuse to believe that. I can't lose her just when I've realized how much I need her. I can't.

chapter twenty-seven

Ginny took me to my parents' house from Logan's, and I went straight to my old room and haven't moved since. I've ignored my own phone for days. Last night, I finally caved and asked for a basic rundown from Ginny, and she said the story blew up, from local news to national, and there was a segment on the *Today Show* dedicated to college bucket lists and the hidden dangers. Oh, and I've pretty much been painted as a sex addict.

Everyone seems to have a say on what my list means—about me, my past. Do they notice the regular innocent college stuff on the list? Nope, only the sex stuff. It's beyond embarrassing. My parents are supportive, but two sex scandals are a lot for them to take, and my mom is getting the brunt of the backlash since it involves her university and daughter.

And everyone is waiting on me.

I've been contacted by every news outlet, even the university newspaper, but I have nothing to say. I just need it to die down, and my life will quietly go back to normal. Ha, no, my life will never be normal again. I'll forever be that girl in the sex video. The girl with the sex list.

I want my lonely, private life back. Before Logan got his hands on my list.

As soon as thought enters my mind, my body aches and a sick feeling enters my mouth, but I refuse to question it. I'm furious at him. It doesn't matter that I miss him. So damn much. But all I see is that video exposing me. Yes, it wasn't really him, but I feel betrayed all over again. It's not fair to him, the logical part of me knows that, because he's a victim too. He deserves better than my resentment. He deserves someone who trusts him completely, who won't doubt him at every corner. We just need to go our separate ways, and all this will go away when the next scandal hits. I burrow into the covers of my childhood bed and tell myself not to cry. Again.

The door to my room slams open and the light flips on, blinding me so much that I put the covers over my head.

"Nope, we're done hiding," my mom says and pulls the covers off me.

"Mom! Stop!"

"No! I'm done letting you mope around. You have an hour to make yourself presentable and get downstairs."

"Why?"

"Because I'm tired of seeing your greasy tangled hair, and you stink. We're having lunch as a family." She leaves, coming just short of slamming my door. I retreat back into the covers for the next ten minutes, fully planning to ignore my mother's demands. But she also kind of scares me. So, I toss the covers off and force myself out of bed.

When I get into the kitchen, my parents are sitting at the table like they're about to stage an intervention. Maybe they are.

"What's going on?"

"We have something you need to see." She slides her phone to the middle of the table. I go and sit down, picking up her phone. On the screen is a paused video of Logan.

I put it down. "I don't want to watch that."

"Too bad." My mom hits the screen, playing the video. Logan looks terrible and wonderful at the same time. He speaks to the camera.

"There was a video posted here that has gotten a lot of attention. It was not posted by me. My phone was stolen, and it was posted by the person who stole it. The suspect was arrested so I hope there will be some justice in all this."

I pause the video. "Trish has been arrested?"

Mom nods. "This morning. She's out on bail, of course."

"Of course." I look back to the phone and continue the video.

"Since that video was posted without my consent, I beg all of you that saved the video to please delete it out of respect for me and Ally. I've been struggling with how to deal with all this and have decided to just be honest. I have a list too." He holds up his list to the camera briefly. "I made it freshman year when I wanted to cross off every clichéd college rite of passage I could. So, yeah, my list is pretty much about sex and booze, but it was also about taking control of my life. I'd had a pretty shitty year and thought this was my chance to live it up. I did some, but not like I imagined, because what I was trying to escape was still a huge part of my life. So, my list got buried in the bottom of a drawer until a few months ago. I found Ally's list and it reminded me of all those silly things I wanted for myself. About to graduate, just like Ally, we struck a deal to help each other out."

He smiles, it's a secret smile. One that I know has to do with the fact that our deal totally fell apart.

"Thing is though, are the lists silly when they represent something important to you? Our lists are so much more than what's on them. They're actually not about that at all. They're about taking back what was lost to us. They're about finding ourselves. About trusting ourselves. Trusting each other."

He pauses and looks away from the camera. It seems like he wants to say so much more but is unsure, maybe?

"Neither Ally nor I deserved to have our privacy taken away so carelessly from us. To have the tender trust we've built tested. I refuse to have our lives defined by this. To be painted in a dirty light. Especially because what came from our lists was something beautiful and special and better than anything listed on it. Go to part two for more."

I click on the next video. "I know Ally and I aren't the only college students who have ever made a bucket list. So, stitch this video if you're willing to share your reasons for making your list. I imagine it's similar to ours. I imagine it becomes more than simple thrills and experiences. That's the beauty in it, isn't it? No one should be judged on what brings them joy. Where or how they find love. Be kind. Peace."

He throws up a peace sign and the video ends. My heart is hammering against my chest. Love? He said love. Did he mean…? I shake my head. I can't believe he did that. I glance at the comments and what I see is all positive. Supporting him…and me. I search and there are tons of videos that stitched his. All of them are very supportive and share their own reasons and experiences.

"This is amazing," I say and realize I'm crying.

A tissue is held out for me, and as I take it, I realize that neither of my parents are offering it. I turn to see Logan standing next to me. I jerk to standing. "What are you doing here?"

"Hoping to take you on a date."

"A date? Now?"

"Yep."

"I don't think that's—"

He takes my hand. "It's a great idea. Come on." He leads me out of the kitchen, not giving me a chance to say anything more. I glance back at my parents, and they tell us to have a good time like what's happening is normal.

He takes me to his truck and opens the door for me. This is my chance to say no, to run back to the house and bury myself, and all my problems, back under the covers. Instead, I climb into his truck.

"Where are we going?"

"You'll see."

"Logan, I'm not in the mood for surprises."

"Trust me. Please."

I almost scoff at that but look out the window instead. The thing is, after everything that's happened, I do still trust him. We head toward downtown then turn down some residential streets. He parks and looks over at me. "I haven't told you, but I've been adding to my list. Things that are only for me. Well, except they're mostly about you."

"About me?"

"Yeah, things like *make Ally laugh so hard she snorts*."

"I don't snort."

He laughs softly. "You do, but the point is, I decided to start writing them down. I kind of started a new list. The first one is *take Ally on the date I promised her*."

He nods ahead and I look over and see it—the graffiti park. The same one he told me he would take me to when we were at the hotel bar. I press my hand against my heart. It's racing so fast I'm afraid it's going to burst right out of my chest. The burn of tears wells up in my eyes.

"Logan..." I stop because the emotion in that one word is already too much.

He must realize how much I'm struggling because he grabs a backpack from behind the seat, and I hear the clink of spray cans. "Come on."

It isn't too crowded, and we find a good spot to attempt our own art. We laugh at each other when it becomes clear that neither of us are very good artists. When I hear myself laugh, the sound almost knocks the wind out of me. For the first time in three days, I forget about everything. It's just me. Not the girl I was in high school who took a dare before thinking of the consequences and not the girl in college who was too afraid to take even the smallest of risks. The new me. The woman that's somewhere in the middle.

Suddenly, I know what I want to do. I shake the can and start spraying.

"Becoming is better than being," Logan reads when I'm done. He looks at me. "I like that."

I nod. "It's a quote from a psychologist famous for her work on mindset." I look at him. "I've only been 'being' since that Halloween. Lately, though, I've felt like I was 'becoming' again. Becoming into this new version of myself. A version I was really starting to like. And then everything happened, and I felt lost again."

"Ally," he closes the distance between us and pulls me to him. His eyes roam over my face. "If you let me, I'll be your compass. I'll be your light. Whenever you feel lost, I'll be here. Helping you find your way."

I smile at him and remember Ginny's words. "My beacon."

He smiles softly. "Yeah." He brushes his thumb across my cheek. "Remember the first day we met?"

I know exactly what he's talking about. We hadn't officially met then, but I've never forgotten the moment we shared. "At the RA meeting."

He nods. "I did this really bad dad joke to break the ice."

I bite my lip as I remember. "What do you get when you cross an alien and a college student?" I pause. "Someone from another universe-ity!"

I giggle again and he shakes his head. "All groans and eye rolls except for you. You're the only one who laughed."

"Totally embarrassing." I cover my face with my hands.

"Totally adorable. It was this really quick and loud laugh-snort combination."

I drop my hands. "Okay, I snorted that time. It was mortifying. Everyone looked at me."

"That sound hit me like a punch to the gut. It was so unexpected and funny and…interesting. I looked at you and everything faded away. Your gorgeous green eyes, your flushed cheeks, that hesitant smile as you realized everyone was looking at you…I couldn't look away."

"You stared at me like I was ridiculous for laughing."

"I was looking at you like a guy who was thinking, I could fall in love with this girl."

I attempt to swallow, but I can't with my heart now lodged in my throat.

"My dad told me about the day he met my mom. How the moment he saw her, he knew he needed her in his life. It was the same for me. And it scared the hell out of me. I saw my parents' marriage go from the kind you wish for to full of broken promises. The last thing I wanted to do was meet the love of my life on the first day of my sophomore year of college." He tips my chin up and leans down so we're breaths apart. "But I did."

Emotion clogs my throat, rendering me unable to say a word. He pulls me closer and presses his forehead to mine. I wrap my arms around his waist.

"My parents always shared a pinky promise as their way to say I love you. The end of their marriage, her death...I've always seen it as a result of broken promises. So, I vowed to never make promises. Then I kept making them to you. I had every intention of keeping each one too. And when I didn't, it fucking killed me. It just proved that I had no business going off list with you, even if it's all I wanted." He takes in a shuddering breath and holds my gaze. "I don't know what the future will bring, but I don't want to be afraid of making promises with you. Making promises with you is simply inevitable because I've been falling in love with you for years."

Tears prick my eyes as my breath stalls in my chest. I can't believe what I'm hearing. Love is definitely off list.

"You have?"

He cracks a smile and takes my hand, leading me over to an area of the park we haven't ventured to yet. When we round a corner, I see a cartoon-like drawing of a wolf in a suit. The suit shirt is open slightly at the neck and the shirt underneath is Superman blue. On his long nose sits a pair of glasses and behind them hearts bulge out of his eyes as he looks at the cat next to him. But it's no ordinary cat; it's me, on our first Halloween. With thick bangs, cat ears and whiskers, wearing a black sweater and short shorts. It looks like they're holding hands, but their hands are only linked by their pinkies. It's us, Ally Cat and her Patient Wolf.

"Oh my God." I press my hand to my mouth, openly crying now. No one has done anything like this for me before. "I love it. So much."

He reaches out and wraps his pinky around mine, and we stand there together much like the painting. I rest my head against his arm and just soak in everything he's done and said in the past hour. When I woke this morning, feeling wrecked and broken, I never imagined I'd end the day feeling so whole and content.

Eventually, we untangle and take pictures of the art. I wish I could take that section of the wall home with me.

He takes my hand again. "I'm going to take you home now."

"You are?"

"Yeah, we can finish this date another time. I know it was a lot for you to come out right now, but I want you to know that I'm not going anywhere, Ally. I'll be as patient as you need me to be. But I need you to fight, too. For us. For yourself."

There's so much I want to say. But he's right. First, I need to stop hiding. I can't just 'be' anymore. It's time to become.

chapter twenty-eight

The Toro Times
University Newspaper

#kinkyally in her own words
An exclusive story by Ally Worthington

When your life starts spinning out of control, there are lots of ways to handle it. My way has been to let it spin and ignore it until someone else's life starts spinning and takes the attention away from mine. Every day dawns with a new scandal, so why not wait it out? But then again, let's get real, my day in the spotlight might fade, but it'll never go away. There will always be a reminder that follows me around, popping out of its hiding spot whenever I let my guard down. #kinkyally will forever be associated with me. It's a clever hashtag, but I refuse to let it define me.

In high school, a video of me was taken without my consent. A video that was stolen and made public. I was blindsided. My boyfriend had abused my trust for a game of truth or dare, then someone else thought it would be fun to humiliate us both (though guess who saw most of the backlash?).

I got off social media, moved, and changed my name. I wasn't the same person anymore. I lost all zest for life. I even contemplated ending my life and that scared me. It wasn't easy, but in the end, I asked for help.

After that, I made school my number one priority and got on track to graduate as soon as possible. I took all risks out of my life. I stopped going out. I dated the safe guy. My life was very much eat, sleep, school, repeat.

I found myself months away from graduating, single, and having done nothing a typical college student does. So, what did I do? I got drunk with my best friend and made a silly college bucket list. The list went a little more sideways with every downed margarita, but it was all in good fun. And the next day, that's exactly what I thought of it, a joke that I would never take seriously. Then it landed in the hands of Logan Mackenzie.

Logan and I have known each other for years. We were friends to each other on our most difficult days, but we were also strangers. I was mortified when he handed it back to me. What if he read it? What if he put my list on the internet? It was my worst fear.

Oh, the irony.

To make a long story short, Logan read my list and he was very interested in helping me out. I had no interest in help. I couldn't even remember what was on the list, but Logan did. He took a picture of it. I wanted to kill him, but I also saw how protective he was of it. He sent it to me and deleted the picture (so he thought). I was resistant at first, but Logan is hard to resist, especially after he shared his own list. I'd trusted him with so many things over the years, and knowing we had this in common, I knew I could trust him with this. If I was going to take risks again, it might as well be with someone I considered safe.

You were so not safe, Logan. Far from it.

You're right, our lists are so much more than the items on it. With each one we crossed off, you repaired another piece of my broken spirit. Then scandal comes, and I think it's shattered once again. I'm exposed in every possible way. My worst fear is realized. My list is out there for the world to see, and I'm being cyber-bullied, slut-shamed, and ridiculed all over again. The world is looking at me and speculating about my character, my life, my sex life and the dangers of college bucket lists. All because I got tipsy and had a night of laughs, like every other normal college student. Doesn't that seriously blow your mind? That something so benign became this malignant mass of interest.

But it turns out, my spirit isn't broken after all. No, it's stronger than ever.

That list helped me find life again. I was living in black and white, and now my life has color again. I've laughed. I've cried. I've done things I never thought I'd do in a million years.

And I fell in love. Logan, I love you so much.

You saw past all the "fun" stuff on my list. You saw me, the real me. You've always seen the real me. My drunken list brought us together, and I don't regret one moment we've shared. I'm so sorry I tried to make you believe that I did. Thank you for not giving up on me. I love you and I want to make all the promises with you—off list, on list, no list.

I refuse to hide anymore. I refuse to be shamed because I'm not ashamed. I refuse to be a tragic tale or a victim anymore. I chose psychology as my major so I could help others and I'm starting now. I'm working with the university to create a center and hotline to help students struggling with their mental health due to cyberbullying and social media. The university already has lots of resources and policies in place but feels the toll social media plays in our lives is only getting greater and could use specific attention and a safe space. More information and resources can be found on the university's website listed at the end of this story.

If you're struggling in any way, I hope my story provides some encouragement. That even in your darkest days, a ray of light can be found in the most unexpected places—even a college bucket list.

chapter twenty-nine

Ally loves me.

After two days of not hearing from her, this morning I found a copy of *The Toro Times* right outside of my bedroom. Ally's story and the bravery it took to write it has completely blown me away. I'm so damn proud of her I can't see straight. What I want to do most is kiss the ever-living hell out of her and hear those three words out of her sweet mouth.

I race to campus, hoping she'll be where I think she'll be. As far as I know, she hasn't been to any classes since spring break. As soon as I enter our class, almost every head swivels toward me. Instant chatter starts up, then comes some applause and cheering. Oh fuck. Ally is going to hate this.

I slowly make my way down the steps toward the seats

Ally and I normally sit in. As I close in, she stands and faces me. She looks a little embarrassed, but not completely uncomfortable.

I stop half a foot from her, breathing hard. "Hey."

She grins at me. "Hey."

"So…you love me, huh?"

She tilts her head, a hint of playfulness in her gorgeous green eyes. "Maybe."

"Maybe? Hmmm, that doesn't sound right. Maybe I should quote your exact words." I start to dig out the folded newspaper I have stuffed in my back pocket.

She giggles and stops me. "Yes, yes. I love you. I love Clark. I love the patient wolf. I love *you*, Logan."

Unable not to touch her any longer, I pick her up, pull her against my chest and kiss her like a starving man. A roar of cheers erupts around us that has us breaking apart in laughter.

"I love you, Ally Cat," I say and brush another kiss against her lips. "I love you, Allyson." Kiss. "I love *you*, Ally." Kiss.

We kiss again, and this time all the noise fades away. It's only us. When we finally pull apart, I'm so hot for her I can barely breathe.

I press my forehead to hers. "Ally, I'm not feeling very patient right now."

She laughs. "Your wolf is showing, Logan."

I give her my best wolfish smile. "You know it."

"Well, there are quite a few items left on our lists to tackle."

"I thought we were off list."

"We're making our own list. Together."

"I like that. Let's start now."

I put her down and grab her hand and start leading her out of the classroom, and everyone goes wild with cheers and catcalls. The last thing I hear is Professor Martin yelling that she expects to see us in office hours tomorrow to receive the extra assignment our exit just earned us.

epilogue

Ally
Halloween

Watching Logan take the field in a crowd of cheers always makes my stomach flutter, but today my nerves are on a whole other level as this is his first start of the season.

He was drafted in the sixth round to the New Orleans Revelers, and this is only the second game I've been able to attend. I went to his debut game and there was no way I was going to miss this one. We made a pact that no matter how busy our lives were, we were going to find a way to be together on Halloween.

I yell and clap zeroing in on his number as he runs across the field. As the team starts to gather on the sideline, he looks up, scanning the area he knows we'll be seated in. I raise my arms and see the moment he finds me. He makes a heart with his pinkies and thumbs and I do the same, it's our version of the pinky promise. He gives me a Heart Bursting smile and it's all I can do not to jump down there and kiss him silly.

He waves at his dad, Miranda, and Brianna who are in the seats next to me. Jack asked Miranda to marry him not long after Logan gave his blessing, and they married this past summer. Until Logan moved to New Orleans, he made it a point to see his dad weekly. Most of the time it was a dinner that included all of us. The first few times we were all together, it was a bit awkward, but then everyone clicked right into place with each other.

Logan and Brianna almost instantly fell into a sibling relationship, which is mostly shit-talking and teasing, but they're also super supportive of each other. Honestly, Brianna feels like a sister to me too. With the three of us all being only children, I think we all craved having that extra person in our lives. And it's been pretty awesome.

"Think he'll introduce us to Malone?" Bri asks me. "God, he's so hot."

"And married."

Bri makes a face. "Why did you have to go and remind me? Can I please have my fantasy?"

"I'm pretty sure Logan won't let you around any of the single players. Apparently, the locker room talk can get pretty explicit."

She leans closer and lowers her voice so Jack and Miranda don't hear. "Maybe I need a little explicit in my life."

I laugh. "Well, you'll need to find it on campus because there's no way Logan will want to contribute to your explicitness."

She sighs. "And here I thought the perk of having a big brother was all his hot friends."

"Um, have you not seen Nate and Wes? Wait, forget I said that. Logan's head would explode if you go there."

Brianna rolls her eyes. "Yeah, not interested. Those two are so annoying. I'm pretty sure Logan made them some sort of big brother stand-ins or something. I saw them at a party once and they chased off every guy I tried to talk to. Wes even told me that freshman didn't belong at parties. Like he didn't party his freshman year. So stupid."

I laugh, but I feel for her. I do know that Logan asked them to keep an eye out for her, but there's no way I'm going to tell her that. Maybe I can get them to back off.

The game kicks off then the defense takes the field. My stomach tightens as I watch Logan jog on. The starting edge rusher is out this week because of an ankle injury so I know Logan really wants to make an impression today and help bring his team the win. I grab Brianna's hand as they line up. The ball is snapped, and the quarterback gets off a quick pass before anyone can get to him. The offense gets two first downs in a row before the defense holds them and now it's third and long. I hold my breath when the play begins, the quarterback quickly scrambling back for a pass play as the defense blitzes. Logan easily breaks a tackle and guns right for the quarterback. My heart starts racing and I'm jumping up and down screaming. QB runs from Logan and throws the ball away just before Logan can take him down. The crowd erupts in cheers.

"Oh my God, he did it. Did you see that?"

"I felt it." Brianna rips her hand from mine and starts shaking it out. "Girl, I thought you were going to wrench my hand off."

"I'm so sorry! I totally forgot I was holding it." I hug her then Miranda and Jack, unable to contain my excitement.

Brianna refuses to hold my hand for the rest of the game and it's a close one until the third quarter then the Revelers take a two-touchdown lead, securing the win. Logan got two sacks and the smile on his face fills my heart with joy. The transition from college to the pros plus maintaining a long-distance relationship has been a big adjustment. To see him this happy really makes it all worth it.

I make my way to the railing at the field as Logan comes to meet me. I lean over and he grabs me under my arms and hauls me over.

"Logan! What are you doing?"

"Kissing my girl," he says as wraps me in a hug and covers my mouth in a searing kiss. It's a kiss meant for the bedroom, not the sidelines, and if it's caught on camera, it'll likely stir up our past drama. But I don't care.

This is us and we refuse to listen to all the judgment and noise, even if it has all died down. It hasn't been easy, but we have each other's back and that's all that matters.

"Okay, you gotta stop or we'll get a flag for indecent exposure," I say pulling away, my breathing unsteady.

He laughs. "Baby, I plan to be indecent with you all night."

I swat at him. "Tame your wolf. We have dinner with your family first."

He groans, but I know it's just for show. He gives me a quick kiss just before his family shows up at the railing and he turns his attention to them.

Hours later, Logan isn't subtle about kicking his family out of his condo. Me and Brianna are flying out early tomorrow since we have school, but Jack and Miranda are sticking around for a few days so Logan will get to see them again.

As soon as the door closes, Logan hefts me up over his shoulder takes me straight to the bedroom.

"Logan! Oh my God! You're crazy!"

He drops me on the bed and takes off his T-shirt and holy fuck, the man takes my breath away. The NFL is no joke when it comes to nutrition and fitness. He has muscles and definition he didn't have a few months ago.

"Jesus, you're so hot."

His smile is cocky as he runs a hand down his defined abs. "You been missing me, baby?"

"You have no idea."

His expression changes from amused to serious. "Oh, trust me, I do." He leans over and pulls off my jeans and panties in one fell swoop. "Fuck, Ally Cat. You have no idea how crazy you've been driving me all day."

He runs his hand up my leg, his fingers teasing my slit. "All I've been able to think of is fucking you while you're wearing my number. I even added it to the list." He pushes a finger inside me, and I arch up and cant my hips, silently begging for more. Yes, we still have a list. We thought it would be a good way to keep us connected while we were apart.

"Fuck…so wet." He groans as he slowly fucks me with his fingers. It feels so good too, but it's not nearly enough.

As if he has the same thought, he pulls away and starts tackling the button on his jeans. "Bra off but keep on my jersey."

I shift to sitting and work off my bra. "Isn't it technically my jersey?"

Now naked, he grips his cock and gives it a long pull as a sexy growl comes from his throat. "My number. My woman. Mine."

I love it when he goes all caveman on me. I toss my bra aside and he grabs me by the legs and pulls me to the edge of the bed then up to standing. He raises the jersey just enough to reveal my breasts then knots it in the back so it'll stay that way. Then he presses me back down so I'm sitting on the edge of the bed.

"Spread your legs, Allyson."

I do and his eyes flare as he sinks to his knees and takes in his fill. "Look at that pretty pussy all wet and ready for me."

God, he can't say things like that. I already feel like I'm going to burst if he doesn't touch me again. He leans in and kisses each of my inner thighs before spreading me even further and kisses me right where I'm aching for him. I jerk as an intense burst of tingles flood me. I tangle my fingers in his hair, urging him to keep going. He moans and the sensation vibrating through me almost does me in.

"Logan…please. I want you inside me when I come."

He lifts his head and places another kiss on my thigh. "I will be, baby." Then he sinks his face between my legs again. His hands come up and gently pinch my nipples as his tongue works its magic and I'm gone. I come hard and loud, my hands curling into his hair as I ride his face.

After my body ceases spasming, he kisses his way up my body, now lavishing his kisses on my breasts. He pulls back and simply looks at me. "I've been fantasizing about this. Your tits wet from my mouth while you're wearing my number. Ally, you look so fucking hot. My cock hurts it wants you so bad."

"Then what are you waiting for?" I move so I'm fully on the bed and open my legs to him. He groans and crawls on top of me, pulling my leg up over his hip then pushes inside me in a quick, hard thrust.

He stops and lets out a ragged breath as his forehead falls to mine. "Fuck, I miss you."

"You miss me or my pussy?"

He laughs and I love how I can feel it all through my body.

"Both." He kisses me. "I just miss this. Being close to you. Hearing you laugh. Talking to you." He slowly pulls out then thrusts back in. "Feeling you come."

I moan and lift my hips up. "More."

He grins and buries his head into my neck, kissing, sucking and licking as he fucks me in slow, hard strokes making sure he's hitting the right spot to make me come all over again. And I do. It's just as strong as the last one too, filling my body in fiery waves.

He groans and shifts, pulling my legs up against his chest before fucking me relentlessly, pushing my orgasm to an intensity that's almost overwhelming. His lusty gaze stays on my chest and jersey until his expression shutters as his climax hits. His eyes meet mine then and we stay locked together making the pleasure coursing inside us even more powerful.

Much later, after we come out of our sex coma, I say, "You were amazing today."

He pulls me further into his side. "I don't think I'll ever forget this game." The emotion I hear in his voice has me lifting up and looking at him. He's staring up at the ceiling, his eyes glassy. "When I got in the car this morning, the song on the radio was my mom's favorite. The song ended right when I got to the coffee shop. After I placed my order, the barista called out the name, Simone."

"Wow, that's crazy. Your mom's name isn't exactly a common name."

"I know. And the weird thing was, no one claimed the drink. It was a pumpkin spice latte, which she loved. She was one of those people that went crazy over them every fall. Personally, I think they're disgusting, but I took it with me. The cup with her name on it is still in my locker." He swallows. "It really felt like she was there with me today."

I reach out and link my pinky with his and he presses his thumb to mine. He looks at me. "Then there was you. I got to wake up in your arms on a game day. You in my jersey. Here with me, on Halloween. I couldn't have asked for a more perfect day, and I never thought this day would ever be that again."

I lean down and kiss him. "It was a perfect day and I'm so glad I was here for it. I love you."

"Love you back." He gently kisses my lips then I move to rest my head back on his chest but the notebook where we keep our running list catches my eye on the nightstand. It wasn't there earlier.

"What other depraved things have you added to the list since last time?" I lean over and grab it, skipping to the last few items listed and immediately see, *fuck Ally while she wears my number.* Then my gaze falls to the next item and my breath stalls in my chest.

Marry Ally

"Um, Logan?" I show him the page.

"Oh," he says and grins as a blush fills his cheeks.

My heart is going a hundred miles per hour. I love those words. But I'm not ready for them, especially when we're living in different cities and have only been dating for less than a year. He reaches up and cups my cheek. "Relax, Ally Cat, that's not a proposal."

"Okay," I say, not sure what else to say.

He sits fully up and pulls me into his lap, taking the notebook from my hands and setting it on the bed. "This morning, the game, coming home to you…I just know I want more of these days. I want all my days to have you in them. So, I added it. I know we're not ready yet, but one day I hope to cross it off."

Tears are flowing from my eyes. Honestly, while I knew we were committed to each other, I wasn't sure he'd ever want to get married.

"Thought you didn't want to get married young," I say, repeating his words from my freshman year.

His beautiful eyes, soft and vulnerable, meet mine. "Ally, you were always a game-changer."

And just like that, my heart tumbles over itself. "Fuck, Logan. How is it possible that you can make me fall more and more in love with you?"

He laughs. "I'm a charming wolf, remember?" He reaches

out and swipes away the tears on my cheek, his expression turning serious. "Have I really freaked you out?"

"No, but you're having an emotional day and—"

"Ally, I didn't need to write it down. It's here." He presses his other hand to his heart. "It's off list."

The man is seriously going to make my heart burst from all the love that keeps swelling inside me. And I need him to know that I feel the same way. I reach over and grab the pen on the nightstand. I pick up the notebook again and add my own item and show it to him.

Marry Logan

"Making a life with you doesn't scare me. You're the best risk I've ever taken. And I want to keep taking them with you."

"Promise?"

"Promise." I press a kiss to his lips, sealing my vow.

He immediately deepens the kiss then flips me over so he's on top of me. He looks at me with his Sexy Danger Combo smile and I know exactly the direction his thoughts are going.

"Good. Because I've got some list ideas that'll probably land us in jail if we don't time it just right."

THE END

a note from the author

Thank you for reading OFF LIST! I hope you enjoyed Logan and Ally's story! If you have time, please consider leaving a review. It would be much appreciated. xoxo

CONNECT WITH CATE!

JOIN CATE'S NEWSLETTER

www.cateashton.com

- instagram.com/romancingcate
- facebook.com/Cate-Ashton-Author-106315095223612
- twitter.com/RomancingCate
- amazon.com/stores/Cate-Ashton/author/B09N2QRZF9? ref=ap_rdr&store_ref=ap_rdr&isDramIntegrated=true&shop-pingPortalEnabled=true
- goodreads.com/Cate_Ashton
- bookbub.com/authors/cate-ashton

books by cate ashton

PERSONALLY YOURS SERIES

YOURS IN LUST

YOURS TO PROTECT

about the author

Cate has been in love with love stories for as long as she can remember. It never occurred to her to be a writer until she realized she was constantly making up love stories in her head and she enjoyed that far more than anything else. So, she put fingers to keyboard and hasn't stopped.

Cate likes her romance with a dash of humor, a punch of emotion, and heaps of heat. When she's not writing, she enjoys spending time with family and friends, finding new places to visit, and curling up with a book (naturally).

Cate resides in Texas and living out her own HEA with her husband, two children, and pandemic pup.

acknowledgments

I wrote this story before the pandemic and after lots of requests led to rejections, I regulated it to the shelf. But I loved it so much and really wanted to see it shine. So, I pulled it back out, made several edits, and it's definitely a better book for it. Through all the years, I had lots of people help this story along.

Abigail Owen – You've been such a help from editor to cover designer to overall supporter, advisor, and friend. Thanks for my awesome cover and indulging my crazy picky and perfectionist ways.

CCDS – Catherine, thanks for being part of the village that helped me get my back cover blurb in shape. Your insights are always so helpful! Susye, thanks for being there in Denver when the journey of this story started. Deb, thanks for always being on hand for great advice and a lending hand. My friendship with the three of you is incredibly important to me and I love that we still make time to see each other even when life is crazy. Love you ladies!

Dolly Jackson – Thank you so much for the edits on the final draft of this story and for your great advice and support!

Shellee – I know you had a hand on helping this along years ago and you definitely helped me get my back cover blurb under control. Thanks for putting up with all my reiterations!

Christina Kirby – Thanks for editing this years ago and being my roommate, travel mate, and support in Denver when I first started shopping this out.

Cheryl Etchison – Thanks for helping me break out of blurb writing circle! I've really enjoyed our write-ups and really going to miss them.

Alaina – Thank you for being a beta reader and giving this story a last look.

Anastasia Novikova. – Thank you for the awesome illustration for my cover that brought Ally and Logan to life.

As always to my family and friends who are always there helping me along as I continue to figure out this journey of publishing. Your support means the world to me.